2014 FIRST PLACE WINNER!
General Fiction
Kindle Book Promo / LuckyCinda
International Contest.

"Kelly's fast-paced novel takes the reader on a flight of fancy couched in realistic, straight-forward and graceful prose that makes the fantastic utterly believable. It's hard to stop reading...fasten your seat belt for an enjoyable flight."

—Kirkus Reviews

"The strong voice speaking from the pages of Winged, by April Kelly, immediately captures both interest and sympathy...with cliffhangers that keep the reader turning pages breathlessly. Winged seizes the imagination because of its unusual premise, but it wins our hearts because it is, after all...the story of the universal need to pursue passions and dreams, often at a high cost."

—Southern Literary Review

Also by April Kelly with Marsha Lyons

Murder In One Take
Murder: Take Two
Murder: Take Three

Cynthia —
Put your seatback & tray
table in their upright and locked
position, then enjoy the flight!
~ [signature]

WINGED

by
April Kelly

Flight
Risk
Books

For Sandy

Keep your chin up and your kilts down
And let the wind blow.

—Scottish proverb

Smile patronizingly at my naming her Angel,
but remember I was only eighteen and my child *was* born
with wings. Well, the doctor didn't call them wings. He
called them a congenital anomaly and recommended they
be surgically removed before we left the hospital.

I had never heard the word anomaly before, and I
only recognized three syllables of congenital, the three that
had gotten me in trouble nine months earlier as two other
twelfth-grade girls and I crashed a fraternity party where I
downed about a dozen drinks that must have been ninety-
nine percent wine and only one percent cooler.

The drugs they gave me during the birth—more to
shut me up than to ease any pain, I suspect—impaired my
ability to detect reactions from either doctor or nurses that
would have indicated I had just expelled a freak. The words
penetrating my mushy consciousness gave no hint there
was a problem: *girl, umbilical, Apgar, turkey sub*. One of
the nurses may have been placing her lunch order.

Three hours later I was stitched up, cleaned up and
sitting up when a nurse brought me a pink wrappy thing
with a tiny head sticking out one end. Immediately upon
off-loading the bundle to me, she gave a tight smile and left.
I had barely enough time to register the features of the
squinched little face before the doctor approached my bed,
his own face fixed in a squinch. It looked better on the
baby.

Once he had pulled the curtain around my ward
bed—broke teenagers who can't even come up with a baby-

daddy name for the birth certificate don't rate the premium accommodations—the doc began a rambling tale about how some newborns enter the world with webbing between their fingers or toes, and that it was customary to do the surgical fixes before they left the hospital.

"So what are you saying? She has duck feet?"

"No, no, no." He seemed panicked by my question. "Her fingers and toes are fine. But she has two very small membranous flaps on her back that we'd like to remove."

"I want to see them."

"I have to discourage that, Miss Fitzgerald. These congenital anomalies are routine for medical personnel, but for a new mother, especially one as young as..."

He might have said more, but I was already freeing my child from the pastel cotton burrito into which she had been stuffed. Once unswaddled, her little arms and legs did a round of slow-motion waving and her mouth opened in a gummy yawn, while the doctor held out a clipboard and asked me to sign the consent form.

I gently turned her over to place her on her stomach on my stomach and saw them for the first time: wings.

It wasn't much of an argument. I had only turned eighteen two months earlier, but I knew I was an adult in the eyes—if not the common sense—of the law, and that I had the right to say no to the mutilation of my child. Frustrated, the doctor left and I was finally alone with her.

Still facedown and sleeping on me, her tiny form rode the rise and fall of my belly as I breathed. One arm curved alongside her head, fist extended, and the rhythmic movement combined with the facedown, arm-out position made me think of Superman flying.

I wish I could say I had some warm and maternal feeling for that little stranger, but I didn't. There was a vague sense of obligation to handle her carefully, but no more than when I had held a puppy or a kitten as a child. No, the only feeling I had was a curiosity about her, an interest in this creature created solely by me. Well, by me and some unknown Sigma Tau Gamma.

The doc had been accurate in calling them membranous flaps. Though they matched the cream and pink of her back, they looked more reptilian than human: rudimentary triangles of skin emerging from either side of the small knobs of her upper spine, then curving and hugging her shoulder blades. I gently stroked one with the tip of my index finger, Brailling the info to my brain. Not as soft as I thought they would be, and with the slightest of ridges along the sides, like piping under the skin. When I slipped my fingernail under one edge and lifted the flap, there was a small amount of tensile strength in it, enough to snug it back in place when I took my finger away.

I gently turned her over, triggering that slo-mo dog paddling of her arms and legs again. Cradling her against me, I took in the brownish fuzz that capped her head, one piece in front almost long enough for my licked fingertip to paste into a curl. I examined the minuscule diaper, deciding it looked like the one worn by the wetting doll I got for Christmas when I was five.

I leaned over to check out the itty-bitty eyelashes, so we were almost nose to nose when she opened her eyes. We both flinched, and I pulled back far enough to focus. The cliché caught me off guard, that intense rush of love that bonded me to her instantly. That alone would have been a powerful enough experience, albeit shared with virtually every other new mother since the beginning of time. But that was only the opening jab of the one-two punch that changed my life forever; the tap that laid me out was looking into her eyes and seeing my own face—twice, tiny—reflected back. Not the face I had then, but my future face, the one that bends over a yellow pad tonight as I sit on this bunk and scribble out my life. Was that future me trying desperately to communicate answers to questions teen me had not yet begun to ask? Before I averted my eyes to break that frightening connection, three powerful thoughts surged into me: one, that this child would save me; two, that I would be willing to give up my own life for her; and three, that I would one day see her fly. All three have come true, but not in any way I could have imagined.

A tall, silver-haired priest was the next person to try to persuade me to have my daughter's wings removed. As I was in a Catholic hospital, I was not surprised to see a priest, but from the embarrassed look on Father Paul's face, he *was* surprised to see a female breast. Hey, what could I do? It was snack time for the kidlet, and an open ward doesn't offer a heck of a lot of privacy.

Father Paul was almost too easy a target. When he speculated that my daughter would be teased by her school chums—he actually used that word, chums—when they learned of her secret deformity, I countered by claiming to be reluctant to interfere with God's plan.

"If He created her this way, how can mere mortals presume to improve on His plan? And she doesn't have a deformity; she has a pair of wings."

"Allison, you can't actually believe they're wings. That defies logic."

"Oh, right. But a pregnant virgin and a dead guy waking up after three days make perfect sense. Sorry, padre, but I'm sticking with the wings theory."

I'm not sure if it was my blasphemy or the sight of my swollen, blue-veined boob as the baby finished brunch and lolled away from it, but the good father stood quickly, scraping back his chair. I'm sure part of him wanted to stay and fight for the soul of a child born to so obviously a lost-cause mother, but I also sensed the larger part of him would be relieved to return to the terminal patients who welcomed his comforting words. I decided to absolve him of my sins.

"I'm naming her Angel."

Camel's back, meet the straw. Father Paul didn't have much of a poker face and, looking appalled, he choked out a tight blessing, then exited ward left.

I had only said it to be a bitch, but when micro girl burped in her sleep and I looked down at the milk bubble inflating and deflating in the corner of her mouth, I figured Angel was as good a name as any. You don't have to believe in God to believe in angels.

I had three days in the hospital getting to know her, learning how to take care of her basic needs, and wondering where we could go when St. Luke's threw us out. Brian's mom and dad had been amazing, letting me stay at their house when I started looking like I was hiding a basketball under my shirt and my own parents ejected me from their vinyl-sided Eden (with detached garage), but Brian was taking early college entrance and I could hardly ask Mr. and Mrs. Haywood to let me stay on with the bambina. Nice as they were, I knew half the reason they invited me in the first place was their fervent, long shot hope that Bri was the father. They clung to the belief that being gay was a phase he would snap out of and that Greg was only his study buddy.

Brian came to the hospital the day after Angel was born, carrying a bouquet of daisies for me and a really inappropriate teddy bear in a black leather onesie for her. That was the day he told me he was leaving for Berkeley the following week. We had been good friends since the tenth grade, and his departure would bring me down to zero in the best-buds department, as Heather and Chelsea—my two partners in the great frat party debacle—had been forbidden to have any contact with me since our drunk and disorderly escapade. Most of the rest of my semifriends had pulled back when my pregnancy became obvious, with the few holdouts falling away after the principal told me I could no longer be a Gettysburg Cougar. (Go, silver and blue!) I think it was less that the other kids were judgmental and more that we didn't see each other every day at school anymore. Face it, the foundation for ninety-five percent of all high school friendships is proximity.

I bonded with Angel, ate instant oatmeal and green Jell-O, and resisted two more attempts by the doctor to change my mind about removing the wings. On the fourth morning we were released. As I stood on the steps of St. Luke's, I didn't have a home, a job, a clue, a high school diploma, a family or friends.

But I had my baby and, thanks to me, she still had her wings.

Jesus, I wish I had listened to that doctor.

The next three years were uneventful for Angel.
For me, however, the treadmill never stopped running on
its highest speed and steepest incline. Bang off the steps of
St. Luke's I improvised a black eye with the aid of Maybel-
line eye shadow in a matte moss green, then talked my way
into a battered women's shelter so Angel and I would have a
place to stay that first couple weeks. Thinking back, I'm
sure the lady who ran the place could tell the boo-boo was
faux, but I must have looked young enough and desperate
enough that she decided to let me in without asking too
many questions.

She did, however, gently encourage me to call my
parents. Something about a grandchild being able to melt
the iciest of hearts. I wanted to believe she was right, but
not enough to make the call myself. With my permission
she dialed my parents and put the call on speaker.

"Hello?"

"Mr. Fitzgerald, my name is Carol Taft and I'm here
with your daughter Allison. She asked me to call and give
you the good news that you have a grandchild."

The faint hum of the speakerphone was the only
sound in the room for too many seconds.

"Are you still there, Mr. Fi—"

"I'm here."

"Well, how do you feel about being a grandfather?"

"You must be mistaken, Miss. I couldn't possibly
have a grandchild because I do not have a daughter."

With a faint click, the connection broke as my father

hung up the phone. Carol looked sad and embarrassed.

"Maybe we can call back later and speak with your mother."

"I admire your tenacity, but you just talked to the soft-hearted half of the team."

Since I was all Angel had, I needed to make something of myself, and after that phone call I knew I would be working solo.

The easy stuff? Getting a job, a place to live and my GED. The hard stuff? Completing two years at a community college, paying for child care on a waitress's salary and tips, and—between work and school—being away from my daughter twelve hours a day.

We had one nasty incident when Angel was around eighteen months old. A new worker at my daycare place took a photograph of her and sold it to the same tabloid that had often carried stories and fake photos of a creature they called Bat Boy. And I don't mean he worked for a baseball team; this fictitious character had vampire teeth and wings like a bat. I was standing in the checkout line at the grocery store one evening, tired after seven hours on my feet, when I saw the headline "Bat Boy's Baby Sister?" There was a picture of Angel wearing only a diaper and sleeping on her stomach. The photograph had been doctored so that her little flaps had scalloped, bat-wing edges.

Luckily, that rag had the reputation of fabricating Elvis sightings, horny Bigfoots, and anal-probing aliens, so everyone probably thought Angel's picture was also bogus. I read the wild-ass, paranoid, hyperbole-posing-as-reportage while I waited forever for the woman ahead of me to unload her cart. And I remember wondering why she hadn't gone through the one-hundred-cans-of-cat-food-or-less line. The most upsetting thing about the tabloid—other than the fact that an innocent little baby was objectified and exploited for financial gain—was that it quoted some small-time fundamentalist Christian evangelist named Billy Harper saying this was a sign of God's wrath. Billyboy predicted more "hideously disfigured" infants would be born with demonic wings and devilish tails in response to society's tolerance of homosexuals, adulterers and, I assumed, skanks who bore babies out of wedlock.

One week later that same "newspaper" broke the story of those gigantic albino alligators in the sewers, so Bat Boy's baby sis dropped off the radar. By then the daycare center had fired the employee who had taken the picture, assured me nothing like that would ever happen again, and offered six months of care with no charge. A financial break like that was a godsend at the time, so Angel stayed where she was without ever knowing there had been a fuss.

Angel's wings remained inert during that first three years, neither bothering her nor interesting her. Our pediatrician checked them periodically for any signs that they might be impacting her growth or mobility. Although they got a bit larger as she grew into a toddler, they looked the same as they had from the start: thin triangular flaps with a slight thickening along the edges.

My pediatrician asked why I hadn't had the flaps removed when she was born and I was too embarrassed to tell him I had bullied a doctor, a priest and several nurses to get my own way, so I claimed I had not been offered the option. He didn't understand how an OB/GYN could have been so insensitive, when the removal would be costlier as she got older, not only monetarily, but in potential psychological damage to Angel.

I began second-guessing my postpartum decision to keep her intact. Even if I made it through junior college, snagged a scholarship to continue toward my degree, and eventually got a job at an accounting firm, it would be years before I could afford to pay for an operation. And by then Angel might be feeling revulsion for the reptilian flaps I had so cavalierly dubbed wings when she was born. And what if my perfect plan for college and career didn't work out? What if I were still pouring decaf refills and serving burger platters ten years down the road? What if Angel had to go through the rest of her life hiding those ugly flaps on her back, all because I wanted to prove something—and I'm not entirely sure what—to those authority figures at St. Luke's Hospital?

These thoughts roiled in my mind at night, and I frequently woke with the aching fear I had made a terrible mistake. Awake and alert, however, I always remembered that first look into Angel's eyes, when I suddenly *knew* I would see her fly one day. Not flying as in being successful or happy—it wasn't a metaphor—but soaring in the sky on the power of her own wings. No matter how much I tried to dismiss the idea of her flying, I always came back to the certainty that one of the other things I "knew" from that first eye contact with her had already come true. She *had* saved me. In little more than a year, I had gone from a drunk seventeen year old pulling train for a bunch of frat boys to a college student and working single mother. I hadn't done it for me; I did it for her. Because of her I had at least the chance of a respectable, successful future. She made me strong.

The second of the three truths I had seen in her eyes—that I would be willing to give up my own life for her—felt true already. If you had asked me back then if I were prepared to sacrifice my life for Angel's, I would not have hesitated before saying yes. If a truck had come hurtling toward the two of us and I only had time to jump out of the way or toss Angel to safety, then she would soar and I would squish. I was *so* naïve. I didn't realize that when the question is called in real life, it is never as quick and easy as a speeding semi. When the time finally came for me to cash that check I had so confidently written before I had even cast my first vote, the process was searingly hard. It cost me everything, *everything,* but I made damn sure the check cleared.

What had made me look away after that link was established? What fear had compelled me to cut off the flow before I learned more, before I got clarification on the knowledge shooting into my soul? There had been an almost imperceptible undercurrent, a darkness that scared me into darting my eyes away from the force of it. When I finally looked back, I saw only the bright, unfocused eyes of my infant daughter.

Sorry. Didn't mean to wander off on a metaphysical tangent. I was attempting to document the practicalities of that first three years.

We lived in a studio apartment, the deposit and first

month's rent paid for by the sale of the diamond pendant my grandmother had given me for my sixteenth birthday. I hated to sell it because it was the last gift I ever got from her—she died from a heart attack four months after my Sweet Sixteen party—but I was relieved to know it was valuable enough to put a roof over my head until I could pull in a paycheck.

After I got my GED and registered at a community college, my schedule became really heavy. Up at five to shower, dress and eat breakfast before waking Angel at six to feed and bathe her. If the weather was nice I might take her for a walk in the park. If not, we stayed in and read books about kittens looking for their mittens and big white bunnies hopping through Carrot Village. At nine I dropped her off at daycare, then caught a bus to school, getting to my nine-thirty class with ten minutes to spare. When my last class ended at one-thirty, I bussed back to a restaurant a couple blocks from the apartment, eating an apple or a sandwich on the way, then changed in the restroom and was taking orders by two. My half-hour dinner break came at five and I used that time to pick up Angel and drop her off at Katie's.

Katie was the thirty-year-old wife and mother who lived with her husband and four young children in a large apartment on the ground floor of my building. Every week-day around five-fifteen, I dropped Angel off at her place. Katie's youngest, Stacy, was almost the same age as Angel, and they became crib friends. I was back at the restaurant by five-thirty, just as the early dinner crowd started coming in. Three hours of meat loaf platters and salisbury steaks later, I clocked out and walked back to my building, where I would pick up my sleeping child and carry her up to our apartment.

Bath time was our happiest time together. Angel loved the water. Or rather, she loved what she could do with it: splash it, drink it, make fart bubbles in it. I always washed her hair first, working up a mound of shampoo lather, then shaping it into a tall pointy-head or a couple of horns, then holding a mirror up for her to see. That was a sight gag she never got tired of, shrieking with laughter each time she saw her bubble-headed self in the mirror.

Shortly after Angel's third birthday, we were enjoying bath time when something different happened. I held the mirror for her to see her latest lather coif, she laughed her screechy toddler laugh, *and her wings moved.*

I thought I must be mistaken. The tub water had given them a split-second's buoyancy, or the mist in the bathroom had played an optical trick. I cupped a glob of lather from Angel's head and put it on my own nose so it slid down and dangled precariously, causing Angel to point and yell, "Bubble boogers!" I sputtered my lips, horse-like, and the froth went flying. She lifted her chin, half-choking on her squeal of delight. Her eyes were squeezed shut, transported as she was by my antics, but I kept my own eyes on her wings. As Angel continued to laugh, the little flaps lifted away from her back maybe half an inch, then up about the same distance. Her squeal settled to a giggle, she went back to slapping her hands on the surface of the water and the wings snugged back into their usual position.

So began the next chapter of our lives.

Angiogenesis is *not* the name of an Irish biblical character. It is the development and growth of new blood vessels in places where none existed before, such as in the expanding belly of a man riding the express train from Endomorph to Morbid Obesity. Or in a pair of previously inert wings.

Dr. Whittaker could neither understand nor explain the sudden appearance of fine red arteries and even finer blue veins in Angel's wings, but he insisted they could not have caused the slight lift and spread I had described to him. He speculated that a contraction of her back muscles had pulled the skin tight enough to cause minor movement of the tiny flaps.

At first the wings only occasionally flared when she was completely happy. Soon, however, they began flaring *every* time she was happy, causing a few amusing situations at playgrounds, carnivals and other venues where children were likely to have fun. The wing flare would lift the back of her shirt, puffing it out for the duration of her giddy moment. Once, she caught the eyes of two park moms as she shot off the end of the slide, shrieking with joy. It was her piercing laugh that snagged their attention, but what held it was the fact that she looked like a mini hunchback in a Smurf shirt.

During the next three years, while I was completing work for my bachelor's degree and taking a part-time bookkeeping job that paid better and was less grueling than waiting tables, Angel became aware of—and fell in love with—her wings.

I made sure Angel had books long before she was verbal, as I had grown up in a household suspicious of any written words not directly attributable to a disciple of Jesus Christ. She loved the picture books with pettable fluffy lambs and quacking ducks, but around age three she began paying extra attention to any book with winged creatures. Fairies, sprites, pixies, even dragonflies fascinated Angel. Once I walked into the bathroom and found her standing on the toilet seat so she could look in the medicine cabinet mirror and see her wings reflected in the full-length mirror on the back of the bathroom door. Not long after, the questions began.

"Am I a fairy?"

"No, you're a little girl."

"Fairies have wings and I have wings. That means I'm a fairy."

"Pigs have noses and you have a nose. Does that mean you're a pig?"

"Hm-m."

"You are a little girl. With wings."

"Do any other little girls have wings?"

"Well, I don't know about all the little girls in the whole world, but I would be surprised to learn there was another girl special enough to be born with wings."

We would continue making Japanese lanterns or baking brownies or coloring, and she would seem satisfied for a few minutes, then:

"Am I a pixie?"

And the whole conversation would start again.

Angel became quite the girly girl and stayed that way through kindergarten, choosing to be a fairy princess three Halloweens in a row. Because her own wings didn't come up to fairy princess size or beauty standards, we bought a set of those little tie-on wings made of light wire and some sheer fabric like voile or organdy. A package of sequins and a spray can of glitter pimped out those wings to such perfection in her eyes that she wanted to wear them every day. After twice finding sequins floating among her Cheerios, I had to limit wing wear to Sunday afternoons at home.

"Did my daddy have wings?"

After a year of the fairy/sprite/pixie inquisition, she finally zeroed in on the line of questioning I dreaded most.

"No, he did not have wings."

"Hm-m."

Could I be so lucky? Could she possibly be satisfied with that? Not a chance.

"Hey, where *is* my daddy?"

I told her I didn't know where he was and she didn't ask anything else. But I knew it was a very short leap from where is my daddy to *who* is my daddy, even for a four year old, so I decided to try to find out.

The doors of the Sigma Tau Gamma house were always open for a cute coed, and at twenty-two I could still pass. Unfortunately, almost five years had gone by since the night of Angel's conception, so not one of the STGs in residence had been around back then. The members of the chapter were all smiles and helpfulness until they realized what I was digging for, then the smiles turned into smirks and the ranks closed. They obviously thought it was their duty to protect prior frat brothers from having anonymous babies pinned on them.

I had enough income for all the basics and a couple extras, but no budget for private investigators or paternity tests. With the frat guys stonewalling, my search had to be tabled.

It would be two years before I learned that after I left the STG house, phone calls went out to every brother who had been in residence five years earlier, warning them of the potential paternity suit that had just been escorted out the door. The plan was to give the alumni ample time to rewrite the past so each was innocent. The fuse on that bomb may have been two years long, but it eventually burned to its end and blew up in their faces.

"Are you *sure* I'm not a fairy?"

"Yes, I'm sure."

"Why?"

"Because I'm a mother and I know everything."

"Mommy, you do not know everything."

"Name one thing I don't know."

"You don't know the name of Stacy's new bunny."

"You mean Sir Crunchalot?"

Her eyes narrowed with suspicion as she tried to figure out how I knew the unknowable. I could have told her Katie had called the night before complaining that the new rabbit chewed everything—carrots, food pellets, even lettuce—with loud crunching sounds that she could hear all the way back in her bedroom. Hence the name. You may think it was unfair of me to let Angel believe I was omniscient, but if I had told her the truth, I would have had to tell her (in the interest of *full* disclosure) that Katie had also asked me if I knew a good recipe for hasenpfeffer.

Angel's first day of kindergarten was less than one week away when she told me she didn't want her wings covered up anymore. For some little girls, it's their hair or pretty clothes they are proud of and want to show off. For Angel, it was her fairy wings. Even though they were the same membranous flaps that had been on her back the day she was born, to Angel they were shimmering, gossamer flappers, like the wings on the fairy tale creatures in her books.

The wings were small, so the modifications for her school clothes were simple. I found a seamstress willing to put what amounted to two very long vertical buttonholes on the back of each blouse, shirt and dress. Realizing how cruel children can be, I figured exposing her wings would invite hateful comments—and I was right—but they only came from a few children. Most of the others, and the teachers, were fascinated by, interested in, or at the very least, immune to the fact that the little flaps poked out of the backs of Angel's tops and flared when she laughed. The few cruel taunts didn't appear to bother Angel at all. In fact, she told me in strict confidence that the other kids without wings were jealous of her.

She may not have been a fairy, but there was no doubt she was a princess. Her dresses and blouses had to have some kind of ribbon, ruffle or embroidery, and her wavy brown hair needed to be set off with barrettes, bows or headbands before she would put one foot out the door of our apartment. It was as if she felt the rest of her ensemble needed to match the beauty of the gossamer wings she believed she had growing out of her back.

Angel remained a girly girl and her flaps were fairy wings through kindergarten and the following summer. Then, when she was in first grade, she checked a book out of the library which contained a picture that shocked her out of her Hans Christian Andersen phase and launched her into her own personal Cretaceous period.

Children are, I think, the most skilled copers
(is that even a word?) on earth. I once knew a boy with a
lisp who studied the thesaurus every night, searching for
words without the letter S, so he could speak and not be
humiliated by constantly demonstrating his impediment.

Wendy, the girl who was my best friend in third
grade, was a bed-wetter. The first time I slept over at her
house I was half-wakened three times during the night by a
soft buzzing sound. When I asked her about it at school the
next day, she claimed not to have heard anything. Then
when she stayed over at my house the first time, I came
awake enough at the sound of the buzz to see her slip out of
my room and into the bathroom. A few moments later I
heard the flush and I feigned sleep as she crawled back into
bed. Two more times that night she got up. Several weeks
later, when Wendy was sure I wouldn't betray her, she told
me her shameful secret.

So, at age eight, this poor kid set a tiny alarm clock
to go off at midnight, two and four every night of her life.
She did it at sleepovers for the obvious reason, and at home
because her mother thought she wet the bed deliberately
and berated her for it every time it happened.

A third-grader, unable to seek psychological coun-
seling or get checked for possible organic sources of her
problem, is resourceful enough to come up with a fix that
salvages her pride, even if it doesn't deal in any way with
the underlying issues. Now *that's* impressive.

The most extreme childhood coping mechanism—

short of suicide, that is, which I consider more a surrender to horrific circumstances than an attempt to survive them— is multiple personality disorder, and it is almost always triggered by battering and sexual abuse. Rather than being the deliciously dramatic, half-crazy stuff of television and movies, MPD is really a creative and effective survival tool. By spreading the horror over several different people, the child makes bearable the unthinkable. Splitting out into multiple personalities also lets the child create a "protector" character to do the job the actual parents or caretakers are not doing.

Survival techniques like these are sometimes the child's only hope of living through truly grotesque circumstances. When the child grows up, however, and escapes the situation that necessitated development of the coping mechanism, he or she may be unwilling or unable to let go of the device that once prevented a slide into an abyss.

Some of us are fortunate. The survival skills we develop don't stand out and alarm people, but still have the power to get us through to the next day or hour or minute. And sometimes those skills may be capitalized on, rather than hidden or abandoned, once we outgrow the immediate need to survive.

For me it was numbers. More specifically, counting. From the moment I learned how to count to ten, I used numbers to calm myself, to get myself through to the other side of a bad incident. At first it was just counting to ten over and over. As I learned to count higher, though, merely *counting* didn't have the power to keep me safe, so I came up with counting patterns. Simple ones at first, then more complex. Counting by threes. Then counting ahead seven numbers, dropping back three, counting ahead another seven and continuing the stutter-step climb to safety. *One two three four five six seven four five six seven eight nine ten seven eight nine ten eleven twelve thirteen ten eleven twelve thirteen fourteen fifteen sixteen thirteen...* The more complex the pattern, the more engaged my mind, the more detached I was from reality, and the safer I felt.

My first calculator was a sanity-saving revelation. I could unobtrusively play with it and, as long as I kept a few books nearby, my parents assumed I was doing schoolwork. I built intricate numerical pyramids with that calculator, stretching my mental capacity, amusing myself, ensuring my emotional survival.

Here's one you can try out on a friend. Hand them a calculator and ask them to punch in this sequence: one-two-three-four-five-six-seven-nine. No eight. Then ask them to select any number from one to nine. Let's say they select seven. In your head you multiply seven by nine and get sixty-three. Tell them to multiply the original sequence by sixty-three. When they do, the display screen will show the number they selected—in this case seven—all the way across the screen. If you make sure the original sequence is correct, multiply their number choice by nine, then ask your friend to multiply the original sequence by the product of their chosen number and nine, the resulting pattern on the screen will *always* be an eight-digit string of the number they chose.

After developing numerous (ha!) exercises like that, I moved into numbers as words. It started when I realized the number sequence three-nine-one-three-five spelled the word *siege* when I turned the calculator upside down. From there I progressed to longer words—*water hoses*: five-three-five-zero-four-zero-two-four—then phrases—*high five*: five-one-four—and finally simple sentences—*I see*: three-three-five-one. My all-time favorite was the declarative sentence *"I ate two hogs."* I'll let you figure out how to do that one. Hint: you'll use seven digits.

Just as my protective walls grew thicker and taller when I added calculating to counting, they strengthened exponentially when I phased in computing. Numbers are virtually unlimited in the virtual world, as are the games, sequences and tricks you can make them do.

If counting was tryptophan, then calculating was marijuana and computing was heroin. My mantra was: stay cool, calm and collected with counting, calculating and computing.

All this is taking the long way around to explain why I became a CPA and why there are so many numbers in these pages. Even now, at forty-three, I am calmed by numbers; they make me feel safe.

Zero is *always* the painful starting point, the terror, so every number advancing away from zero is a step toward safety. Three may take me out of the immediate danger zone; oh, but eleven is a much more secure location. And since zero was the flashpoint, I inevitably counted up and away from it.

When I watched launchings from Cape Kennedy, the countdown to lift-off unnerved me. The roiling clouds of smoke, roaring engines, trembling rocket and falling-away support tower all symbolized for me the chaos waiting at the wrong end of any numerical sequence. Counting up is escape; counting down is an inexorable approach to a dark, terrifying place.

The creature that killed Hans Christian An-dersen with its bare hands (claws?) was a turkey-sized fly-ing reptile of the late Cretaceous Period called pteranodon. Pictures of its fossilized remains and a photo of a recon-struction—courtesy of the New York Museum of Natural History—appeared in a book called *Let's Visit the Dinosaurs* by Harvey C. Sharrett, which Angel brought home shortly after she entered first grade.

Turkey-sized is actually a bit misleading. If you served pteranodon for Thanksgiving dinner, there would be the usual number of drumsticks and the normal amount of breast meat, but anyone desiring a wing would have a twenty-five-foot span of finger-licking-good eating.

Angel was an average student, except for reading. When she began first grade, she was already reading at a fourth-grade level, something I attributed to her obsession with her wings.

Disappointed that I was not available twenty-four-seven-three-sixty-five to read to her, Angel had been forced to partner with *Sesame Street, The Electric Company,* the "Jamie Knows a Word" videos, and others so she could learn to read about her beloved sprites, elves, pixies and fairies. Oh, she still enjoyed attaching herself to me like a barnacle on the couch at night while I read her the adven-tures of Perian the elf king and his fairy queen Yanna for the one hundredth time, but by age four she could read that one all by herself, along with most of the more junior fairy tale books I had bought her.

I continually fed her reading habit, but it became harder and harder to find child-friendly versions of the classic tales. I don't know if the brothers Grimm took that last name before or after collecting their stories, but you would be hard-pressed to find darker concepts in the writings of Stephen King and Clive Barker. A boy buried alive in "The Stubborn Child" reaches his hand up from the grave, only to have it struck by his mother until he withdraws it back into the dirt. The twisted, incestuous king in "Thousand-furs" makes an erotic pursuit of his only daughter. A little girl guilty of nothing more than curiosity is burned to death in "Mother Trudy." A newly married queen roasts and eats her stepchildren while the king is off at war. Trust me, bad-dog Cujo has nothing on the giant slavering wolf in "The Hunter's Prey."

By omitting the rapes, murders and cutting-out-of-beating-hearts, I pared down the fairy tale reading to an amount Angel had mastered by the end of kindergarten. A child of two can hear *Good-night Moon* a gazillion times without getting tired of it, but an intelligent six year old who has read "Snow White and Rose Red" fifteen times gets restless and needs new stimuli.

So I was not surprised to see the half-dozen books she brought home from the library of her new school. There was a book on honey bees, a biography of Harriet Tubman, two Nancy Drews, a beginner's guide to origami and the previously mentioned book on dinosaurs.

That evening we dined at Gravitinos, a spaghetti joint in our neighborhood, celebrating her successful first week of first grade.

"Well, after five days what do you think of Miss Lerner?"

"She's *so* nice and she wears blouses with flowers on them and she lets us take the ferrets out and play with them at recess and their names are Hecky and Jecky. Hecky is the boy. And she is *so* pretty."

"Jecky?"

"Mom! I was talking about Miss Lerner."

"Sorry. I didn't mean to insult your ferret-loving, flower-wearing teacher."

Angel gave me a warning scowl, crunching down on a piece of garlic toast, dropping a gentle shower of buttery crumbs down into the ruffles on the front of her dress.

"She's nice and she's pretty. That's good." But my daughter was not inclined to rejoin a conversation with someone who could make light of her first teacher crush. I would have to use cagey mom skills to draw her back in.

"Is Miss Lerner prettier than I am?"

"You're not pretty," she responded matter-of-factly.

"Thank you very much. And did I mention you're paying for your own meal?"

"You know what I mean. Mom's aren't *supposed* to be pretty. They're just supposed to be moms."

"Where's that waiter? I may have a glass of wine after all."

She patted my hand, as if to reassure me that coming in second to Miss Lerner didn't mean I would lose *all* her affection. I waited until she was engaged in a struggle with a particularly large skein of spaghetti before surreptitiously wiping the garlic butter off the back of my hand.

After we walked home, I settled in to pay bills and Angel went to her bedroom to read. Ten minutes later she came charging back, frantically calling for me. I was out of my chair and halfway across the room when she thrust the book at me.

"Look! Wings like mine! Page eighteen. How do you say it, Mom? How do you say its name?"

I took the book from her trembling hands and saw my first pteranodon. I pronounced it for her, going by what I knew to be the pronunciation of ptomaine and pterodactyl, then we sat on the couch and read the text. Pressed up against my side as she was, Angel's quaking communicated itself to my own body, and we vibrated in sync through the paragraphs about pteranodon, her eyes never leaving the photo of the reconstructed flying reptile.

"They're like my wings," she breathed. "They look *exactly* the same."

Well, they certainly looked more like her tiny flaps than the wings of queen Yanna and her elf-king husband, but from the quavering of Angel's voice and the trembling of her hands, I knew she was having an epiphany. I noticed her own little wings were lifting and falling against her back in time with her rapid breaths. She wasn't happy or joyful; she was excited.

From that moment on, it was intensity of thought that caused her wings to pulse and flare, and almost overnight Angel morphed out of her babyish, girly ways and into a serious, focused child. She didn't deliberately set aside her frilly clothes and fairy-wing fantasies, she just left them behind. Her new obsession, though, was every bit as consuming as her old one. I finally had to buy Sharrett's book on dinosaurs for her, as the school librarian told her she couldn't check it out again after the fifth time.

Angel had previously shown only normal interest in using my computer, but suddenly it became a window onto information about pteranodon, and I had to set limits on her computer time. Over the next three years she was frequently exposed to online predators but, since they had all been extinct more than sixty million years, I didn't worry.

What excited Angel most about pteranodon was that it had flown without having the keel-like breast bone to which the powerful muscles of flight are attached in most birds. Dr. Whittaker had patiently answered her questions over the years about the possibility of flying, once showing her a diagram of a bird's skeleton compared to a child's skeleton. The narrow sternum of the child was the perfect construct for rib support, but looked flimsy compared to the proportionally larger plate-and-keel design of the bird's sternum. Even if Angel had had muscles leading to her wings (which she didn't), there was no underlying support system for them. The explanation had disappointed her, but she could see the logic in it when she compared the two skeletons.

Pteranodon didn't need the heavy breast keel because it didn't flap its wings to fly. It was a *glider*. Most likely getting a running start on the ground and heading down an incline, pteranodon would catch the slightest air current with its twelve-foot-long membranous wings and lift off. Angel had never truly given up the idea of flying, even in the face of Dr. W.'s skeletal demo, and now she had a bit of fuel to feed the flame of that desire. The fact that Angel's flaps were still only about three inches square was merely a technicality in her mind.

She would be nine years old before she gave up on pteranodon the same way she had let go of all the lovely flying pixies and fairies. In the intervening three years, she anxiously waited for her wings to grow into wide, reptilian gliders, sometimes trying to stretch them by reaching each hand over the top of the opposite shoulder, grabbing her little flaps, and pulling on them.

During those three years two men entered my life, one for an explosive short burst and the other for the long haul.

As a brand-new certified public accountant, I was hired by Kleinman, Schwartz, Merrick and Dodd, an accounting firm large enough to offer plenty of room for advancement. Nobody expected me to bring in new clients—doing scut work for the senior accountants was more what they wanted from entry-level people—but within two weeks, I had an appointment on the books with someone who had never done business with the firm before.

His name was Mark Dennison and he showed up for that first meeting with his fiancée. He and Sharon were set to be married in December—this was October—and they wanted to optimize the tax advantages marriage would bring them. They were a delightful couple to deal with and by the end of that first meeting I had been hired to research some tax loopholes they might be able to take advantage of before their wedding, and had a tentative offer to do their first joint return the following spring. We booked a second meeting for the next week, shook hands all around and said our good-byes.

My immediate supervisor was out on compassionate leave—I had not even met him yet—so I went to *his* supervisor to report my score. If Mr. Fletcher was surprised or impressed he didn't show it, but the next day I was asked to join Mr. Dodd, one of the partners, in his office where I was asked how I had managed to lure Mark Dennison in as a client. I told Mr. Dodd truthfully that Dennison had been a cold walk-in.

"So you've never met him before?"

When dealing with strait-laced guys like Mr. Dodd, I was always tempted to say things like, "Well, I may have boinked him that summer I worked as a carny stripper," but I resisted the urge for the sake of my job.

"No, sir. Should I have?"

"Not necessarily. But we've been trying to get his family's business for more than twelve years. His father won't budge from Bellingham and Carter and, up until now, the son has run all his work through them, too."

That's when I learned that the Dennison family was old money. So old it was *olde*. Mark's account alone would be a profitable addition to the rolls of Kleinman, Schwartz, Merrick and Dodd, and with the addition of Sharon Wells' current and future income management—it turned out she was the heiress to an armored car company fortune—they would be among the firm's top income-generating accounts. If I didn't screw up.

In retrospect, it was smart that I didn't make the carny stripper comment. Mr. Dodd had been sizing me up to decide if he felt comfortable letting me test the Dennison waters alone. I assured him things could not have gone better with the couple, and that I felt confident I would further cement the relationship at our next meeting. After having done some research late the previous evening, I discovered a perfectly legal way for Mark to shelter several hundred thousand dollars before the end of the year.

Mr. Dodd nodded his head thoughtfully, then said he was willing to let me proceed with Mark Dennison by myself.

"Mr. Evans will be back from leave next Monday. I will bring him up to speed on this, but I expect you to keep him posted about all the ongoing aspects of your dealings with Mr. Dennison."

"Of course."

"And if you should encounter even the smallest of roadblocks, let Mr. Evans know immediately."

"I will."

"If Mr. Evans should be, for any reason, not available, please call me and apprise me of the situation."

What is it about old guys that they need to hear the

word yes five different ways before they believe you understand them? I felt like a dried piece of chewing gum trying
to wrench itself off the bottom of a theater seat just getting
out of his office.

On Monday I arrived to find several not-so-subtle
changes in my office. My perfectly adequate chair had been
replaced with a leather executive chair and there was a
short, striped couch with side table and matching armchair
where the two client seats had been. A couple of serious
pieces of art now hung on the walls where the inexpensively
framed lithographs had been before. Soft light filtered
through the shade of what appeared to be a genuine Tiffany
lamp. A note on my desk said, "Miss Fitzgerald, let's put
our best foot forward for the Dennisons." It was signed,
Bradley M. Dodd, C.P.A. Surprisingly, the "o" in Dodd had
not been turned into a smiley face.

Like magic the scut work was absorbed by the rest
of the team, so I was able to focus on preparing for the next
day's meeting with Mark and Sharon. Shortly before lunch
a ghost popped into my office.

"Hi. I'm Charlie Evans."

I stood and put out my hand. "Allison Fitzgerald.
It's good to finally meet you, Mr. Evans."

"Charlie, please. I've decided to forego the whole
Mr. Evans thing until I become a partner."

"Right. Plenty of time to be a stodgy tight-ass then,
huh?"

It was only a small smile but it communicated that
he was amused rather than offended by the comment.

"They kind of are, aren't they? May I sit?"

I swept my hand toward the new furniture and he
sat down.

"Well, technically, I'm your supervisor, but rumor
has it you've already reeled in a very big fish all by your
lonesome."

"I'd love to take the credit, but I didn't even dangle
a hook in the water. That sucker flipped out of the lake and
landed right in my lap."

"Right-time, right-place scenario?"

"That's what I'm guessing."

"You have everything under control?"

"I'm pretty sure I do. The next meeting's tomorrow morning and I have a couple plans to show them, each of which could be very advantageous. And they're supposed to bring in the stuff I need to start preplanning their first joint return. Copies of everything are on your desk."

"Good. If you hit any snags or want to bounce an idea around, I'm always available." With that he stood and crossed to the door.

"Thanks, Charlie. I realize how important this is. You can assure Mr. Dodd I won't let the firm down."

"Oh, he already knows that. He believes in you."

"He said that?" I was genuinely surprised.

"Didn't have to," he replied, pointing toward my new lamp. "It took me three years to get one of those from the old tight-ass."

The ghost of Charlie Evans slipped through the door and out of my office.

From gossip in the break room, I already knew a few things about Charlie: he was thirty-one years old; he had a little boy named Nicholas; and his wife had been killed in a single-car crash six weeks earlier. Here's what I knew about him from that first encounter in my office: he was tall and gaunt, and he looked closer to forty than thirty. There were puffy pouches under his sad-looking eyes and he was working very hard to keep his grief from spilling out onto the people around him. His smile was forced, as was his "banter," but he seemed grateful to be treated normally, instead of as a fragile man who has suffered a devastating loss. I liked him.

Mark Dennison showed up alone for our meeting, saying something about a last-minute rescheduling of a dentist appointment for his fiancée. Nothing about that sounded strange and I laid out the two tax strategies I had researched, as a perky young woman ducked in and brought us coffee—another bit of insurance from Mr. Dodd, I assumed. It was after we had finished our coffee and Mark had given tentative go-aheads on the two tax proposals, pending Sharon's approval, of course, when I realized he was looking at me. Really *looking* at me. I may have then blushed or given some other indication of noticing how he was studying me, because he suddenly looked down, ostensibly to check the tax papers he held, and seemed slightly flustered. Under other circumstances I would have been both flattered and interested. Mark Dennison was wealthy, personable, and an easy eleven on the gorgeous meter. This was no ordinary boy-meets-girl scenario, however, and I did *not* want the situation to get sticky.

As a client, Mark was very likely my ticket to success. As a potential romantic interest, he was a minefield. I reminded myself that it had only been a look after all, and that I was most likely reading into it things that weren't there.

We finished up by briefly going over the information I would need to plan the combined filing for Sharon and Mark next year. I asked for another week to study the material, and we set up the next meeting. When we shook hands before he left, Mark held onto mine a little longer than necessary, long enough to look into my eyes and say quietly that he looked forward to seeing me again.

"And I'm looking forward to seeing both of you next time." I tried to smile warmly, efficiently and without any hint of come-on.

I thought about going to Charlie, but I didn't want to set off an alarm when the fire might only be in my imagination. How stupid would I sound implying a guy as rich, attractive and engaged as Mark Dennison was interested in me? Mr. Dodd might kick me off the account or, worse, he might tell me to seduce Mark to keep the account. I finally decided I wouldn't mention it to Charlie unless Mark showed up for the next meeting without his fiancée. That look had probably meant nothing.

So there I was, the queen of all numbers, and yet I somehow forgot that nothing *always* equals zero.

Midday Wednesday was quiet. Most of the employees had gone out to celebrate somebody named Bernie's fortieth birthday at a pizza parlor. I didn't know who Bernie was—although I had been asked to kick in five dollars for a gift—and I had not really had time to make any friends at the firm, so I stayed behind to eat in peace and do a little more work on the Dennison account.

I entered the break room with my lunch, where I found Charlie flipping through the Yellow Pages. He looked up in surprise.

"Oh, hi. I thought everybody went to Bernie's lunch thing."

"Turns out Pizza Hut was overbooked, so I volunteered to be bumped for ten bucks and two future pizzas of my choice. Is the smell of tuna going to bother you?"

"No. Sit, sit."

I sat at the table and unwrapped my lunch while Charlie continued paging through the phone book with a frustrated expression. It was obvious he could not find something he needed, but I wasn't sure if an offer of help would be welcome. Finally, though, he looked across at me.

"Allison, you have a child, don't you?" He asked the question hesitantly.

"Yes, a daughter."

"How old?"

Where was he going with this? "Angel is six."

"Does she still do the Halloween thing?"

"With a vengeance."

"Oh, good." He seemed very relieved. "Maybe you can help me then. Where do I rent a Halloween costume for my little boy? I've called three places and they all say they only carry adult sizes."

It was suddenly painfully apparent that Charlie's deceased wife must have handled the domestic side of their life and insulated Charlie from the niggling little things like Halloween costumes.

"How old is your son?"

"Nicky's four."

"And what does he want to be for Halloween?"

"Batman."

"Piece of cake. I know an exclusive boutique that'll have Batman costumes out the wazoo." He eagerly picked up a pen to jot down the name. "It's called Wal-Mart."

"Wal-Mart rents costumes?" Sadly, the surprise on his face was genuine.

"No, they sell them. Nobody rents kid's costumes; it's cheaper to buy."

"Huh. Who would've known?"

"Pretty much everyone else in the country." He smiled sheepishly and I could not help feeling protective of my poor boss as he took his first stumbling steps toward being a good parent.

I looked up at the sound of Mark Dennison's soft knock the next day and realized with a sinking heart that he had come alone again. He gave me a shy smile as he stepped inside, then asked if I minded if he closed the door. *One two three four five six seven eight...*

"It gets so stuffy in here, I'd rather leave it open." I hoped my tone was breezy enough not to offend him or to tip him off about how uncomfortable I was.

It seemed for a moment that he would still close the door to my office, but then he dropped his hand from the knob and crossed to the couch. I would have to speak to Charlie immediately after the meeting ended and get some advice about how to deal with the situation while it was still in the embryonic stage. As long as Mark didn't make an overt move and I didn't acknowledge that anything other than business was going on between us, we could both get out of this unscathed and I might not blow my big chance.

When he spoke, he did it quietly enough that no one walking past my office could possibly have heard.

"Allison, we need to talk."

One two three four five six seven eight... My heart was pounding and I was wishing I had asked Charlie to sit in on the meeting. I did *not* want to hear another word from this man, but I didn't know any way of saying that without risking losing the account. He must have taken my petrified silence as a willingness to hear him out. *Nine ten eleven twelve thirteen fourteen...*

"Seven years ago I was in residence at the Sigma Tau Gamma house at the university. I was there the night you were assaulted."

*Fifteen Sixteen Seventeen Eighteen...*I kept counting as I got up, crossed to the open door and gently closed it. I continued as I went back behind my desk and sat. Though we were safe from being overheard now, I spoke as softly as he had.

"Why are you here?"

Mark's eyes looked haunted and I could see he was trembling. "First, to say I'm sorry. I am *so* sorry. I have no excuse for what I did to you. There is no excuse. And the only explanation I can give for participating in such a truly despicable act is that I was twenty-one, privileged, and I thought I was untouchable."

He looked down at his hands, seemingly humiliated by his admission. It wasn't anger I felt; it was a flood of ugly memories from that terrible night so long ago.

"I was seventeen, intoxicated, and I thought I was worthless." I don't know if it was the words themselves or the pathetic image they portrayed, but his shoulders and chest made tiny, convulsive moves. He still didn't look up, but I saw tears dropping onto his crumpled hands.

"You said first. What was second?"

"What?" he asked, finally looking up at me.

"You said first you wanted to say you were sorry. That implies there is a second thing." He shook once in an effort to get himself back under control while I waited.

"I understand you became pregnant from the incident."

Reaching for the framed photo of Angel that I kept on my desk, I hesitated before turning it around. Mark moaned when he saw it and dropped his face into his hands. He quietly sobbed and I silently counted. By the time he pulled himself together enough to continue the conversation, I had counted myself into enough of a calm to continue it with him.

"The second thing is that I'm willing to take a DNA test."

The door stayed closed for more than an hour, and I'm sure people were beginning to wonder, but there was much for Mark and me to discuss. Among the first things I asked was how he knew my name to track me down. That's when I learned about the warning that had gone out two years earlier after my visit to the fraternity house. Phone calls were made to Mark and eight other men. *Jesus, could it really have been nine?* The event had been experienced in a drunken stupor and I had been suppressing the memories for seven years, so details like the number of participants were freshly horrifying.

Mark's remorse was genuine, so why had it taken him two years to come forward? He told me his response to the phone alert had been to set up a retroactive alibi for the night of the incident, as did most of the other alumni with whom he had contact. Once they were all sure they were covered in the event of an accusation, they went on with their lives as though nothing had ever happened.

That didn't really surprise me. What *would* have surprised me was learning that the same men who'd been willing participants in a gang bang had consciences that caused them to feel one fraction of the pain I had lived with so long.

"Six months ago, after Sharon and I got engaged, we had the 'full disclosure' conversation."

"You *told* her?"

"No, I wasn't even man enough to do that. The point of the talk was for each of us to be completely honest about any baggage we were bringing to the relationship, but I rationalized not telling her because I had ensured it could never resurface in my life and impact the two of us. I'm sorry; this must be hurtful to hear."

It *was* hurtful to hear that a life-changing event for me could have been so insignificant to the others involved, only a detail to be "taken care of" and forgotten. I wanted to know how Mark had come to this moment where he now felt the mirror image of the guilt and pain I had carried all these years.

Sharon Wells had taken the soul-baring conversation much more seriously than had Mark, and she disclosed that she had been raped while still in college. Nothing about her demeanor or behavior had ever given him reason to suspect her life had been anything less than privileged perfection. Watching her break down as she described the attack and the emotional damage it had caused her, Mark felt helpless. When he asked her why she had not reported the rape to the police, she laughed. He was stunned. As a young lawyer, he believed in the rightness and near infallibility of our legal system, so he was not prepared for her to tell him she had made the same choice many women make after an attack. She had opted not to risk being re-raped by the police taking down her "allegation," submitting to the violation of an exam so that graphic descriptions of her bruised and torn parts could be entered into a trial transcript, and then being humiliated by the questions of an aggressive defense attorney—not only about exactly when her panties were torn off, but also how hard she tried to fight off her attacker, and what precisely was his penis shoved into and when. And that would be the prelude to innuendo about her prior sexual partners and experience. All of this would have played out in front of however many people were in the courtroom, presumably quite a few in addition to the press, since she was the only daughter of a wealthy and powerful man.

Mark had never heard the woman he loved speak with such bitterness. He felt hatred for the worthless piece of shit who had caused Sharon such shame and pain, then gotten away with it. And for the first time, he felt he had more than an abstract understanding of the consequences of a sexual assault. An airplane crash is only another news headline unless someone you love is in 14-C when the plane goes down.

That night Mark had been unable to sleep, knowing he was no better than the stranger who had raped Sharon. Mark was walking around freely, had suffered absolutely no consequences from his participation in an assault on an underage female who had been plied with alcohol until she was incoherent, and had even been prepared to lie to make himself appear to be the victim of a false accusation in the event that poor girl ever got up the nerve to seek justice.

For all Mark knew, Sharon's rapist could be doing the same thing. He might be eating in the same restaurants, playing golf at the same club, attending the same fundraisers and social events as Mark. Who would know? Not one person in a million would guess Mark Dennison was capable of committing a sexual assault and then strolling away to his successful future without even a glance back at the little rag doll who had been hustled out of the house as soon as enough coffee had been poured into her to enable her to stagger to the prepaid taxi the frat brothers had thoughtfully called for her.

It had taken him two more sleepless nights to work up the courage to tell Sharon everything, and he half expected her to call off their engagement. Once again, however, this young woman he had believed he knew so well surprised him. She let the engagement stand, conditional on his finding a way to make at least partial restitution.

He had traced me through a private investigator, and was trying to find a nonthreatening way to approach me, when I was hired at Kleinman. Sharon came up with the idea of calling on me as prospective clients, going with Mark to the first meeting because he was afraid to face me alone. Then she told him he had to do the rest by himself.

And just like that, my brilliant score didn't seem so brilliant anymore. They hadn't sought me out because I was a savvy accountant; it was only a way for Mark to get close enough to be forgiven for his sins. No wonder Mr. Dodd had been so inquisitive about how I had brought in

Dennison and Wells. They could afford the best—hell, he already *had* the best, Bellingham and Carter, the most successful accounting firm in the city—so why would he seek out this entry-level accountant at Kleinman, Schwartz, Merrick and Dodd? Well, now I knew exactly why, and I would have to think of a way to explain losing the account as mysteriously as it appeared to everyone I had acquired it. And how had I convinced myself that I had won them over by uncovering those tricky little loopholes? Had I really thought his father's accountants didn't know all those obscure tax maneuvers?

Mark had answered all my questions, and I believed he had answered them truthfully and completely. Now it was his turn to ask me a question.

"Did you have anything in particular in mind when you went to the Sigma Tau house?" I must have looked surprised, because he hastily clarified. "The second time, I mean."

"I wanted to find Angel's biological father." It was the first time her name had been spoken in the room, and it hung there, personalizing the situation even more painfully for him.

"Don't worry," I said. "I'm not looking for a pipeline to your family's fortune."

"Oh, God, no! I didn't mean..." He was embarrassed again and, in all fairness, I had spoken with anger and defensiveness. "I just wanted to know what you would, I don't know, think was fair or right or something if it turns out I'm her, uh. I mean if I'm the one."

He was trying so hard to put right what could never be changed, and I couldn't hate him. It was time for me to suck it up and cut him the slack I thought he probably did deserve.

"Look, Mark, apparently there's only a one-in-nine chance you're the bio-dad to begin with. And even if it turns out you are, I'm not going to cause any trouble. I'm making a good salary now, so I'm not trying to leech off anyone else. All I ever wanted was for my little girl to know who her father is."

We worked out the practicalities of the DNA test,

and he assured me the lab he used would be discreet. I only realized after we had shaken hands and he had gone, that he meant it as a reassurance of *my* privacy and protection, not his own.

My nerves were too frayed for me to begin formulating the story I would tell Mr. Dodd when he asked me how I had let Dennison and Wells slip away. I decided to go out for lunch, as much to avoid having to talk to anyone in the firm as to get myself calm. I picked a Chinese restaurant because, usually at those places, you can order from the menu by numbers. Hey, every little bit helps.

I felt tired and unravelled after lunch, so I stuck to my office, marking time until I could go home and think everything through. About four-fifteen, as I was staring at the wall clock, wondering if the minute hand would ever move, my boss appeared in the doorway giving me two thumbs up and as sincere a smile as a ghost can manage.

"You were right about that little costume boutique."

I was happy to be distracted, and relieved he hadn't come by to ask how the meeting had gone.

"So you got Batman all kitted out, then?"

"Well, once we got there he changed his mind about Batman. Decided to go as an actual bat."

"At least your kid wants to be a mammal. Mine's going as a flying reptile."

My confused mood lifted. Charlie had made his way to my couch and flopped down on it, and suddenly we were nothing more than two single parents sharing funny stories about our kids. And five o'clock came in about ten minutes.

The following week I learned two things: one, that Charlie didn't have a clue about the dos and don'ts of trick-or-treating and two, that Mark Dennison was *not* the biological father.

After advising Charlie not to let Nicky eat anything that wasn't in its original wrapper, and telling him to hold Nicky's hand all the way up to every single door, I finally asked him to join Katie and me as we made our annual gleaning of the simple carbohydrates. Joshua, Katie's youngest, was nearly four, so I figured he and Nicky would hit it off. As always, Stacy and Angel would be paired up. Katie's oldest three, all boys, would be along for the candy haul, not the companionship. Halloween fell on a Friday that year, so Pete wouldn't be joining us—her husband still worked the second shift because it paid better—and Charlie would be able to learn the ropes without too much pressure.

I had told Katie about Charlie's recent loss, and she just folded him into the group in a way that precluded any awkwardness on his part. ("Here, Charlie, hold this while I tie his shoe." "Charlie, would you run up there and tell Joey to get back here and stay with the group.") He was made to feel included and useful. Seeing him relax during our two-hour walkabout, I realized how tense he must have been, worrying that he would mishandle Nicky's first motherless Halloween.

The surprise was that Nicky and Joshua did not automatically buddy up. Josh was frightened by all those witches, skeletons and vampires that kept racing by, trying to load grocery store-sized paper bags before the freebies started drying up around nine or nine-thirty. The year before he had been too young to have a clear understanding of what was going on, and the following Halloween he'd be elbowing his older brothers aside to be the first to the doorbells, but that first year Charlie and Nicky joined us, Josh was clingy and not very sociable. He rode Katie's hip most of the time, hiding his face in her neck when some sweet-looking older lady commented on how very realistic his lightsaber looked.

Stacy and Angel kept some distance between them, as Stacy was still in the princessy stage, while Angel had fully embraced her inner reptile. Stacy was worried the pteranodon wings would snag her frothy tutu. Pete had cleverly built them with two pull cords that Angel could yank on when she wanted the Naugahyde flappers to extend out to their full span of three-and-a-half feet.

Nicky and Angel were the odd couple of the evening. She lorded it over him a bit, as her custom-made dinosaur wings put his Wal-Mart bat wings to shame. Rather than being intimidated, Nicky was fascinated with her costume, inspiring her to flap open her fake wings even when she wasn't trying to hustle a little something extra from a candy pusher.

Angel bossed Nicky around—not in a patronizing or mean way, but in an almost parental style—especially when she saw he was not going to seriously challenge her in the wing department. Only four, he was too young to harbor any aspirations toward alpha maleness, so he didn't chafe at the bossing. In fact, the little guy seemed to welcome it. I think Nicky had been rudderless since his mother's death, especially with Charlie walking on eggs all the time for fear of further scarring his son. Angel showed him the correct way to hold his bat-embellished plastic pumpkin so that none of the precious cargo spilled, and Nicky, assuming she had been around the Halloween block a time or two and knew what she was doing, eagerly followed her instructions. When a plastic skeleton alongside a path leading up to a house suddenly rattled its bony arms and made a ghostly moan, the boy flinched, so Angel took his hand and led him

on toward the candy grail. As she did, we heard her say the
skeleton had frightened her, too, when she was his age.
Charlie and I exchanged an amused glance as she went on
to assure him he'd be used to all this by next Halloween.

Back at Katie's, the three oldest fled to their room
to gorge and play video games. Once Angel's pteranodon
wings had been shed, she and Stacy were best friends again
and they sat together comparing and swapping their stash.
Joshua and Nicky were both so worn out from excitement
that even the sugar high couldn't keep them awake. Not
sure of the protocol, Charlie was about to leave with his
half-asleep son, but Katie put the two boys in Josh's bed
and announced it was time for the grown-ups to have some
treats.

When Pete got in around eleven-thirty, Charlie and
Katie and I were still at the dining room table, piles of pis-
tachio shells scattered around an almost-drained bottle of
wine. Pete cracked open a second bottle and the four of us
sat up talking until after one.

It was the first time Charlie had socialized with
anyone since his wife's death, and he told me much later it
was the first night he felt he might one day be a halfway
decent single parent. And later I realized Halloween had
been the night when Charlie Evans stopped embracing his
ghost-hood and began the long process of reclaiming his life.

The night was good for me, too, a much-needed dis-
traction. Earlier that day Mark Dennison and Sharon
Wells had come to my office with the sealed DNA results.
We opened the envelope together and saw the data that
ruled out Mark as Angel's father. I thought we'd have a
cordial handshake and they would walk out of my life, but
this surprising couple kept on surprising. Mark asked my
permission to call the rest of the possibles on my behalf and
see if he could persuade any of them to submit voluntarily
to testing. I didn't think he would have any more luck than
I had, but I thanked him for being willing to try and gave
him my blessing.

Sharon then asked if I had looked over her finan-
cials for next year's filing. I was stunned.

"You're staying?"

"Unless you'll be uncomfortable having us on your client roster."

I looked at Mark. His smile wasn't pitying or in the least bit noblesse oblige, but I still could not believe it.

"Look, if you're doing this out of some sense of guilt or obligation, you really don't have to." I looked straight at Mark. "And I can't guarantee I'll find every microscopic tax advantage your father's accountants would."

"Probably not. They're real barracudas," he replied.

"Not to mention boring old farts," Sharon added. "I'll trade the couple extra dollars they might save us for the advantage of having someone young and hungry on our side. Assuming you still want to handle our accounts."

I had been so close to going to Charlie before the meeting, to notify him about the imminent departure of Wells and Dennison from our firm. The only reason I had not was that Charlie was going trick-or-treating with us that night, and I didn't want to upset him before his public debut as a single dad.

I still had no idea who Angel's father was, but I did know Mark was a decent man who would continue his self-imposed penance by trying to find out.

Angel remained fixated on pteranodon for the rest of first grade, then all through second and third. I kidded her about Stacy being her BMF—best mammalian friend—while pteranodon, or "Pterry", as we had started calling it, was her BRF. She hung in there, waiting for her wings to grow large enough to catch the air currents and glide through the clouds. She had faith, in spite of Dr. Whittaker's scientific explanations of the impossibility of it ever happening, despite the fact that her flaps remained tiny, growing only marginally larger with her own childhood growth spurts, and despite the knowledge that all her flaps ever did was lift slightly and flare out when she was intensely focused on something. She believed with all her heart she would fly one day.

The summer she turned nine, that summer between third and fourth grade, Angel's life changed dramatically. One Saturday I couldn't find her after I had put lunch on the table. She didn't answer me when I called, so I stepped into the backyard to look for her. She wasn't on the swing set or trampoline, but I shouted her name again anyway.

"Angel!"

"I'm up here."

I followed her calm voice with my eyes, then staggered to one side and had to grab a crossbar of the swing. Angel was sitting on the peak of the garage roof. My heart raced as I realized first, that she was sitting sideways on the roof peak—if she had been straddling it, I would have at least felt she was safe from slipping down and off before I could get to her—and second, that there wasn't a ladder propped against the back or sides of the garage.

"Please don't move, Angel," I managed to choke out through a suddenly dry mouth. "How did you get all the way up there?"

"I flew." She said it so calmly, so matter-of-factly as she gazed up at the sky, I was afraid she would stand and sail out into the air.

"You *flew?* Are you sure?"

After a pause, her shoulders sagged and she looked away from the sky and down at me. When she finally spoke she sounded weak and sad.

"The ladder's in front."

I raced around to the front of the garage and found Charlie's ten-foot ladder leaned up against the small space between the open roll door and the edge of the roof. I checked that the feet were set securely, then climbed as quickly as I could. From the top of the ladder I could see down the roof line where Angel still sat sideways, now with her arms folded onto her knees and her face down on her arms, a picture of desolation. I prayed the traction of her tennis shoes on the shingles would be enough to prevent her sliding off before I got to her.

After hauling myself over the roof edge on my side, I didn't even try to stand. I straddled the peak, then scooted myself a few inches at a time toward my daughter. As much as I wanted to start counting so I could quit shaking and concentrate on getting to Angel, it was more important for her to stay calm than me.

"Stay right there, kiddo, I'm coming. A few more feet and I'll be there. Good thing I have jeans on; this roof is ro-ough." I tried to sound relaxed, almost sing-songy. The last thing I wanted was for her to hear anything in my voice that would indicate she was in trouble. So, I babbled, hoping even ridiculous words, said calmly enough, would spin out like a silken rope and hold her tightly until I got to her.

"Wow, you can see right into that bird's nest in the tree. Pretty great view from here. I should get Charlie to move some lawn chairs up."

When I was finally close enough to grab Angel and pull her to me, I gathered her in, my chin snugging down over the top of her head to pin it to my chest, one arm snaking around her waist, the other scooping under her knees. She folded herself against me and began quaking with sobs.

"I'm never going to fly, am I? These stupid wings are useless. And they're ugly! I hate them, Mom. I really, really hate them!"

I rocked her and soothed her as she cried out the loss of nine years' worth of hopes and dreams. She cried out the betrayal she felt, first from the fairies and pixies who had promised her gossamer wings to let her flit through enchanted forests, and now from Pterry, who had made her believe she could one day soar through the sky on powerful, leathery gliders.

If I had any doubt about the depth of her loss, the intensity of her emotions, I had only to look down over her shoulders where her tiny, useless wings slapped frantically against her back, three or four beats a second.

The Sharrett book went up on a shelf in her room where it remained untouched for the next nine years, and pteranodon was not mentioned again in our house. That Halloween, Angel went as Abe Lincoln.

What had triggered her disillusionment?

If there was one galvanizing incident or realization, Angel never shared it with me. More likely it had been the cumulative effect of three years' of tumult and upheaval in her life.

Not all the upheaval had been bad. Charlie's and my wedding day had been a joyful day for everyone. Katie was my matron of honor, with Brian flying in from San Francisco to be a "bridesman"—at least he wore a tuxedo and didn't insist on the same pale peach gown Katie and Charlie's sister wore—and Angel was the flower girl. After the fact, we all referred to Nicky as the ring dropper, as our six-year-old ring bearer had been unable to keep that band of gold on its little satin pillow for more than three steps at a time as he walked down the aisle.

By the time we got married, Angel adored Charlie. She decided the wedding officially entitled her to call him Daddy and he could not have been happier about it. She had become close with Nicky during the year after Charlie began dating again, acting as my co-babysitter when he was out with someone. Katie and I had been Charlie's wardrobe advisors, post-date analysis team, cheering squad, sounding board and shoulders to cry on after he bravely reentered the dating game. He won some rounds, lost some rounds, but never came up a big winner. Not one of the women he went out with ever made it far enough to be introduced to Nicky.

It was Katie who finally pointed out to him that he was just floundering around. She advised him to take some time off from dating so he could figure out what he was really looking for, then target only women who had the potential to fill those needs. He agreed it was a good idea, and three weeks later he walked into my office, took my hand and gently pulled me to my feet. There was no declaration of undying love, no passionate kiss. Charlie simply folded himself around me with his chin snugged over the top of my head. As I put my arms around him and pressed my cheek against his chest, I felt completely safe for the first time in my life.

Our first official date was my first date ever—unless you count going to the prom with a gay boy when you're seven months pregnant a date—and it was as romantic a first date and as sweet a first kiss as I could have fantasized about as a high school girl. It took less than a year for our two families to blend seamlessly, so the wedding was only a formality everyone wanted to experience.

Never having had a father, a sibling or grandparents, Angel was ecstatic that saying some words at a fancy party could provide her with a real dad and a little brother who adored her all at once. And when she learned ten months later that she and Nicky were going to have a baby sister, her life seemed perfect. Except for having wings that couldn't fly.

Maybe because every other thing in her life was

changing and moving forward, Angel became acutely aware
that her wings were the same useless appendages they had
always been. Maybe up on the garage roof Angel finally
accepted the reality that she would never fly. I don't know.
I only know that something broke in her that day.

From then on, Angel wanted her wings covered up.
Of course, their flaring was a problem, so she began wearing Lycra halters that were like sports bras without the
cups, and these kept the flaps inert under her clothes. Her
wings had never been a daily topic of conversation around
our house, but now they were never mentioned at all. She
was old enough to shower and dress by herself, so it was as
though they had disappeared. Nicky had the hardest time
putting her wings out of his mind; he had always loved
them, and liked to try to grab them when they were rapidly
slapping against her back.

The day I climbed up onto the garage roof to bring
my Angel back down to earth I was five months pregnant.
The distractions of my job, my family, a baby on the way
and a child in crisis fully engaged my brain. If somewhere
inside I remembered that first look into Angel's eyes, that
belief I would see her fly, the memory had been obfuscated
and supplanted by the practicalities of real life. It had been
a long time since I seriously thought those first feelings
about Angel were true visions.

When Charlie and I discussed the situation a short
while later, *I* was the one to suggest the surgical removal of
the wings. The two of us contacted Dr. Whittaker, and he
referred us to a plastic surgeon with whom we scheduled a
consultation before talking to Angel about a possible future
without wings.

After watching her slink around for months with
her wings hidden, after being warned with a hard look if
one of us so much as mentioned their existence, we were not
prepared for the vehemence of her objection to having them
removed. We had laid out the surgical solution obliquely
and sensitively, but the moment she understood what I was
suggesting, and what Charlie was supporting, Angel burst
into tears and shouted at us that she would run away before
she let anyone cut off her wings. She slammed her bedroom

door shut before Charlie and I could react.

Charlie called to cancel the presurgery exam we had scheduled, and I went to assure Angel we would never force her to give up her wings. I held her, rocked her, soothed her, all the time remaining puzzled by the contrast between her actions over the previous months and her true feelings about the wings.

Late that night I woke up with the answer. Just because you lack the ability to be a prima ballerina, you don't let somebody cut off your nondancing feet.

Mark Dennison had been true to his word. In the twelve weeks following his own paternity screening, he persuaded three of the other eight men to submit to DNA tests voluntarily and, when those turned up negative, he went after the remaining five.

Three of those five eventually caved under pressure from the national Sigma Tau Gamma organization, which, understandably, wanted to avoid the public disclosure of a crime having been committed at one of their chapters. Again the results were negative.

Eight months after the process of elimination began with Mark, two men remained untested. One was a money manager at a large investment company, one was a gastro-enterologist, and they both flatly denied they had been part of the original incident and refused to be tested. When threatened with legal action—predicated on the deliberate cover-up, which was still within the statute of limitations— both men challenged Mark to go ahead and try. They were confident they had rewritten the past skillfully enough to avoid any prosecution.

Since I wasn't looking to make the results part of a paternity suit, Mark felt he could employ methods which might not hold up to rigorous legal scrutiny. To that end he exerted pressure on the money manager by going over the guy's head, dangling a chunk of the Dennison fortune in front of the owners of the company, then withdrawing it when he "discovered" one of their key people was a man he had had a problem with back in college. As expected, the man's bosses, desperate to have a crack at the portfolio, pressured him into making nice with Mark. Alone with the guy, Mark made it clear what constituted making nice in his book. The test was negative.

And then there was one. After failing to persuade the ninth man—the gastroenterologist—to cooperate, Mark finally acquired the DNA illegally, bribing the hygienist at the man's dentist's office.

Each time results came back, Mark brought them to me still sealed, then left. That final time I asked him to stay while I opened them, as we both assumed we had come to the end of our search. And, of course, the end of Mark's penance. I opened the envelope to find the results were once again negative. Not one of the nine men who had been my collective "first" was Angel's biological father. I had been a virgin before that night at the fraternity house and a celibate afterwards.

"I don't understand," I said. "Is there a chance the lab made a mistake? Maybe not with this one, but with one of the others?"

He looked miserable. "I don't think so."

"Then how? Immaculate conception?"

"There's another possibility."

"What?"

Mark looked embarrassed, and I could tell he was reluctant to say whatever was coming next.

"What could possibly be worse than knowing I had sex with nine strangers while I was drunk?"

"There might have been others." He couldn't even look at me when he said it.

"Others," I echoed, stunned. "I thought we had a complete list of brothers in residence at the time."

"We did. But sometimes in a frat house there are visitors. Alumni are always welcome to spend a night or two. A brother will occasionally have a friend stay over. Or a friend of a friend." His voice trailed off.

"Oh, my God."

"There wouldn't be a record of who else was in the house at the time."

I slumped down in defeat, still trying to absorb the

idea that there was no way even to guess at how many had participated. I shuddered.

"Look, Allison, this isn't necessarily a dead end. I could go back and talk to everyone again. See if someone remembers any—"

"No," I cut him off. "No. I'm not going to let my life continue to be an episode of the *Maury Show*. Today it ends."

"I'm sorry."

"Don't be. You've already done so much to try to find the answer for me."

"I don't mean just about not finding Angel's father. I mean about, well, originally."

"Twenty-one is young and reckless. Seventeen even more so. We made mistakes; we survived. I promise you I have no anger or resentment toward you."

"If there is anything, and I mean *anything*, Sharon or I can ever do to help you, please call on us."

I knew he was sincere, but I was done with asking him to help me. From now on we would only see each other once or twice a year and it would be strictly business.

Angel had been asking me for some time who her father was, and I had assured her I was trying to track him down. Finally, I had to tell her we were never going to find him.

"Do you think he's dead?"

"It's possible, but I don't think so."

"Did he not like me?"

"Oh, sweetie, he didn't even know you existed. If he had, he would have loved you very much."

"Did he not like *you*?"

"Unfortunately, he didn't know *I* existed either."

Angel nodded thoughtfully, not as if the concept confused her, but as if she were mulling it over carefully.

"You know who I like?"

"Who?" I asked.

"Charlie."

"Now that is a coincidence. I like him, too."

That was our last conversation about her biological father. Maybe I underestimated the impact of learning so young that she would never have a "real" father. Maybe—if only in a small way—the disappointment of not knowing her other parent dovetailed into the disappointment in her wings, contributing to her rooftop meltdown a year later.

Shelby Leigh was born in November, and Charlie encouraged me to cut back on work hours. Kleinman and company had long since bumped me up to supervisor of my own small group of neophyte accountants, feeling I was key to holding onto the Dennison account, and wanting to keep me happy with generous raises and bonuses. Charlie was by then perched on a secure rung of the corporate ladder just below partnership, so we were doing well enough for me to relax a little. I began working one day a week at the office, and three days at home. It was nice to spend time with the new baby, time I had not had with Angel.

I was twenty-eight years old and I had a beautiful home, a great job, three wonderful children and a husband who made me feel cherished and safe. After a long, rocky start my life had acquired a comforting normality.

It lasted three years.

Those three years brought changes to each one of us, but they were, for the most part, gradual and positive changes.

Shelby blossomed into a playful, happy toddler with Charlie's soulful eyes, my full pouty lips, the same brunette curls as Angel, and with Nicky's dislike of anything green besides frosting. Her personality, however, was all Shelby. She was loving and accommodating, but she was nobody's doormat.

Nicky joined a soccer team when he was eight, and showed an immediate talent for the game. I don't think Charlie missed a single match over the following two years. Nicky still adored his big sister, although as Angel neared twelve she had less tolerance for his hanging around, and was relieved when soccer began taking up more of his time.

Angel's grades came up and stayed up, something I attributed to her decreasing focus on her wings. Without those fairies and dinosaurs occupying most of her thoughts, there was finally enough brainage left over for school work.

Charlie, who had been such a ghost when I first met him, thrived in his father role. From a man who believed children's Halloween costumes were rentals, he had evolved into the superdad who could braid hair and tie bows just as well as he could patch bicycle tires and play video games.

As for me, I savored those peaceful, happy times, but probably not nearly as much as I would have if I had only known that first the peace would disappear, then the happy.

One of the great things about Charlie was that he made sure he spent alone time with each child, forming a special, individual bond outside of the general family dynamic. With Nicky it was soccer practice. Shelby was his regular assistant when he made the Friday night pizza run, and they always got there early enough to share a soda and gossip while waiting for the order to come up. He had a movie date with Angel once a month, and it always tickled me to hear him discussing the latest teen flick with her, analyzing and debating the finer points of each movie as though he were dissecting a Truffaut or Kurosawa film. In other words, he took it as seriously as she did.

That was Charlie's everyday approach to being a dad. On special occasions, though, he always found a way to heighten the experience for the child involved.

Angel's twelfth birthday was approaching, and she and I were planning a Saturday afternoon pool party for her and fourteen of her closest friends. Charlie, meanwhile, was doing his own secret planning. He wouldn't even tell me what his surprise was, claiming I was a security risk. All Angel and I could get out of him was that he would take off from work come Friday—the day before her big party—and the two of them would be leaving on a little adventure. No amount of cajoling on my part could get anything more out of him than that she needed to be ready to leave at seven in the morning and the two of them would be back by late afternoon.

I could tell the outing had been a success when they pulled into the driveway. The car had barely come to a stop when Angel catapulted out of her side and began running toward the house, calling for me. I could see something in her right hand, and I figured it must have been one heck of a gift to get that kind of reaction from our ordinarily composed preteen girl.

She nearly crashed into me as I stepped out the front door.

"Mom! Mom! I know what I want for Christmas!"

"Thank God! I hate last-minute shopping and it *is* already June."

"Look at the pictures," she said, waving a handful of

photos in front of my face. Taking them, I noticed Charlie sauntering toward us, a big satisfied grin on his face.

"I went hang gliding! It was awesome! It was like flying. Like I always knew it would be."

I looked at the photos, which had obviously been taken by a camera fixed to some part of the hang glider. They showed Angel in goggles and a helmet, strapped into the apparatus and stretched out prone in the air. A few inches above her was a man—presumably an instructor—in similar gear and positioned as she was. Behind them in each photo was a different aerial vista.

Charlie got to the porch before I had looked at all ten shots.

"I took some with my own camera, too. The plane towing her into the air, the landing, the UFO that almost sucked her up."

But Angel wasn't even listening to him.

"Can I have lessons, Mom? Please? The brochure says most people can solo after five or six tandem flights."

"Do I have to give an answer right now? I mean, I'd like to talk it over with your dad first."

"I know they're probably expensive, but I won't ask for anything else, I swear. Not until I'm at least..."

"Forty?"

"I was going to say fifteen."

"Give me the brochure and I'll look it over after your party."

"Dad has it," she said, taking off into the house and calling for her brother. "Nicky! Guess what I did?"

Charlie sheepishly handed me a trifold brochure. "I was pretty sure she'd like it, but I had no idea she would go nuts like this."

"Are you kidding? You tapped into the mother lode of all her fantasies."

The pool party was a success in my opinion. No one drowned; no one cried; nobody got into a snit. But all Angel talked about the whole time was her hang gliding the day before. And though she squealed with delight when she opened my gift to her—quarter-carat diamond ear studs she had been eyeing at the mall a few weeks earlier—I knew it was Charlie's gift that had rocked her birthday world.

He and I discussed the lessons and, although they were a hundred seventy-five dollars each, we decided we could afford them. The biggest hurdle was that the hang gliding place was a two-and-a-half-hour drive away, so if we gave her this as a Christmas gift, I would be driving five hours each time Angel had a lesson. Shelby would be old enough for pre-K by then, so we decided to go ahead.

Angel's one dream her whole life had been to fly. Maybe hang gliding would be able to soften her three-year-long disappointment in her own wings.

We told her Sunday night she would get the hang gliding lessons for Christmas, with all the usual parental caveats about grades, chores and behavior. She pronounced us the winners of the best-parents-in-the-world award, then darted out of the room to call all her friends and tell them the news.

Parenting 101: never promise your child something you cannot deliver.

When I called the hang gliding place the following morning to inquire about any package deals they might have on lessons, I was told they wouldn't instruct anyone under the age of sixteen. Angel was welcome to come back and take as many tandem rides as she liked, but would have to wait four years to train for a solo flight. When I told him most *thoughtful* businessmen would have included that detail in their brochure, he snottily responded that most *responsible* mothers wouldn't want their twelve year olds flying around the sky on their own.

I waited until the next weekend to tell Angel, and she was, as expected, crushed. I found myself wishing she would hurry up and discover boys, as even the angst and drama of adolescent crushes was preferable to her obsession with flying. Her mood stayed subdued for six weeks, partly because she was embarrassed at having made such a big deal about the lessons with her friends.

Then, about two months after her birthday, Angel's outlook darkened dramatically. She was suddenly snappish with Nicky, impatient with Shelby, sullen with Charlie, and downright bitchy to me. And when I went into her room one afternoon to put away laundry, I found her curled up on her bed, weeping. I hoped the sadness would pass, as with her previous disappointments, but I had completely misread the situation.

The morning after I'd discovered her crying, she waited to come down from her room until she heard Charlie leave for work with Nicky, who was being dropped off at a friend's house for the day. Shelby had already eaten breakfast and was happily singing to her three favorite stuffed animals in the next room. I was washing breakfast dishes when Angel came slinking into the kitchen looking pale and jangled. She came up behind me, putting her arms around my waist and leaning her head against my back, a taller version of the way she used to hug my knees and press her face into the backs of my thighs when she was a little girl and needed me.

"Mom?" She said it so softly I had to turn off the water to hear what came next. "I think I got my period."

And she erupted into tears again. We had long since had "the talk," and she knew what to expect—in the abstract—but the reality of that first time bewildered her. We got her set up with everything she would need for the next few days, making a drugstore run for sanitary products and an over-the-counter remedy for cramps. In the car on the way back to the house, she made me promise not to tell Charlie. The entire situation seemed to cause her acute embarrassment, which I hoped would lessen over the new school year when, presumably, most of her friends would be going through the same thing.

By November she had developed enough for a first bra-buying expedition, as the Lycra halters weren't able to do the job anymore. I was forbidden to come into the fitting room with her, although I was allowed to give opinions about bras while they were still on hangers and, of course, to pay for them.

By December Angel had sprouted her first pimples, tiny and sparse in the eyes of all but their host. To her they were craters, volcanoes, the end of civilization as she knew it, so all she wanted for Christmas was an expensive skin-clearing system she had seen advertised. It was endorsed by an older teen girl who acted in a television series Angel liked, so she was certain it would work. Charlie and I were skeptical, but since the distractions of puberty had pulled her focus off flying, we bought the stuff and hoped for the best.

By February the skin program had done its job. Angel's skin was mostly clear and smooth again, with only the occasional Krakatoa to send her rushing to the mirror and dabbing on two or three additional blemish creams.

Everything appeared to be progressing normally: the periods, the budding breasts, her complexion. So I was surprised when Angel nervously approached me one Saturday morning after Charlie and Shelby had gone with Nicky to a soccer game.

"Mom?"

"Sí?"

"Uh... I think I have a problem."

From her tone I knew this was more serious than a homework issue. "Are you all right?"

"There's something wrong with my wings."

19

We went back to her room, where she took off her shirt with her back to me. The band and straps of the bra pinned her wings to her back in the same way the halters had for the past several years. It had been more than a year since I had seen Angel's wings, but they looked at first like they always had. When she reached around and unhooked her bra, the wings sprang free, assuming a more relaxed configuration.

She hugged her shirt to her chest to keep herself covered as I moved closer. The wings were larger than when I had seen them last, but that didn't surprise me; they had grown incrementally, if very slowly, almost from birth. What *was* unusual was that their shape was different.

When Angel was born, her flaps were equilateral triangles of skin, attached for about a half-inch line to her back, a line theoretically cutting off the tip of that third point on the triangle. Point one aimed for the spot where her arm joined her shoulder, and point two vectored toward her hip bone.

The joint lines on her upper back were now five or six inches long, and if you imagined the lines of the wing edges continuing until they had made those third points deep in her back, the angles would have been much more open than the old 60° angles. They looked closer to 90°. The sides going up toward her shoulder from the top of the line of attachment were still short, maybe six inches, and the up-pointing angles were smaller than 60°. The biggest change, though, was the longer length of the wing edges that dropped from the top angle point to the bottom one. How had she been able to keep these so well hidden?

I put my hands on her shoulders and turned her so her back caught the light streaming in from the window, noticing now what the dimmer light of the room had not revealed: the color of the wings no longer matched the skin on Angel's back. They had become a sick-looking muddy brown. And, as I moved in for a closer look, I realized the color was not the only problem.

Both wings were covered with small bumps that appeared to be inflamed. I lifted each wing to check the other side and found the same thing. Whatever it was, it had not spread to her back—the skin underneath both wings was clear. I tried to keep alarm out of my voice.

"How long have they been like this?"

"I don't know. Maybe a couple of months."

"Does it hurt?"

"No, I can't feel anything. I saw them when I got out of the shower one morning and I thought they were just pimples. There were only a few then, so I put a clean sock over the end of my bath brush and rubbed zit cream on them. But it didn't help, and then more and more started showing up. What do you think it is?"

The last thing I was going to tell her was the first thing I thought of, about a conversation I had had with Dr. Whittaker when Angel was still an infant. According to him, people born with nonfunctioning organs run a much higher risk of developing pathology—a medical euphemism for cancer—in the organ. That's why so many people who are born blind eventually opt to have their eyes surgically removed and replaced with artificial ones.

"It's most likely only a reaction to laundry detergent or your bath soap. Or maybe your bra straps are chafing them. Probably nothing, but I'll call Dr. W. on Monday to set up an appointment."

"You really think it's only a rash or something?" She sounded so relieved.

"Well, that or the egg pods some alien impregnated your wings with while you were sleeping."

"Oh, you're a real laugh riot, Mom."

"I'd better start working tonight. It's going to take *forever* to knit that many little baby sweaters with four arms each."

From the roll of her eyes, I knew I had gotten her mind off what was going on with her wings. But the rest of that weekend was hell for me.

On Monday the doctor examined Angel's wings. He took swabs for a lab, but was able to rule out certain horrors on the spot: smallpox, herpes, flesh-eating bacteria. Unable to put her wings under a microscope, he used a magnifying glass for a closer look at the ugly bumps.

Some of the nodes were tiny and hard, but closed. The majority were large—maybe half the width of a pencil eraser—with openings. And a few were swollen and had their openings occluded with a dark brown substance Dr. W. dutifully scraped and packaged for the lab.

He noted the size change since Angel's last physical, and measured all the angles and edge lengths. Finally, he took a couple digital photos to send to a colleague of his who he said might have a better idea what was going on.

The lab analysis would take several days, but Dr. Whittaker told us he felt confident the answer would turn out to be something easily remedied, like an allergic reaction to laundry soap or a bath product.

Angel was visibly relieved to hear him suggest such mundane possibilities. I think she took comfort in the fact that those ideas had been my first response, too. If a mother *and* a doctor have ruled out anything major, well, nothing major could be happening, right?

I kept Angel home from school on Tuesday and Wednesday, and we cut slits in some of her old shirts so her wings could air out while we waited for answers. The smaller bumps got larger; the larger ones became inflamed and swollen; and the unidentified brown stuff clogging the biggest bumps threatened to start oozing out any minute. Whatever it was, it was progressing rapidly.

The Thursday morning call from Dr. W. was at first a relief: fungal, viral and bacterial causes had been ruled out. There was no cancer, plague or communicable disease. But with all they could rule out, there was still nothing they could rule *in*. Then he said his colleague—the one to whom he had sent the photos—thought he had seen it before, but needed to examine Angel's wings to be sure. Dr. Dolan had agreed to meet us at Dr. W.'s office at two o'clock that day.

Dr. Dolan was a charming, elderly gentleman with a full head of white hair and a matching moustache. I assumed he had been one of Dr. Whittaker's medical school instructors or mentors. He gently examined both of Angel's wings, then took out a jeweler's loupe to look more closely at the bumps. Angel and I waited patiently and respectfully until I couldn't stand it another second.

"Dr. Dolan, do you have any idea what this is?"

"Yes," he replied solemnly, taking the loupe away from the surface of the wing he had been examining. Angel turned, hugging the paper gown to her front, ready to hear the worst. "The nodes themselves are inflamed follicles. You'll note that they group generally into wide lines across the wing. These are called pterylae, or tracts, and the bare spaces between them are apteria."

Count on a doctor to drone on in bio-babble when all you want is the bottom line. "Are any of those things dangerous for my daughter or communicable to other people?"

"Oh, no. No. No."

"Then why do some of them look infected and ready to pop? And what is that brown stuff in them? Should we be concerned about that?"

"The nodes are swollen, I agree, and the presence of the matter clogging the openings indicates they *are* ready to rupture, but not to evacuate a toxin. All the follicles will eventually swell, become impacted, and then contract hard enough to begin expelling neossoptiles."

Could the man be any more exasperating?

"And in plain English, what are neossoptiles?"

"Feathers."

Feathers, so streamlined and simple in appearance, are actually complex examples of natural engineering. Think of a feather you found on the ground and picked up when you were a child. If you pulled it through your fingers in one direction, it was a smooth, sleek plane, but pulling it the other way, your neat plane split and separated, giving it a raggedy look. The remedy was to pull it back through your fingers the right way, magically knitting the gaps and smoothing the plane.

A feather is comprised of one long, central shaft, the bottom part of which—the part below the feathery stuff—is called the calamus or, more commonly, the quill. The upper part of the shaft is the rachis, from both sides of which extend the numerous rami, or barbs, that adhere tightly to each other and form the flexible plane of the feather.

How do these barbs stick together? Well, extending outward on both sides of each barb are smaller barbules, which help join it to its adjacent barb in a taut weave or web. Each of those thousands of barbules is covered in tiny projections called barbicels, which adhere to each other so tightly that air cannot get through. And the barbicels can do that because they are covered in microscopic hooks called hamuli. Think Velcro on a reverse pyramid plan.

It is important that the plane of the feather—which is actually known as the vane—is impenetrable by air, as feathers serve only two purposes: as insulation and as an aid in flight. If the microscopic hamuli have hooked together all the barbicels, and the minuscule barbicels have fastened all the barbules, and the tiny barbules have united the barbs, and you throw in a light coat of oil, the feather is not only airproof, but waterproof. Water birds have special oil glands near their tail where they can rub their beak, coat it with the avian equivalent of hair gel, and then preen their feathers to make a natural rain barrier. That same preening, sans oil, can lay all the many parts back in place, just as a child's hand can smooth a feather long separated from its previous owner.

In 1936, someone who obviously had too much time on his hands counted the feathers of a whistling swan: 25,216. In 1949, someone on a tighter schedule counted a female ruby-throated hummingbird's feathers: 1,518. Most songbirds have between 1,100 and 4,600, and a nine-pound bald eagle carries one-and-a-quarter pound of feathers.

Some birds hatch prefeathered. Others have only what is called natal down: long, soft filaments which are replaced by feathers as the hatchling grows. And some are altricial, meaning born naked and sprouting feathers only in their later development. Like hummingbirds.

Or my daughter.

Dr. Dolan was, as you may have already guessed, not a medical doctor. His Ph.D. was in ornithology, but Dr. Whittaker had been hesitant to tell me that beforehand, in case his suspicions were unfounded. It certainly explained the dispassionate, professorial drone as the man explained what was happening with Angel's wings. He very much wanted to track her "case" and write a paper on it for an ornithological journal, but I put him off by telling him I would have to discuss it with my husband before I could give an answer.

What I wanted to say was, "Go to hell; she's not a science project," but I needed to keep him interested enough to stick around and give us an idea of what we could expect in the immediate future, wing-wise.

And what was Angel doing during all this? Trying to keep the smile off her face. She was squinching her eyebrows and nodding seriously as Dr. Dolan spoke, but I knew my daughter well enough that I was sure she had not heard another word after the pronouncement that she was growing feathers. Every previously abandoned flying fantasy was flowering anew in her mind.

Angel got dressed in the exam room, while Dr. Dolan and I talked in the office. He assured me that what was happening was normal—well, normal if Angel had been a woodpecker—so I took his card, told him I would call him with an answer about the paper he wanted to publish, then left with my daughter.

Outside of the medical building, before we even got

to the parking lot, Angel shrieked with joy. I had not heard such a purely happy sound from her in years. She grabbed both my wrists and conducted a short orchestral piece using my arms as batons.

"It's happening! It's finally happening," she sing-songed.

I could see tears welling in her eyes, and knew it had cost her plenty to sit in that room and nod thoughtfully while the bird guy droned on. Everything she had ever dreamed of was coming true. If feathers were beginning to grow, then her wings would begin to grow. If her wings grew, then they could fly.

Well, she did get two out of three.

18

There were numerous practicalities to consider and decisions to be made, so we sat down as a family to let the two youngest know what was going to be happening with their big sister's wings. Shelby had gotten an occasional glimpse of Angel's wings, the concept of bathroom privacy not having fully registered yet in our three-year-old's brain. Nicky, who had taken Angel's hiding of her wings as a personal rejection years earlier, was now too old, too cool and too involved with his own interests to do more than casually acknowledge their reappearance.

Once Shelby had been put to bed and Nicky had gone to his room, Charlie, Angel and I worked out the logistics of everything else. Our first consideration was Dr. Dolan's request. Not wanting Angel's life to become some kind of freak show, I was resistant. But Angel wanted to keep Dolan on her team. A mother and father were acceptable guides through the wilds of normal puberty, but Angel was going to require the expertise only a guy like the professor could provide. And, as Charlie pointed out, her situation was unusual enough that any other expert we consulted was going to want to do the same thing.

Charlie examined the forty-page glorified pamphlet Dr. Dolan had given me to look at: *The Quarterly Journal of Ornithology, Vol. XIX, Issue No. 3.* It seemed harmless, and had a small enough and specific enough circulation not to present a problem. And if it bought us the expertise we would probably need, Charlie thought it was a good idea. So, the motion carried.

Ornithologists: 1, Mothers: 0.

Our next topic was the wings themselves. Many of Angel's seventh-grade peers had never seen them, as they had been covered for three-and-a-half years. With only two months left in the school year, and her wings looking so ratty at the moment, Angel opted to keep them hidden for a little longer. We would watch what developed over the summer, then talk about debuting the wings at the start of eighth grade.

Angel gave Charlie and me each a long, emotional hug before going to her room. He was genuinely moved to feel the distance between them evaporate. In that sweet hug, however, I read: *Ta-ta, stalwart parents. You've been great, don't get me wrong, but now it's time for me to move on. I'll write if I get the chance.*

Charlie and I talked for hours, always coming back to the fact that Angel was just an ordinary child, and we wanted to maintain a normal life for her. Or as normal a life as we could maintain for a girl who appeared to be on the verge of developing a pair of feathered wings. We didn't want her photo in the newspaper; we didn't want reporters snooping into her life; we had seen the havoc wreaked on the lives of the rich, the strange and the famous, and we didn't want that for our daughter.

We had no way of knowing that when the press invaded our lives, it would be Angel who courted *them*, not the other way around.

Time and events accelerated rapidly after that, and I'm trying to keep everything clear in my mind as I tell you the story. Oh, I understand you've heard the story— *everyone* has heard the story—but no one has ever heard the whole story, the real one that Angel and I lived.

Now is when I turn down the background volume for expediency's sake. Please know that although I won't be writing much more about Charlie, Nicky, Shelby, my job or any of the other important parts of my "normal" life, they were always there. They always existed, and even if it sounds as though everything I thought, said or did revolved around Angel, know that I never stopped loving Charlie or being a good wife to him. I never stopped loving and caring for my other two children. That all three hate me so much now is entirely my fault, my responsibility.

Before Charlie came into my life, when Angel and I were still in our "you-and-me-against-the-world" phase, we had nicknames for each other, names trotted out and used when we were in especially silly and carefree moods. For some reason lost to my memory, we affected British accents when we used those nicknames.

"I say, Fish Lips, would you mind passing me the garlic bread, old chap?"

"Not at all, Peanut, my dear," I would respond. "And by the by, you have a spot of sauce on your chin."

"Pip-pip." She would swipe with her napkin. "Is it gone, old bean?"

"Yes. Jolly good show, Peanut. Clean as a whistle."

"Thenkyew, Fish Lips."

"Think nothing of it, guv."

There were three important points to the game. One, you wanted to be sure you were loud enough that the waitstaff and nearby customers could enjoy the accent, which I must have picked up from old *Benny Hill* reruns. Two, you had to use the other person's nickname as often as possible and in as silly a context as possible. Three, and this was the most important one, you couldn't giggle, snort, laugh, snicker or in any other way break character. So the goal, of course, was to make the other person do exactly that. As soon as one of us broke character the game was over.

By the time she was three and a half, Angel could do a pretty good bad British accent, and we treated not only other restaurant patrons to our routines, but shop girls, people in the grocery store line, those in the seats near us on the bus and poor, patient Dr. Whittaker. We didn't do it every day—we were *artistes,* for crying out loud, and couldn't be expected to perform constantly—but when we did, we thought we were a laugh riot.

I was Fish Lips. Long before full lips were so fashionable that celebrities were willing to have their own butt fat injected into them to plump 'em up, I had lips that were either lush and sexy (if you were a guy working a move) or shameful and indecent (if you were my mother).

Angel had been dubbed Peanut by Katie's husband Pete when she was only eighteen months old and "no bigger than a peanut." She wasn't *that* tiny, but Pete was working off the memory of his own three boys—all hefty as sandbags by a year old.

Once all her baby fat was absorbed, Angel became a very slender little girl, not to the point of looking malnourished, but definitely appearing delicate. That fit nicely with her early fairy/pixie/sprite fantasies, as you could almost believe the tiniest pair of gossamer wings would be able to lift her off the ground.

By the time dinosaurs ruled her world, she was a wiry and boyish nine year old, but the shortest in her class. Dr. W. assured me her height and growth rate were within the normal range, albeit at the low end of the charts.

When she began developing feathers on her wings, she was just past twelve-and-a-half years old and was four feet nine inches tall. She grew one more inch before her thirteenth birthday, and then all height broke loose. Between thirteen and fourteen she grew four inches, to five feet two. Between fourteen and fifteen she grew five-and-a-half inches, sometimes crying in her bed at night when the very real growing pains in the long bones of her legs were stronger than the two aspirins I had given her. Then there was a slowdown, and she topped off at five feet nine by her sixteenth birthday, two inches taller than her mom.

She was small-boned and delicately slender, but her weight was always only an estimate because, as the wings grew and the feathers sprouted, they, too, gained weight. Her total at sixteen was one hundred thirty pounds, fifteen to twenty of which we estimated was wing.

The early feathers were not like the ones I described previously. They were down—little puffs of dull brown fluff—and like a Frederick's of Hollywood marabou boa, they shimmied in the slightest breeze. Angel would sit at her desk doing homework, wings dangling over the back of the chair, and Shelby would sneak up behind her and blow on the down to watch it dance.

"Try not to spit so much when you blow, Shel. I have to sleep in these."

Shelby would squeal with delight, then run out of the room, leaving her long-suffering big sister to her work.

Everyone at Angel's school adjusted quickly to the downy wings when she started eighth grade. It may seem strange now to think she didn't attract more attention, but everything about her, her family and her life—with the exception of the wings—was so normal and ordinary that not one person ever thought of turning her over to the freak police or clandestine government agencies.

Dr. Dolan published the first of four papers in the bird journal and, as Charlie had predicted, the subscribership was so small and specific that nothing came back to affect us. Dr. Dolan used the name Laura instead of Angel, so those who read the article didn't know who she was, and those who knew who she was never saw the article. For a scholar, he had a pretty sweet style to his writing, not dusty and dry, as I would have guessed. That first article began with the following paragraph:

> *Hair, skin, fur and scales are body coverings, each gracing the form of multiple species of mammals, reptiles and fish. Feathers, however, are exclusive to birds. No other creature of the sea, land or air has for these past millennia worn feathers. Until Laura.*

The summer after eighth grade, around the time she turned fourteen, Angel went into a snarky, weepy mood for a few weeks, and then all her fluffy down fell out. Dr. Dolan identified it as a normal molt, and based his second paper on it.

The new growth was real feathers, not down, but the color was still the same dull brown. By then the wings themselves were changing, the top angle softening into a curve, and the bottom one staying sharp, but lengthening until the tips of the last feathers brushed the tops of Angel's thighs.

The lines where the wings joined Angel's back were long enough—maybe eight inches—that she could no longer wear a regular bra. We found a halter bra with a single strap that went around the back of the neck, and a bandeau that hooked around her waist. Since she was such a sylph, Angel's breasts were quite small, and the bra was worn only occasionally. Most days she just popped on a pair of flesh-colored circles with sticky backs, a little item we found on a website catering to exotic dancers. I offered to order her the purple-sequined set with the tassels, but she slitted her eyes at me in disgust and said, "As if."

Jeans and skirts were not a problem, but tops were. We found a seamstress who helped design a pattern for shirts and blouses that would keep Angel decent and warm, but let her wings hang free. They were big enough by then to be too much for our earlier solution—simple, buttonhole-stitched slits—so the new design had a piece in back that was wide enough to cover the space between her wings. It was sewn to the collar or neck, then it dropped to below the wing joint, where it attached to the rest of the garment with Velcro.

The summer after ninth grade, Angel went into another dark mood, which Nicky was quick to identify as PMS—premolt snarkiness. The feathers dropped and new ones grew in, but not with the same uniform brown color. The new feathers formed indistinct horizontal bands beginning with the darkest brown at the top, and lightening over two additional bands until the bottom feathers—by then trailing to midway between her rear end and her knees—grew in a rich, caramel color.

17

A year later, by the end of the third molt, Angel's wings had attained their full, dramatic size and breathtaking plumage. For the first time, Dr. Dolan asked if he could accompany his article with a photograph and, since he had been so helpful guiding us through the changes, we agreed.

A simple white backdrop was set up in our garage so that Angel would stand out in sharp contrast. Charlie and I insisted on maintaining her anonymity, so her face was turned away from the camera in the side shot. The shot from the back was no problem, as only her brown curls were revealed. She wore jeans and her pasties, but she held a towel to her front as the shot was set up. Right before the photo was taken, I stepped in and she handed me the towel.

Dr. Dolan had agreed to give us final approval on what photographs he could use. Angel was only sixteen and, even if the journal's readers didn't know who she was, we didn't want anything iffy being published.

In the end, the profile shot was eliminated because if you looked hard enough, you could see the side of her left breast. Ever the practical naturalist, Dolan settled for a three-quarter angle—which still gave a pretty good idea of what the wing looked like from the side—and the shot from the back that took in the full-length glory of both wings.

It was that last photograph, never published in anything other than an obscure little ornithology journal, that brought our world crashing down.

Two years later, *Newsweek* **magazine would**
call her wings "a shimmering cascade of cognac, honey and
liquid gold"—not a drink *I* would order, but a reasonably
accurate description.

After Angel had been through that first molt and
grown real feathers, she was ecstatic. The fact that they
were a uniform mud brown didn't bother her, as her long-
term goal was flying, not showing off. The second molt left
her with faintly differentiated bands of color running hori-
zontally across her wings which, since she carried them but
didn't often see them, once again was of little importance to
her. It was after the third molt—the summer she turned
sixteen and the feathers grew in like those of some exotic
falcon—that Angel began to understand and appreciate the
full visual impact of what she routinely called her "big
honkin' set of wings."

So, what did they actually look like, these wings of
cognac and gold? Imagine yourself flying, then look down
on a large bird in the air below you, its wings outstretched,
then isolate one wing in your mind. That squarish part adjacent to the body is covered with layers of contour—or
flight—feathers called secondaries. The contour feathers on
the other half of the wing, the triangular section that points
away from the body, are called primaries, and they are the
longest feathers, gradually increasing in length until the
very longest one at the wingtip.

The leading edge of the wing, the edge that knifes
into the air in flight, marks the beginning of a series of

overlapping bands called coverts, and they are classed as
primary or secondary, depending on their placement on the
wing. Angel had three sets of secondary coverts on the section of her wing that attached to her back. The first set
along the leading edge—her lesser secondary coverts—were
a deep, glowing bronze that tightly overlapped the warm,
cognac-hued band which made up her median secondary
coverts. The medians, in turn, snugged over her greater
secondary coverts—feathers in a smoky topaz color. After
the three coverts, there was a solid plane of secondary
feathers going back to the trailing edge of the wing, a plane
of brilliant golden topaz. The colors were clearly demar-
cated, but one eased into the next the way different colors
in a rainbow do, so there was no shock of contrast between
the deep bronze and the bright topaz. Not so with her primaries.

The pointy outer half of Angel's wing had only one
set of primary coverts, and they matched the bronze of the
leading-edge secondaries, but with no intervening bands of
graduated color, the sudden expanse of golden topaz was a
visual shock. Or would have been if anyone had ever seen
it. Since the wings could not spread on their own, that
dramatic feather show could be seen only if someone lifted
the end of one of Angel's wings and held it out to one side.
We did that a couple times after the amazing feathers grew
in, Charlie or Nicky doing the hoisting, with me positioning
mirrors so Angel could see. Nicky would act unimpressed,
making some sophomoric joke like: "What do KFC and my
sister have in common?" Shelby and Angel would chime in,
"Boneless wings." In the beginning we oohed and aahed
and, in the case of little Shelby, stroked, but eventually we
accepted the wing art as reality and went about our lives.

Folded down in their natural state the wings still
had impact, but with the bronze feathers accordioned together in a narrow band along the outside edge, the effect
was more like bold blonde highlights on a brunette.

If you looked at Angel from the back when she was
standing still, her wings conjured up an image of a tall,
elongated heart, the top curves rising above her shoulders
in narrow parabolas like the ones at the top of a harp, and

the sides swooping down to meet at a point ten inches off the ground. The darkest feathers framed the bright center of the heart, and the two longest primaries crossed above her slender ankles like tiny golden swords.

Those stunted triangular membranes of her birth had transmogrified into massive wings with breathtaking plumage, and suddenly those original little flaps were no more than a dimly recalled blype on the radar screen.

We had no idea we were so close to a precipice from which there was no retreat, and so we went about the practicalities of our own lives. For Charlie and me, those practicalities revolved around work and family. He had gone out on his own, taking the Dennison/Wells business with him, and I was by then a shadow partner in his new accounting firm, limiting my hands-on participation to two full days a week and the occasional meeting with prospective clients.

Nick roared into high school going out for pretty much every sport they offered. He was beanpole tall, like his dad, but more athletic, and addicted to the thrill of competition. He lost as graciously as he won, the game itself being the most important to him, whether it was soccer, baseball, basketball, or football. Ultimately, it was soccer and basketball he pursued, being a little too hyper for baseball and a little too reluctant to be flattened by a charging wall of boy meat for football.

Shelby entered first grade wanting to sample the whole range of whatever her library, her teachers and her peers had to offer. I recalled her sister's intense single-mindedness, so at first I saw Shelby as unfocused, but came to realize her broader approach was healthier and much less likely to bring her the disappointments Angel's narrow interests had brought her.

Most of Angel's adjustments had to do with her wings. Because of their size, sleeping on her back was no longer an option, and let me tell you, feathers don't keep *themselves* smooth and pretty. Having neither the beak nor the flexibility to preen them, Angel depended on me to keep them presentable.

She showered normally, washing the wings with a handheld aimed over her shoulders, but she lacked the oil glands to keep the feathers shiny and flat. After trying numerous products and approaches, we finally settled on Pam nonstick spray in olive oil. I would spritz her feathers every Sunday night, wipe down the full length of each wing with paper towels, and she was good to go. Before she left for school every morning, she would spray cologne—she was enamored of my No. 4711 in those days—over her shoulders, where it would settle on the feathers and mask any residual olive oil smell.

Sometimes in gym class or horsing around with her friends or even moving in her sleep, Angel would break or bend a feather, so I learned the falconers' art of imping. My first efforts were structurally sound but aesthetically weak, so I practiced on the loose feathers I was constantly picking up off our carpets, and before long I could repair a broken or shredded feather well enough that you could not detect any sign of prior damage.

Angel socialized but did not date. She had a large group of friends, both male and female, which reconfigured into smaller cadres for mall forays, movie outings and the inevitable pool party at our house every Saturday from the end of May until the middle of September. Stacy was still ostensibly her best friend, but as they now went to different high schools, there was an inevitable loosening of the bond between them.

To sit in cars, classrooms and theaters, Angel had to pull the ends of her wings forward and to the sides of her thighs. If the seat was small or had arms, she had to tug them even further forward and upward, then cross the tips over her knees. Football games were easier for her, as the open design of the bleachers allowed her wings to hang naturally.

Despite her active social life, Angel found plenty of time to study. Her grades were excellent, so I never monitored the books she sat up reading at night, or the pages and pages of notes she made. She also spent a fair amount of time on her computer—which Charlie and I *did* monitor—but she never wandered onto the usual teen cyber hangouts, selecting more science and math-oriented venues. Again, we assumed her good grades were the result of all the diligent studying. Only later would we realize the A's and B's had been an artful obfuscation. She raced through her schoolwork, making sure she did everything necessary for a stellar report card, in order to have plenty of time left over for her own scholarly pursuits. She and the professor e-mailed each other several times a month—nothing to be concerned about—as he was gathering information for his fourth article.

Our suburban household was a picture of domestic tranquility.

The knock on the door which set everything else in motion and changed our lives forever came during Easter vacation, and everyone was home except Charlie. Angel was cleaning up the breakfast dishes, Shelby was gathering her things for a sleepover, and Nick was finally up and in the shower. I was closest to the front door, so I was the first to meet the man on our porch.

Clean-cut, thirties, casually—but expensively—dressed, he extended his hand toward me.

"You must be Mrs. Evans. Hi, I'm Jeremy Tucker and I would very much like to talk to you and Mr. Evans about your daughter." He pumped my hand and flashed a disarming smile.

"My last name is Fitzgerald, Mr. Tucker, and what business could you possibly have with my daughter?"

"Perfectly logical you should wonder," he said, my chilly response not dampening his pluck. He pulled out a business card and extended it to me. "I represent a company which may be interested in offering a substantial—"

"Who is it, Mom?" Angel asked, coming up behind me. As I turned to tell her to go back inside, she stepped forward and was framed in the open doorway when Jeremy Tucker got his first look at her.

"It's nobody important. Why don't you go help your sister pack her duffle bag."

Angel's eyes held Jeremy's for a second, then she slowly turned around and walked back into the shadow of the entryway. As she made her turn, I heard the sharp intake of air from our caller.

"Jesus," he breathed, "it's true."

With Angel safely back inside, I took the opportunity to read the business card he had handed me.

Jeremy Tucker
Vice President, Advertising
WHISPER, Inc.

This information was followed by the usual phone, fax, cell, and e-mail contact information. Whisper, Inc. was a genuine major corporation, but that was no proof the card or, indeed, Mr. Tucker himself, was genuine.

"Do you know that for less than fifty dollars, I could have my local Kinko's design and print business cards proving I was the prime minister of Venezuela?"

16

He was still dazed from his first look at Angel, and all the slickness had evaporated from his demeanor. From cocky glad-hander to humble supplicant in a heartbeat.

"Mrs. Evans... I'm sorry, Ms. Fitzgerald, I'm begging you, literally begging you and your husband to meet with me. I assure you it will be to your daughter's benefit. Check me out with the company, ask any questions you like, set the time and place you feel comfortable with, and I'll meet you anywhere, anytime. Please."

Still holding his card, I stepped back inside the house and quietly closed the door.

"Why didn't you find out what he wanted while he was here?"

"That's what *I've* been asking her," Angel responded impatiently before I could answer Charlie.

Nick had been requested to go to his room so the three of us could talk after dinner. I would have preferred speaking to Charlie alone, but Angel had been upset all day about my closing the door on Jeremy Tucker, and was in no mood to wait out some pointless, parental talkfest.

"When a man I've never seen before starts asking about my *underage* daughter," and here I shot a hard look at Angel, "well, sue me for erring on the side of caution."

Moments after Tucker got back in his rental car and drove away, Angel had found the business card and begun speculating wildly about his reasons for coming.

Whisper was an American success story founded by twin sisters fifteen years earlier. As newly graduated high school girls from a blue-collar family, they didn't have the money for college. Their grades weren't high enough and their parents' income wasn't low enough to qualify for any scholarships of substance, so Susie and Anne Schultz started their own business.

The Schultzies, as they were later called, bought several bolts of jewel-toned Thai silk from a discount fabric warehouse, then designed and sewed fifty samples of their first lingerie item: an edgier interpretation of the classic babydoll sleep set, which they called "Dirty Babies." The local stores almost immediately sold out of the seditiously named—but adorably designed—nighties, so the Schultzies brought in two other seamstresses and knocked out another twenty dozen units.

The company's original name was Silken Whispers, as their mother had advised them to keep quiet about what they were doing in their room with her old Singer. If their father found out, she said, he would have a conniption. The name was shortened to Whisper when the Schultzies went public six years later with a company founded on two key principles: natural fabrics and cool designs.

The Whisper line included everything from panties and bras to robes and pajamas, from stockings and slippers to loungewear and evening clothes. Their basic line was one hundred percent cotton, and their other items were all in natural fabrics. Even the velvets eschewed the common, cheaper polyester and went for either cotton velvet or the more luxurious silk velvet. The Whisper line was hip, high-quality and reasonably priced. Within a couple years there wasn't an upscale mall in the country that did not have a Whisper store.

Nothing in the Whisper line was sleazy or cheesy, no crotchless or peek-a-boo numbers and although they did offer lingerie in the classic trinity: white/beige/black, their signature colors were always the rich, vibrant jewel tones of those original bolts of Thai silk.

Susie Schultz was the businesswoman, Anne the designer; the women themselves were not flamboyant, but they became the darlings of a set that was. Anne was asked by a young actress to design her dress for the Academy Awards and, although the twenty-something star lost the Oscar to an older (and much more talented) British actress, her dress got press for weeks. In a veritable sea of women whose voluminous breasts were being served up on tiny trays of fabric, the young actress had stood out in a fitted version of the classic Chinese sheath that covered her from chin to ankles. It was white-on-white brocade, with long, tight sleeves and a mandarin collar. She *was* covered, but definitely not demure, as she appeared to have been melted and poured into the dress. When she stood and posed, it draped decorously, but when she walked the long slit on the

side opened and she flashed about two yards of leg. What
made the heads turn and the paparazzi click, however, was
the six-foot-long, blood-red beaded snake whose forked
tongue licked onto the mandarin collar, and whose three-
inch-wide body wrapped around the actress—sapphire-eyed
head aimed at her throat, body slithering across her chest
and under her left arm, then crossing her back in a steep
angle and terminating in the tapered tail that edged down
one side of the slit all the way to the hem. That dress had
launched the eveningwear branch of the Whisper empire.

In addition to being wildly successful, Whisper was
an environmentally aware and socially enlightened company. They never used foreign sweatshops to bring costs
down, they donated twenty percent of profits to charities
benefiting children and animals, and they were frequently
cited among the greenest corporations in America.

In other words, there was not a single bad thing you
could say about Whisper without wandering outside the
boundaries of truth.

After Jeremy Tucker left, I went online to verify
that the numbers on the card actually belonged to Whisper.
Then, without a lot of hope I would get through, I made a
call to Susie Schultz. After a switchboard and a soft-voiced
secretary, I was passed to an officious executive assistant
named Clark, who told me Ms. Schultz was in conference.
He then asked me the nature of my business with her.

"I'm the mother of the girl with wings."

If he had only continued in his snippy manner and
reluctantly agreed to take down my number for a possible
return call, I would have hung up and thrown Jeremy
Tucker's card away. Instead, I heard a soft "Ohmygod,"
then he told me he would put me right through to Ms.
Schultz. And he did.

We spoke for less than ten minutes, but she assured
me Jeremy was one of her most trusted employees and that
he spoke with her voice in the matter of my daughter.
Whisper was considering offering her a lucrative modeling
contract, the specifics of which Jeremy was authorized to
discuss with us.

While I had been online and onphone, Angel had

been in her room, apparently doing her own research. I told
her what Susie Schultz had said, and she told me she knew
why they were interested in her. Whisper was poised to
launch a new line called "Wings," whose name came from
the innovative new bra design that replaced underwires
with beautifully stitched wings that joined at the center,
then flared out beneath the cups, giving the support of an
underwire, but with a fresh approach targeting young
women and teens. The matching panties also had V-shaped
wings, but they were only decorative.

We laid out all we knew and all we were guessing
about for Charlie, so we could decide whether or not to call
Jeremy Tucker. Angel, of course, was eager to meet with
him. Charlie wanted to talk to the guy, if only to ask how
he had learned about her. I was the only one holding back,
a warning bell sounding in my mind, telling me something
wasn't right. Feeling outnumbered, I took a final shot at
curbing Angel's enthusiasm.

"So out of nowhere, you've decided you want to be a
supermodel?"

"No, Mom, I want to be a super*duper*model. I want
to shoot heroin, sleep with rock stars, and die of terminal
shallowness before I'm twenty-one."

"Hey, don't get in your mother's face," admonished
Charlie. "It's a legitimate concern. You've never shown
even the slightest interest in anything like this."

"That's because up until now modeling was about as
realistic a goal as flying. But if somebody's going to offer
me a buttload of money that I can put toward my higher
education, I can stand around in my undies as well as the
next girl."

We discussed things for another half-hour, but it
was already a foregone conclusion that we would meet with
Mr. Tucker.

At our meeting the following Saturday, Jeremy confirmed what we had already learned about the new Wings line. He then repeated what Susie Schultz had said about the possibility of a contract offer. The only new information he gave us was that Whisper wanted to do a test shoot before committing to anything.

"After all, this is the only photograph we've ever seen of Angel," he said, pulling a print from his briefcase and handing it across the table. It was the back view of Angel in her jeans, one of the two that had appeared in the ornithological journal.

"How did you get this picture?" Charlie asked.

"It was sent to the Schultzies by a man claiming to have photographed Angel for some scholarly magazine." He could see Charlie was not happy to hear that. "Uh, he said he had done the shots at your house, at your invitation. That's how we knew your address. Is that a problem?"

"Yes," I said, "but it's a separate problem."

Throughout the meeting, which we had at a local café, Angel didn't say a word. If anything, she seemed disinterested, in sharp contrast to her vehemently expressed desire for the meeting in the first place. Jeremy Tucker kept glancing over at her, as if gauging her interest level, but she did little more than smile noncommittally.

We agreed to a photo session with the understanding that I would be present the entire time and that all film, video or electronic images of Angel would be either returned to us or destroyed in the event we did not move forward with some kind of business arrangement.

In the week before the shoot, Charlie spoke to Dr. Dolan about the photographer he had vouched for and brought into our home. We didn't know the guy's last name, so Charlie asked Dr. Dolan to find him for us. The professor seemed genuinely upset that Angel had been outted by a person he had introduced into our lives and said he would try to reach him.

When Dr. Dolan called back two days later, he had bad news for us. The photographer's phone had been disconnected and, when he had gone to the man's apartment, the landlord said he had moved and left no forwarding address. Dolan sounded sincerely apologetic, saying he had used the same photographer on several previous occasions without any problems.

Charlie and I decided the photographer was a dead end for the moment, but agreed to tell Jeremy that if the company received any further communication from the jerk, to get contact information and let us know.

When the next weekend rolled around, Angel and I showed up at the studio address we had been given, where we were greeted by an effusive Jeremy. As he walked us through what would be happening, he told us the hair, makeup and wardrobe people were all local, but Whisper had flown in their own photographer. They weren't looking for perfection, only an idea of how Angel might come across to the public.

An hour of face painting and hair fussing turned my willowy girl into a facsimile of a model. She was not asked to wear anything skimpy or diaphanous, but rather was put into a beautiful, slinky gown of golden silk. I was sure it had cost a fortune, so I was surprised how nonchalantly they took a pair of scissors to the back of it to accommodate the wings. For back shots they put her in a pair of their own company's jeans, and then the photographer, Rick, asked her to spread her wings.

From over her shoulder, Angel replied, "They don't spread."

There was a huddle with Jeremy, Angel, Rick and me, during which I explained the whole wing thing. They didn't spread, flutter, flap or fly. The best we could hope for was a slight lift and flare, which would happen only if Angel were very, very excited about something.

Both men turned to Angel, who looked as unexcited as a person could possibly be. Then she spoke.

"My wings *can* be manually lifted and spread. If you would like to ask a couple of your people to hold them out, you'll get an idea of how they would look if, say, a clear filament was threaded through each wing and they were winched up from either side."

"Wouldn't that hurt?" asked Rick.

"Nope, they have no nerves and no sensation. But we'd have to be careful not to damage any feathers."

She must have seen the shock on my face, because as soon as the men stepped away to assign wing-raising to two crew guys, she leaned in to me and whispered, "What's the big deal? I got my ears pierced when I was twelve, and *that* hurt."

She made perfect sense, but my uneasiness sprang from more than a concern about a couple pinholes being punched in her wings. How had she been able to come up with a fix like that so easily? Unless, of course, she had thought through much more than she was letting on to me.

For the test shots, Whisper made do with photos of Angel with her wings spread majestically, courtesy of two men named Eddie and Dave. I know Eddie was one of the production assistants, but Dave looked like a promotional poster for a tattoo parlor. I assume they were cropped out of the final photo.

Two weeks went by before we got another call from Jeremy. He wanted to fly in the next day and talk to us about a contract for Angel.

The meeting was at our house, and Angel, who had been bouncing off the walls with excitement since his call, was once again aloof, subdued and mysterious during the opening niceties.

"Okay, the Schultzies see potential in the photos we took. They would like to sign Angel to an exclusive one-year contract to be the face of our new Wings line, and they have authorized me to offer one hundred thousand dollars for the first year, with the company having the option to renew for a second year at one twenty-five."

Charlie and I were stunned. We had no idea their offer would be so high. Angel, on the other hand, raised one eyebrow and smiled at Jeremy.

"You're kidding, right?"

He hesitated for a beat, trying to figure out if Angel was bowled over by the amount or was dismissing it. He pretended he thought it was the former and kept up his chipper demeanor.

"No, I'm dead serious, both on the original amount and on the second-year bump."

He waited with a sure and expectant smile as Angel stood up. "In that case, my parents and I don't have anything more to discuss with you. But thanks for coming by." She slowly turned and began walking out of the room.

If I had been surprised by the amount of the offer and shocked by Angel's immediate and cavalier rejection, I was completely blown away by the realization that she was *playing* him, turning so he got the full wing treatment, then practically sashaying toward the door to the hallway. Did my daughter really think she could swim with the sharks?

Apparently she could, as Jeremy sprang to his feet before she could leave the room.

"Wait!" She stopped and turned back to him with a questioning look on her face. "Angel, wait. What is it you don't like about the offer? The exclusivity? The amount?"

She shook her head and smiled helplessly, as if sorry to disappoint him. "I don't like any of it." She started her wing-flashing turn again, the puppet mistress pulling the strings to make him move. And he did.

"Okay, okay. What *exactly* were you hoping for?"

I could see the slight lift and flare of her wings; she was getting off on the orchestration of her own destiny.

"Two hundred fifty thousand for one year."

He barked out a laugh of disbelief. "A quarter of a million dollars?"

Angel didn't even blink.

"With all due respect, Angel, you have absolutely no experience and, for all we know, no ability as a model. We'll be taking a big risk hanging a new advertising campaign on a sixteen-year-old amateur."

By this point Charlie and I might as well not have been in the room. We were only spectators at a high-stakes poker game, and our daughter was about to show Jeremy Tucker she had a bigger pair than he did.

"With all due respect, Jeremy," she said, using his first name for the first time, and not any too respectfully, "without me you *have* no campaign. So if you want to hire a 'professional' model and stick some phony wings on her, you go right ahead. And I will entertain one of my other offers. Then you can launch your campaign with your bogus wings, and I'll be in magazines and on TV representing an airline or a car company or a soft drink, and all the world will be asking, 'Why didn't Whisper get the real thing?'"

15

He sank down onto his chair, understanding he had overestimated his bargaining power. Angel must have realized this, because when she continued, the steel had gone from her voice and she sounded almost conciliatory.

"Now, I don't think I'm uneducable, Jeremy. I think you can teach me to strut a runway, suck in my cheeks and practically *drip* ennui. So, what's it going to be? A real model or real wings?"

Three months after that I was in Machu Picchu
watching my barely recognizable daughter lean out from
the top of an eight-thousand-foot-high peak, wings spread
as if she were about to launch herself off the mountain and
swoop down over the citadel of the Incan ruins.   That I
knew invisible wires secured her to the rock like a barnacle
didn't make it any easier on me for the thirty minutes it
took to get the shot.   I didn't relax until the director had
made the call and three burly men scrambled up from the
other side of the peak, two to unhook her wires and one to
throw a heavy cloak around her and brace her against the
wind until the helicopter got back up to them.

    We had signed the contract the end of May, a few
weeks before Angel turned seventeen.   She had gotten the
quarter million and a mutual option on the second year.
She had given exclusivity on images of her and her wings to
Whisper for the duration of the contract.   As she was still a
minor, I was hired to accompany her on the twelve photo
shoots, each not longer than seven days, for a fee of three
thousand a shoot.

    Whisper had waited impatiently while Angel went
through her summer molt, and then scheduled her to be in
Peru for the second week of August.   The last week of July
and the first week of August were spent making her over
into someone whose face, hair and body matched the exotic
standard set by her wings.

    Her hair went from short, curly and brunette to a
long, wavy cascade of honey blonde.   Eyebrows were dyed to

complement the hair and then shaped into full arches that winged up at the ends. Her almost perfect teeth were bleached to movie-star brilliance, and a slightly crooked incisor was veneered into absolute alignment with its neighbors.

Colored contact lenses would be used for the photo shoots, so she was fitted by an optometrist—Whisper decided to go with a different vivid color each month. Her long, acrylic fingernails would be painted to coordinate with the contacts each time.

Angel was very slender, but Whisper thought she looked "soft," so they sent a fitness trainer to work with her starting two days after we signed the contract. By the time we left for Peru, her legs were shapelier and her abdomen was like the head of a snare drum. No muscles bulged anywhere, but as she moved her arms you could see the cuts of her biceps and triceps.

Whisper planned twelve jaw-dropping photographs for their campaign, each one showing Angel—wearing only the signature Wings bra and bikini panties—perched on some ledge or peak as if she were about to fly away or had just landed. It would be November before all the monthly fashion magazines came out with the Machu Picchu photos, the same month Whisper debuted a billboard saturation of the entire country.

By the time the public saw those first ads, we had completed the layout atop an iceberg in Patagonia, the shoot on Easter Island, and were heading for Ayers Rock in Australia. Returning from Down Under with a little over three weeks until our Brandenburg Gate assignment, we were hit by the full force of Angel's sudden celebrity.

Charlie was overwhelmed. While we had been shrimping on the barbie, he had been fielding calls from movie studios, news outlets, talk shows, agents and men's magazines. We put a recorded message on our telephone declining all offers and requesting they not call back. We switched to cell phones and Nick and Shelby were strongly warned not to give out their number to anyone other than a trusted friend. We tried to maintain normality in the face of a tidal wave of crazy.

Interest in Angel remained manic that entire year, though the *immediate* frenzy abated slightly, especially when she refused all interviews, invitations, propositions and marriage proposals. Each month, when the newest ad hit the stands and was plastered across fifteen thousand billboards, the buzz spiked for a week or so, then dropped back to a simmer.

Our favorite two marriage proposals that year were from a fabulously wealthy oil sheik *and* his twenty-five-year-old playboy son. Remember, in the ads Angel did not look like the high school senior she actually was; she looked like an exotic and sensual supermodel. The sheik sent her a four-carat sapphire ring to match her eyes—or rather the contact lenses she had worn for the Peru shot—along with his proposal. Playboy son, not wanting to be upstaged by his fifty-year-old dad, had a Sceptre 6.6S delivered to our house. Angel didn't even have a driver's license, but Nick begged her to keep the flashy little sports car so he could drive it when he got his learner's permit. Fat chance.

The high-dollar gemstone and the high-performance roadster were returned to sheik and son, with a note from Charlie telling them his daughter was not yet of legal age. Apparently there is no Farsi translation for jailbait because Angel received two more pieces of jewelry, a full-length lynx coat and a Swiss chalet from the crude oil boys before they gave up and turned their attention to Hollywood's latest starlet woman: a blonde best known for exiting a limousine with knees akimbo, providing a third possible answer to the question, "Boxers or briefs?"

When Angel was around other people on our trips she played her part to perfection. A mysterious beauty who rarely spoke and always appeared cool and desirable. Alone with me in whatever tent, hut, flat or trailer we had been assigned for that few days, she was a fast-maturing version of the gawky teenager I had been mother to only a short while before. Angel worried that *I* worried all the money, fame and anonymous adulation would change her.

"Charlie called. He said the lawyer still can't figure a way to get that chalet out of your name," I said.

"Was that papa sheik or junior?"

"It was pop's response to junior's endangered coat."

"Yeah, those wacky oil dudes," she laughed. "Now if one of them had sent me a *camel,* I might have at least gone out to dinner with him. I mean, a camel would have shown so much more creativity than all those big honkin' diamonds."

"Although diamonds have less of a rep for stinking to high heaven and spitting wads of phlegm."

"You just wanted a rich son-in-law who could afford the best nursing home for you in, what? About five years?"

"I hadn't thought I was that transparent."

"Meanwhile, your poor, wingéd daughter would be tied to a perch in Saudi Arabia alongside a couple vicious gyrfalcons. To be allowed out only when the sheik wanted me to hunt giant snakes among the dunes."

When Angel pronounced winged with two syllables, she was going for bathos. She sighed melodramatically, the back of her hand on her forehead in a Victorian pre-swoon pose. A moment later she snorted with amusement.

"You think the oil dudes really believed I could fly?"

"All I know is they were willing to pay a heck of a lot to find out."

I was treated quite well by the representatives of Whisper and all the members of the crew, but only because I was the mother of the talent. To them I was a necessary item, kind of an ambulatory prop to be kept track of and moved out of the way when the camera began shooting.

And then in Germany, about four hours before the shoot atop the Brandenburg Gate, Angel kneeled down to tie her tennis shoe and Jeremy Tucker stepped on the end of her wing, breaking her longest trailing primary. He heard the crunch and lifted his foot, horrified. All the crew around us went silent as Angel slowly rose. I think they were expecting some diva tantrum, and I know Jeremy was worried he would not be able to get his "money shot." Angel and I had anticipated this happening sometime, so when she gave me the look, I rolled into our prearranged routine.

"Step away from the wing." They were used to the occasional polite request from me—never a command—but I must have sounded authoritative because everyone pulled back. I went down on one knee to examine the damaged feather, shaking my head in mock concern, while Angel managed to look stricken. I stood and turned to a petrified Jeremy.

"Give me an hour and I'll see what I can do," I said softly, keeping any hint of confidence out of my voice. I put my arm around the back of Angel's wings and ushered her over to the nearby trailer.

Once inside, Angel flopped onto the couch, damaged wing up.

"Okay, Big Mama, your turn to shine."

"I don't know why you won't let me teach one of the crew how to do this," I replied, reaching for the case with my imping needles and spare feathers.

"Are you kidding? These people place no value on anything that comes easy to them."

"Adverb."

"*Easily* to them."

I went through the plastic bags until I found the one labeled Golden Primaries, then held feather after feather against the broken one until I had an exact match.

"Like when Jeremy offered us a hundred thousand dollars. I knew if they got me for that they'd never see me as a *really*, really valuable asset. These people *want* to pay too much for everything."

I carefully cut away the crushed end of the feather, being careful not to snip any barbs on the remaining shaft. I selected a two-inch bamboo peg, which I had prewhittled into a soft, triangular shape, then checked it against the opening in the shaft, took out an emery board, and started sizing it to fit.

"And you were sure he would cough up the quarter million?"

"Jeez, no. You could have knocked me over with a feather when they did."

"Cute."

"Couldn't resist," she shrugged. "I didn't have any idea what they would offer, but I knew it would be a lot less than what they were willing to pay."

"So, if he had said fifty thousand..."

"I would have asked for a hundred. Hey, for all I knew he was going to say *ten* thousand. I would have demanded twenty and figured I had hit the jackpot."

I slid my bamboo needle into the shaft, got a tight fit, then removed it and started to work on the replacement feather, cutting so the barbs of the new six-inch tip would knit perfectly with those on the shaft of the old primary.

"Well, I think someone else on the crew should know how to do this. What if I croaked?"

"You? You're only thirty-five."

"Yesterday you said you were tossing me into a nursing home in five years."

"Okay, okay. I'll wait until you're totally decrepit, say fifty."

"Thanks for not sugar-coating it."

I took the emery board to the other end of my bamboo needle, sizing it to fit the shaft of the new tip.

"Seriously, kiddo, this is all very funsy, but I'm not going to bounce around the world with you for a second year. You'll be eighteen when this contract ends—"

"Mom," she interrupted, "there isn't going to *be* a second year."

"Are you joking? They *love* you. Of course they'll exercise their option."

"It's a mutual option, remember? I'm not going to exercise mine."

Every time I feared Angel might become the victim of some powerful force, I learned she was the one manipulating and controlling that force. I checked my fitting, then got out the glue. "You never intended to give them a second year, did you?"

"Nope."

"But you're letting them think it's a sure thing."

"Why not? They're making the assumption that a brainless teenager and her power-hungry stage mother would be—"

"Hey!"

"—and her saintly mom will succumb to money, glamour and celebrity. But we're smarter than that."

"Maybe one of us is, but it ain't moi. Hold still."

I glued the imping needle, then slipped it into the shaft of the old primary, being very careful not to get any glue on the barbs. I blew on it and waited sixty seconds for a bond.

"No, I decided up front I was willing to give fame and fortune one year and one day, but that's all."

"Your contract is for exactly one year. Where do you come up with the extra day?"

"That's going to be the day I work for someone else."

"Who?"

"I don't know yet."

"You know what your problem is, Angel? No self-confidence." Her laugh made her wing twitch. "Hold still again. Almost done." I put glue on the protruding end of the imping needle, then carefully fitted the new feather onto it, twisting it into alignment.

"Look, Whisper is getting their money's worth, me being the only girl with wings and all, but those billboards and full-page magazine ads are also promoting little old me. At the end of the year I hold an auction and whoever bids the highest amount gets me for one day only."

"What if the sheik outbids corporate America? Does he get a twenty-four-hour wing job?"

"God, Mother, you are so depraved. If you weren't the only imper on the set, I'd have you flogged."

"It's done," I said, standing up to put away my imping equipment. Angel pinched her cheeks to redden them, then tried to get her eyes a bit watery. She wanted the waiting crew to believe whatever we had done in secret had been stressful on her, possibly painful. They treated her even more like a precious piece of rare porcelain after that, and when they saw the perfect golden primary feather tipping the end of her wing, a little respect and awe spilled over onto me.

Although we traveled the world that year, we
didn't actually see much of it. One day would be spent on
the Schultzies' private jet—two for places like Australia and
China—one day recuperating, one or two days shooting,
depending on weather, equipment malfunctions and local
coups d'etat, then at least a day going home. Angel later
referred to that year as her "if-it's-Tuesday-I-must-be-on-a-
mountain-in-my-skivvies" tour.

Not all our stories from that time were funny ones.
A sad young man in a large pair of homemade wings posted
himself outside our yard one morning holding a sign that
read "I love you." He never tried to approach the house, but
on the third morning we asked the police to move him off.
He came back two more times before Charlie was finally
forced to get a restraining order. The man had a history of
mental illness, but his mother saw Angel as the origin of all
his problems and complained to the local newspapers about
our unsympathetic treatment of her harmless son.

A late-night comedy program lampooned Angel in a
nasty little sketch featuring a tall, skinny comic (male) in
big granny panties, a slutty looking bra filled with about
twenty pounds of fake boob, and a set of wings that looked
like they belonged on a vulture. "She" played Angel as a
moron, an assumption the writers must have based on the
fact that she never spoke in public or gave interviews. Or
maybe the mean-spirited sketch was a response to Angel's
refusal to host the show.

The most vile attack against her came from a group

called The Brotherhood Of The Lord. Evidently Angel was going straight to hell and, from what we gathered from their nearly unintelligible website, it was because she was young, beautiful and posing in her underwear. Angel read the vituperative comments posted about her, then turned to me and said, "I guess this means they'll be leaving me out of their prayer circle, huh?" I was glad Nick had deleted the postings calling her an abomination and her wings an affront to God and every Christian. It's a good thing Jesus rose from that tomb; if not, he'd be spinning in his grave from all the hateful things said and done in his name.

All things considered, though, it was a positive year. Angel had banked a small fortune. We had never found a way to give back the Swiss chalet, so we finally sold it for more than two million dollars. Angel had also assured herself a steady stream of income without ever having to model again. Her one-day job was a *Vanity Fair* magazine photo session, which paid one hundred thousand dollars for the cover shot that later became one of the best-selling posters of all time. Angel negotiated for a small percentage on the posters, and those checks still arrive at the house every quarter.

All the photographs Whisper had taken were from the front so their product could be seen. The undersides of Angel's wings were a uniform golden color—striking, to be sure—but nothing like the banded magnificence of the backs. The first published picture to show the backs of her spread wings was the *Vanity Fair* cover, and it is still my favorite.

The photo shows her standing in a sunlit meadow full of wildflowers. She appears to be naked (she wasn't) and her arms are stretched up and apart in a wide V. Her head is thrown back, the Lady Godiva hair extensions cascading between her wings and tapering down to the backs of her knees. Her back is arched, her wings spread wide, the sunlight adding an extra glow to each of the separate bands of color. Her fingers are apart as she reaches up, as if beckoning some unseen being. All those elements would probably have ensured spectacular sales figures on their own, but the creative forces at *Vanity Fair* had taken it one extraordinary step further, with the addition of a shadow on the meadow—the shadow of a winged man flying overhead.

I have that poster taped to the wall here, and the intervening years have not lessened the beauty, sadness, romance and power of it. I want that poster to be the last thing I see before I die.

Angel graduated with her class, thanks to a couple of terrific tutors and an understanding principal who had agreed the prior summer to work around Angel's travel schedule. Although she had missed at least four days a month for all of the twelfth grade, she ended up with a 3.4 grade-point average, and I assumed she would be heading to college in the fall.

I had begun urging her to apply to a few schools the previous November, but she put me off again and again. Suddenly it was June and she didn't have a placement. She was molting and depressed, but I didn't think I could postpone speaking to her about it.

"If you wait any longer it's going to be too late for this fall."

"Don't worry, Mom; I have everything planned out."

"What does that mean? Are you taking a year off before college? I could understand it if you did; you've had a grueling twelve months."

"Look," she sighed impatiently, "I'm not going to college. Not now, not ever."

That really pissed me off. "So your reason for doing this whole Whisper thing, the reason you dragged me all over the planet for a year, that was all a lie."

"I *never* lied to you," she insisted.

"You told us that money was for college!"

"No. *You* said it was for college. *I* said it was for my higher education."

With those words, I understood the puppet mistress had been working *my* strings this whole time. She had never—not for a second—given up on the idea of flying and, if there were any possible way to do it, Angel now had the money to make it happen.

Angel asked Charlie to handle her money after she received the first check from Whisper, and he had shepherded her growing fortune with the same care he gave his other clients. After the *Vanity Fair* shoot, she warned us she would be making a number of large expenditures over the summer, and asked Charlie to have two hundred thousand dollars available for her to draw on immediately.

Within six weeks she had bought Shelby the horse she had been begging for since kindergarten, prepaying two years of boarding at a stable less than thirty minutes from our house.

Sixteen-year-old Nick was given his first car, not the Sceptre of his auto-erotic dreams, but a brand-new Jeep Wrangler with enough chrome to make him happy. The catch, Angel said before handing him the keys, was that he had to drive Shelby to her riding lesson every Saturday.

Charlie's gift was also a car, the Mercedes he had been talking about buying for years. One morning he stepped outside to retrieve the newspaper and there it was at the curb, sleek and silver, with a beautiful interior of burgundy leather that was soft as a glove. A huge white bow topped the car, so Charlie knew it had not been parked there by a rich neighbor. The note on the steering wheel read: "Daddy, Go ahead and have a midlife crisis. You've earned it."

My gift was a one-week stay at a luxury spa where I was pampered, fed, manicured and massaged. At least I *thought* that was my gift until I got home from the spa and walked into my brand-new kitchen, complete with the forty-eight-inch Wolf stove I had wanted for so long.

All the gifts were thoughtful and lavish, and I don't want to sound cynical, but I believe Angel intended those unexpected presents to divert each one of us—to ensure our attention was on our own interests, not hers.

13

She said she didn't want to move out of the house, but needed to feel more independent, so she asked if she could have a two-story detached garage built next to the three-car garage already attached to the house. She would have a small apartment on the top floor and put a full gym on the bottom floor. That way Nick could put the Jeep in the old garage and move his weights and benches over to the gym.

Charlie and I were not ready to have her go out on her own yet, so the apartment sounded like a good compromise. We wanted to pay for the construction, but Angel said it would be unfair to use money that could go into Nick and Shelby's college funds when she had so much money and would be the primary user of the new apartment. The Schultzies, having gotten over their pique at Angel's refusal to sign for another year, had approached her about putting out a calendar using the original twelve photographs from the Wings launch. The up-front money from that would be enough to pay for the addition.

Permits were acquired, and the garage/apartment combo was completed by the middle of September. Angel had state-of-the-art exercise equipment installed in the gym below her apartment, and all of us used it.

Weekday mornings Charlie drove to work, and Nick and Shelby took off for grades eleven and three respectively, leaving me alone in the house and Angel up in her apartment. I had offered to continue doing her laundry, but she insisted she was old enough to relieve me of at least that small responsibility. She voiced it as a favor, but I heard it as a warning—her space was *her* space, and even a well-meaning mother with folded laundry to put away was not welcome uninvited.

Oh, Charlie and I had been up there a couple times, once for the grand unveiling of her all-Ikea furnishings and decorations, and once for her first dinner party. Shelby, Charlie and I were the only guests, as Nick preferred to be off somewhere else with his friends. That worked out fine because Angel had only four chairs in her tiny dinette set. We ate Chinese take-out, and Shelby asked if Jasmine (her horse) could move into Angel's old room. Charlie staked his claim on the space for a media center and man cave.

It had been a wonderful family evening, but we had not been invited back, and Charlie couldn't understand why that bothered me so much. Hadn't Nick had a "Keep Out or Die" sign on his bedroom door for years? And didn't Angel join us for dinner nearly every night? He made perfect sense, of course, but I was still uneasy. Maybe Charlie's arm's-length attitude was the result of his having no suspicions about what she was planning up there, and maybe my unease was the result of being absolutely sure I knew what was going on.

I was working out in the gym seven months after the Whisper tour ended. Angel had left earlier in a taxi for yet another mysterious day-long outing. I knew she would have locked the door to her apartment, the one at the top of the outside staircase, but there was an interior door and a set of stairs going straight up from the gym so Angel could come down and exercise in rainy or cold weather without having to grab an umbrella or a coat.

I got off the treadmill and went to the stairs, hating myself for needing confirmation of what I already knew in my heart. At the top step, I tried the door and found it unlocked; pushing it open, I stepped inside.

Have you ever seen one of those TV crime shows where the detectives go into a serial killer's apartment and see the walls covered with evidence of his insanity? Giant photos of someone he is stalking; grisly mementoes of prior crimes; Satanic altars with burned remnants of God-only-knows-what. Producers always light those rooms to cause maximum shock, maximum creepiness. Sunlight filtered in through two large windows, bathing Angel's living room in a soft, uncreepy glow, but it was still a shock.

There were cutaway pictures of different airplane wings, graphs of load-to-lift ratios, dozens of books on birds, a Cessna flight manual, charts with long equations that meant nothing to me, photos of a bat skeleton, and one very large drawing of a wing that looked a lot like Angel's. The drawing was dotted with scribbled notes, curving arrows and lots of measurements.

I touched nothing, but crossed to her desk to check out whatever was in plain sight. A business card from a tattoo and piercing parlor with prices jotted on it. A yellow pad whose top page had several of Angel's usual feather doodles, the circled words "Shelby's b'day," a grocery list, and the name Jack with underlines and a phone number. There were also two books on the desk, *Why Bees Can't Fly: How an Insect Did the Impossible* and the well-worn copy of Harvey C. Sharrett's *Let's Visit the Dinosaurs*.

Why did it bother me so much, seeing the proof of Angel's continuing obsession? On some level she had lived within a flying fantasy since she was three years old, but it never really worried me before. Her wings aren't practical, I had always told myself; she was safe. Safe from what? I was suddenly trembling and counting, desperately trying to keep something at bay, some dark memory. Or vision.

When she was with us, Angel was her same old wise-cracking self, but as the months passed, she spent less time with us and more up in the apartment. She had her own phone line, her own kitchen, and sometimes it was hard to remember she still lived with us. Once or twice Charlie and I had gone for walks late in the evening and seen lights on in the gym. We would walk over to tap on the window and wave, and Angel would look up from her workout and wave back with a smile.

Her story was that she had gotten hooked on working out with weights during the time Whisper had provided the personal trainer and wanted to continue a maintenance program. Charlie believed her, but I had secretly looked in those downstairs windows many times when he was not with me, all those nights I said I wanted to step outside for some fresh air. The personal trainer had done total workouts to get Angel in shape for the photo shoots, but now she did only upper body work. Always upper body.

She had had a wide-grip press bench built especially for her, with a normal-width padded support for her hips, shoulders and head, but a narrower section under her back. Her wings hung down on either side of the bench, dragging the floor as night after night she pressed the weighted bar up over her chest. She used a pull-down machine for triceps presses and lats, and twenty-pound dumbbells for biceps curls and pect flies.

In May Angel asked if she could bring someone over for dinner one night, and Charlie and I knew the gender of the invitee from the way she asked. She had never been on a date (to my knowledge) and she had never brought a guy home to meet her family, so I made sure we were all a little more presentable than normal and that the meal was closer to chef Rachael Ray than Chef Boyardee.

That was the evening we all met Jack. At twenty-eight, he was closer in age to me than to Angel, and I thought he was a little *too* slick, but everyone else liked him immediately. He was almost as tall as Charlie, very fit and movie-star handsome. He knew instinctively how to give a winning first impression to each family member.

I watched from the kitchen as Angel introduced him to Charlie.

"Jack Emrys. Very nice to meet you, sir," he said, striking exactly the right balance of manliness, confidence and respect as he put out his hand.

"Emrys," pondered Charlie, shaking his hand. "Is that a Welsh name?"

"Welsh, Gaelic, Irish or made-up. It all depends on which of my father's brothers you ask." *Close to his family, check.*

Lured by the smell of dinner, no doubt, Nick made an entrance from the stairs.

"Jack, this is my brother, Nicky."

"Nick," Nick corrected Angel for the thousandteenth time.

"Dude, my big brother called me Stinky until I was twenty-five."

"How did you get him to stop?"

"I killed him."

Nick honked a laugh at the deadpan delivery. Jack couldn't have won him over faster if he had been wearing a Korn T-shirt. *Can relate on a puerile level with teens, check.* Two down, two to go.

Angel brought Jack into the kitchen, where he closed his eyes and sniffed the air.

"Wait, don't tell me. I know that smell." Two more quick sniffs, then: "Food?" Charlie and Nick both laughed, and Mr. Charmypants flashed his deep blue eyes and sparkly smile at me.

"Nice to meet you, Stinky."

He laughed, but Angel burned me with a warning look. "Mom, play nice."

Right then Shelby came in and Jack bowed from the waist.

"And *you* must be Miss Shelby. Enchanté," he said, taking her hand and bussing the back of it. "Jack Emrys at your service."

Shelby looked up at Angel and said, "Okay, he can stay," before crossing into the dining room. *Can be courtly if required, check.* Three down, one to go.

Jack declined a drink when Charlie offered—God, the guy was scoring right and left—asking if there were any iced tea instead. Angel poured him a glass from the pitcher on the table.

Everyone helped carry food to the dining room, Jack taking the heavy platter of beef tenderloin out of my hands with a helpful, "Let me get that for you."

"So, Jack," Charlie asked after the platters had completed their first tour of duty, "what do you?"

"I'm a flight instructor at Lawrence Airport." *Has a job, check.*

"Cool," Nick commented.

Shelby looked at Angel, and in complete innocence asked, "Are you going to take flying lessons from him?" I stiffened slightly as I waited for her response.

"No, I can't fit in the cockpit of his teeny, tiny airplane," she replied, jerking her thumb up over her shoulder. "Big honkin' set of wings, remember?"

"Oh, yeah. I forgot."

Jack talked to Shelby about her horse, Nick about basketball, and Charlie about investments. I didn't engage in any of the chitchat, but I thought it wasn't that obvious. As the table was being cleared, he came up next to me at the sink when no one else was in the kitchen. I took the glasses from his hands, thanked him, then glanced up and saw his face looking serious for the first time since he had arrived. He pitched his voice low so only I would hear him when he said, "I like her very much. And you do *not* have to worry about me." Ah, he was a mind reader, too. Before I had the chance to react, Shelby ran into the kitchen, waving a picture of her horse, and Jack went back on auto-charm.

"Jack, look! This is Jasmine."

He glanced from the photo to Shelby several times, then nodded, "Mm-hm, I see the resemblance. Right here around the eyes." She snatched the photo away from him and scowled, but I could tell she was loving it.

Jack and Angel left and walked to her apartment.

"He seems like a really nice guy," Charlie offered, perhaps sensing my reticence.

"I agree, he does *seem* like one."

"Come on, Allie, give him a break."

Five minutes later, as I was turning off the lamps in the front room, I saw his car pull away from the curb and drive off. He was alone.

So, on his first try, Jack Emrys scored four out of a possible four.

Throughout that summer, Jack was a presence, even when the man himself was not in sight. Sometimes his car would be at the curb when Charlie and I got up on Saturday morning. More frequently, it would pull away on a Friday night with Angel and her folded wings crowded into the shotgun seat and not return until late on Sunday or early Monday.

12

When he interacted with anyone in the family, Jack was always perfect—charming, helpful, polite, funny, interesting—maybe too perfect, I thought. Charlie continued to tell me my harsh evaluation of Jack was unfair, right up until a night in late September when he came home from the office edgy and irritable. I asked if anything was wrong, but he insisted he was fine. I backed off, as the behavior was so unlike Charlie's usually easygoing self. He would come to me when he needed to.

I was reading when he came in from the bathroom, sat down next to me on the bed, and kind of slumped his shoulders.

"I have a problem."

"I figured," I said, taking his hand. "What is it?"

"Well, I'm torn between parental responsibility and client confidentiality."

Uh-oh. "I believe the ethics ruling would be that

Dad trumps accountant every time."

He didn't look convinced, but it was enough justification to keep him talking.

"Okay. Angel called today and asked me to transfer a large amount of money to her checking account."

"How large?"

"Two hundred fifty thousand."

"That's large. But, remember, she did the same thing the beginning of last summer when she bought you and Nick the cars and—"

"No, something was different. She originally said two hundred, then she turned away from the phone and said, 'What?' Her hand was over the receiver, but I could hear Jack talking in the background. When she came back on the line, she said I had better make it two-fifty."

"*That* doesn't sound good. Did you do it?"

"She's nineteen and it's her money. She didn't ask for my advice, so I didn't think I had a choice."

For Charlie it was a big disappointment, but I had half-suspected Jack was some sort of con artist all along. He was just too much of a swashbuckling paladin to be true. We discussed whether we should both speak to Angel, or whether Charlie should go it alone with Jack. Either way was likely to backfire on us. For all we knew, Jack had his hooks in Angel deeply enough for her to choose him over us if it came to a showdown, which would give him unchecked access to her money. And if you have ever challenged a teenage girl on her choice of partner, you know we worried Angel would choose him over us even if Jack didn't ask her to.

There seemed to be no winning position, so we kept quiet and waited, agreeing, though, that if Angel made any more large transfer requests, we would step in. Charlie wasn't sure he could still pretend to like the guy, but that turned out to be a non-issue. Angel and Jack kept to themselves more and more. They were gone—we assumed to his house—two or three weekends a month, so it was November before we all sat down again and had dinner together.

At Thanksgiving I noticed her wings were perfect. Angel hadn't asked me for help with them all summer, and

I assumed Jack was doing her imping and maintenance.

The holiday proceeded normally, and if Jack noticed Charlie and I were a little cooler to him than we had been earlier, he didn't let on. He kept up a lively conversation with Shelby, discussed college athletic scholarships with Nick, and helped with the clean-up. Soon after dinner they left in Jack's car, and we didn't see Angel again until the following Monday when she said she wouldn't be spending Christmas with us.

I understand it is natural for parents to be reluctant to let a child go off to start an independent life, and I'm not claiming what I felt didn't have at least a bit of that in it. The greater part of my feelings, though, had to do with my unease about Jack, my sense of his being a danger to Angel. I realized I was waiting for a shoe to drop.

Three days after Christmas, Angel came home and invited Charlie and me for dinner in her apartment. She did not want Nick or Shelby to come, but said she would have a pizza delivered to them at the house. We had our suspicions about why she wanted to see us, and it was a toss-up which we dreaded more, the thought that she might tell us Jack had ripped her off and dumped her, or that she was going to marry him.

Either one of them would have been a shoe. But what Angel dropped was a bomb.

"Okay, I need to warn you about something that's going to happen, so you aren't completely blindsided."

If her opener had been designed to put us at ease, it failed.

"I'm issuing a press release on January third, and there's a good chance it's going to generate a lot of media attention. Maybe even more than the Whisper thing."

My heart sank; I knew what was coming.

"What's going to be in the release?" Charlie asked with hesitation in his voice.

"An announcement that I'm going to fly." *Ka-boom!* "No parachute, no net, no tricks. I intend to become the first human being to fly."

"How?" I wanted to know.

"Well, it's tricky, don't get me wrong. But I've been

researching and working for a year, and I'm confident I now have the solution. I want to go through every step of it with you and answer all your questions, because when the time comes I don't want either of you to worry."

The word surreal gets tossed around so often these days that it has lost much of its impact as an adjective. When a reporter describes the large turnout for a club opening as surreal, and a heavy rain in Los Angeles is called surreal, the word is devalued to the extent that when you find yourself in surreal circumstances, you feel the need for a modifier, if only to explain how surreally surreal those circumstances are. Listening to your winged daughter tell how she intends to pull off a stunt no human being has ever accomplished? *Muy* surreal.

First, Angel played us a video tape of some grainy old Air Force films from around 1961, showing an X-15— one of the many experimental rockets the U.S. tested on its way to a bona fide space program—being launched from a B-52 bomber. The X-15 had no lift-off capabilities, so it was suspended under the wing of the much larger plane. Once the B-52 reached altitude, the rocket was dropped in the air, the bomber cleared out of the way, and the X-15's jet engine fired up. Over years of testing, the drop-and-launch system was perfected.

When the tape ended, Angel turned to us, eager now to tell everything, after so many months of secrecy.

"A few months ago I bought a plane. It's smaller than a B-52, but then I weigh a lot less than the X-15."

Her attempt at levity was lost on Charlie, as the full impact of what she was proposing to do sank in. He stood up, looking grim.

"This is insane. You can't possibly try something this stupid."

"Dad, it is not stupid," she patiently explained. "If you'll just let me—"

"Have you lost your mind?! Your wings DO NOT WORK!" In twelve years I had never before heard Charlie raise his voice in anger.

"We have a way around that."

"*We?* You mean you and Jack? Did that son of a

bitch talk you into this?"

Now Angel was on her feet. She may not have been as tall as Charlie, but her anger, her righteousness and her rapidly vibrating wings gave her a presence that instantly commanded the room.

"*No*body talked me into *any*thing," she spat back. "Jack works for me! And he has spent every day for the last three months helping the engineers modify *my* airplane."

Charlie met her glare with his own for a moment, then turned to me for help. The only sound in the room was the shussing of feathers, as the big wings continued their grand mal gavotte. Angel's destiny was upon her at last, that promise (threat?) I had seen in her eyes when she was barely four hours old. I knew Charlie thought he was right, and I knew he felt I should be shoulder to shoulder with him in a stand against what he surely thought would be our daughter's suicide.

When I turned my eyes away from his, he stormed out of the apartment, slamming the door.

"Et tu, Mom?" The puppet mistress was locked, loaded and ready to fire. I shook my head slowly.

"No."

"You don't think it's insane?" She sounded sarcastic, but her wings were winding down and her anger was cooling.

"I think," I said, choosing my words carefully, "it is inevitable."

I listened to her plans for an hour, then agreed to go out to the airport and look at her plane the week after New Year's. We ate cold Chinese take-out and, by the time I left, I felt we had regained much of our old closeness. She sounded relieved when I told her I was not at all worried, that I believed she would fly.

There were six stairs down to the landing, eight to the ground, forty-two steps to the side door of the house, twenty-three to the stairwell, ten stairs to the second floor, eighteen steps to the master bedroom, seven to the bed and thousands upon thousands of numbers until dawn.

The media fire was slow to kindle. The UFO crowd found Angel too ordinary, and the mainstream suspected it was all a hoax. One scurrilous rag reprinted the Whisper photograph of Angel "taking off" from the Great Wall of China, alongside an article that began: "Has-been supermodel Angel Fitzgerald, in a pathetic attempt to gain back her lost celebrity..." Has-been? She wasn't even twenty years old. A lot of people were still angry with her for not giving them interviews two years earlier, when she had been modeling's flavor of the month, so she had to fight for every bit of coverage she got. At the end of January she received a call from the Larry King show, and she hoped it would herald the end of her being treated like a novelty act.

Her appearance on *Larry King Live* was scheduled for February eighth. She decided to take Jack because, even though he wouldn't be on the air with her, he would be nearby to confirm or explain any of the aeronautical or technical details for the host and his staff. I warned her that I had seen the show a number of times and that King could be tricky, but the puppet mistress was, as always, confident she would be the one pulling the strings.

"Don't you think I know Larry King doesn't give a fat crap about me flying?"

"Gerund."

"About *my* flying. The whole reason I'll be there is to justify him—his—showing all those pictures of me in a bra and panties or naked."

"You weren't naked on that *Vanity Fair* cover."

"No, but I *looked* naked. And what the public cares about is not what you are but what you appear to be."

"If you know he's going to do that, why go on the show?"

"Because I might get only one shot at flying and, if this first flight turns out to be too difficult to duplicate, I need to be sure it is well documented."

"In other words, the more people who know about it, the less chance there is someone can claim after the fact that it never happened."

"Yes. So I do Larry King, I graciously go along with the exploitation, and I wedge in whatever I can about the upcoming flight."

"For all you know, King may have a copy of your medical files proving your wings aren't practical. He may accuse you of being a fake."

"I hope he does. Because then he'll have to give me a chance to explain how I'm going to do it. That's really all I want."

The show was not a disaster, but it did lead to one.

TRANSCRIPT (excerpt)

LARRY: Now, your last name is Fitzgerald,
        but your father's is Evans?

ANGEL: Charlie is technically my stepfather,
        but he *is* my dad.

LARRY: So Fitzgerald is your biological
        father's name.

ANGEL: Uh, no. It's my mother's.

LARRY: Well, that sounds like a road we don't
        want to go down, so let's talk
        about this whole flying thing.

He was responding to her very obvious discomfort with the topic, because if he had asked one more question along that line, he would have come across as playing too rough with a kid just out of high school. The fact that the subject was even touched on rattled Angel enough to dull the polish on her presentation—both of herself and her flight plans.

Once home, she apologized for inadvertently letting a can of wigglers get opened on national television. And even though it was the weakest of her TV appearances, it got the fire started. Interview requests began trickling—and then flooding—in, each appearance giving Angel more credibility. Not necessarily as a girl who could fly, but as a sincere young woman who was interesting to listen to and easy to look at. All the trappings of her stint as a model were gone by then. Her hair was back to its natural color, its natural curl, and was chopped off below her ears. For interviews she calculatedly wore a quasi-military looking jumpsuit. With her short, dark hair, her scrubbed young face and her flier's outfit, she was likened to Amelia Earhart. Even interviewers who didn't believe she had a chance in hell of flying showed respect for her earnestness and the thoroughness of her plans.

11

Angel was completely open about every aspect of her plan to fly, as she did not want people thinking she was merely the architect of a large, dramatic illusion—a female version of the magical Davids, Copperfield and Blaine. She came across as a fierce believer in her ability to do what had been, up to then, impossible.

A few weeks after the Larry King interview, toward the end of February, The Brotherhood Of The Lord, that fundamentalist group which had denounced Angel as hell-bound for her appearances in her unmentionables, decided to wield the sword of the Lord again. Those few lines on the Larry King show about Angel's last name must have given them the idea there were some rocks to look under, some closets to search for skeletons, because the head of the church, a pulpit bully named J. William Harper, declared Angel had been "born in sin and born *of* sin," efficiently encompassing both her demonic wings and her bastardy with the indictment. He didn't say Angel's name in that spew of a sermon, possibly to avoid a lawsuit, but there weren't a lot of *other* young women with wings, demonic or otherwise, so his followers were clear who the target was.

I felt awful that she was being attacked, but with so much good press elsewhere, Angel shrugged it off.

"Mom, the guy's nuttier than a squirrel turd. Who cares what he says?"

Angel spent her time in the run-up to the big event on the road doing interviews, at the airport tweaking the modifications on her plane, or in her apartment with Jack going over the charts, graphs and equations I had once sneaked in to look at, so she and Charlie did not cross paths. I slept in the same bed with him, however, and his anger and concern had not abated. The concern was for Angel; the anger was directed at me.

Neither of us was a shouter or a saboteur, but we still managed to communicate displeasure with—and disappointment in—each other those weeks, then days before April tenth. Our dozen years of marriage had been so happy, so successful, that neither of us had mastered the marital fine art of savaging one's partner with blades forged in intimacy, confession and proximity. We were complete amateurs in matters of domestic discordance, so the best we could do was maintain a rigid politeness between us. He knew I thought he was uncharitably withholding support from his daughter as she pursued the only dream that had ever mattered to her. I knew he thought I had abdicated my maternal responsibility by allowing her to attempt a suicidal stunt. With each person's position so clear, and with neither willing to change, fighting would have been fruitless. So we chose to coexist civilly, if not harmoniously.

And was this a suicidal stunt I was condoning? I didn't think so, and perhaps Charlie wouldn't have either if he had only gone out to the airport with me, seen the plane, listened to Jack and Angel's carefully worked-out plan. It was risky, but not suicidal.

The mechanisms and practicalities of Angel's proposed flight had been revealed to me in January, when I drove to the small airport on the periphery of the city's lower-income suburbs.

The first thing I noticed about Angel's airplane was the name stenciled in six-inch-tall letters between the door and the propeller: Pterry. Second was the pair of cigar-shaped mesh cages—one hanging under each wing—right outside where the struts joined the underwings.

I didn't notice anything odd about Angel as she and Jack came out of the little Quonset hut they had rented. As I walked toward her she stood naturally, her hands in the pockets of her flight suit. She waited to one side while Jack showed me the modifications that would enable Angel to fly without having to lift off on her own.

They walked me over to the Quonset hut to meet the team, three men and one woman ranging in age from about twenty-five to well past seventy. A barrel-chested man with white hair and a Santa Claus beard pumped my hand in greeting.

"Welcome to the pirates' den, Allison. I'm Duncan."

"Nice to meet you, Duncan," I said, "but shouldn't you all be pilots, not pirates?"

"No. Pterry and the pirates. Get it?" I sheepishly shook my head. "No? Neither did Angel. Hells bells, I am just too smart for this room."

"What you are is too *old* for this room," hooted the one woman on the team, a former WASP named Helen.

They were a rowdy, eclectic group of fliers whose expertise and experience had helped Angel craft her plan. After I was introduced to Helen, Buddy, Joel and Duncan, Jack signaled for everyone to pay attention. Angel stood off to one side as she spoke to me.

"Okay, Mom? I'm going to show you something, but you have to promise not to faint, barf or scream."

"Sure, kill my three best moves," I joked, trying to sound less nervous than I was.

"Buddy, Joel, would you do the honors?"

The two men stepped to either side of Angel and took hold of the ends of her wings, gripping the membrane itself to avoid damaging her primaries. As they lifted the wings to their full spread—a twelve-foot span of golden feathers bisected by a slender young woman—Angel's arms rose with them and I saw what she had done.

Around each arm was a pair of three-inch-wide cuffs of woven nylon, one pair at her wrists and the other above her elbows. All four were bolted *directly into her wings*.

"Jesus, Angel!" I sank down onto the nearest folding chair.

"It doesn't hurt. You know it doesn't hurt. Jack had the idea after I told him about the little plastic grommets Whisper put in for the wires that raised them on the photo shoots."

"We needed something more gonzo than quarter-inch plastic," Jack explained. "The wings have lift, massive lift. We know, we've tested them and they are damn near perfect aerodynamically. What they don't have is control, no way to adjust their aim into the wind."

Angel nodded at Buddy and Joel to lower her wings.

"Mom, I know I can't lift them myself, but once an air current breaks over the front of the wings, my arms will control them." Her voice became an emotional whisper. "I can fly."

Jack unbuckled the cuffs for her and I spent the rest of the day absorbing the information all the pirates were eager to share. I examined the grids on her wings where the cuffs attached. For each of the four grids, she had been pierced nine times, three rows of three holes, laid out in a six-inch square. Each piercing was reinforced with a steel grommet, and lightweight bolts passed through them into a matching square of five-thousand-pound-test nylon webbing. The webbing held the straps which passed through the eyes of Angel's cuffs. The effect of her arms being cuffed to the wings was similar to the stretch of bones reaching out into the wing of a bird. Looking at the inner wing from up close, you could see the four large nylon patches, but on the backs of her wings the bolt heads were hidden among her feathers.

Never one to overlook a detail, Angel had made sure the squares of nylon webbing bolted into her wings closely matched the topaz hue of her feathers. No one looking up at her from the ground would notice them.

Jack told me the cage into which Angel would be tucked for take-off and ascent was modeled after the "dove glove" used by magicians to keep a bird hidden, safe and still until its release during an illusion. This one was six feet long and constructed of rigid titanium bands in a mesh. The forward end of the narrow cage was a hollow cone to protect Angel's face from any dust, gravel or debris that might kick up on the taxi or lift-off.

Angel would be weighed in full gear an hour before take-off, and an exactly matched weight of ballast would be loaded into the second titanium cage. They had decided on common potting soil packed into burlap sandbags for the ballast, as the bags would burst on impact with the ground. The burlap was biodegradable and the soil was, well, dirt, so no one could accuse them of littering. The ballast would be dropped seconds before Angel's cage door was sprung, long enough to make sure there was no girl/sandbag midair collision, but not long enough to unbalance the plane before the wing loads were equalized.

Her coppery-brown flight suit for the big event was made of soft, woven synthetic with good insulating ability. It had been custom-designed for Angel, with a wide gold belt and gold stripes down the outside of the legs. There was a glamorous, show-bizzy look to the suit, but its main purpose after protection was to cover the harness she would have to wear to keep her lower body from dangling straight down while she was gliding through the air. The harness had to lift only the weight of Angel's hips and legs, so it was fairly light, more like a system of interlocking grosgrain ribbons. The harness would hold her legs straight out behind her like a heron in flight. As she prepared for landing, she would squeeze the sensor built into her left glove, which would trigger the release of her legs in increments of fifteen-degrees. The fail-safe was a remote control Duncan would hold, to be used only if he saw Angel descend below a hundred feet with her legs still straight.

There was no quick release built into the cuffs on her arms—too much of a chance they would pop off in flight, Jack said—so Angel would have only her wings and legs to balance herself when she landed. In case of a rough landing or a roll, she would be wearing a cleverly designed helmet. It was titanium, custom-shaped to fit against Angel's skull, with a thin layer of porous rubber between her head and the metal. What made the helmet remarkable, though, was the fact that it was covered in synthetic brown curls that precisely matched Angel's hair. She knew most people have fantasized about flying at least once in their lives, and when they do it is not with helmets and harnesses. People dream of flying free, like birds, and Angel intended to be the embodiment of that dream.

The venue would not be the little airport. Too expensive to buy it out; too likely a plane would wander into its airspace in the middle of Angel's flight, the pilot not knowing about a closure. No, she had booked the hang gliding field where Charlie had taken her for her twelfth birthday. She would have it for three days, day two for her flight, days one and three for the set-up and knock-down of portable bleachers capable of holding five thousand people. The local NBC affiliate would have a crew on hand to record the historic event. Angel hoped by then to have at least one cable network agree to carry the live feed, but if that didn't happen, she would still have video to supply to the news outlets.

I drove home feeling reassured that every possible precaution had been taken, every eventuality considered. I wanted to explain it all to Charlie, to assuage his fear and

heal the rift between us, but he didn't want to hear anything about it. He also refused to watch her TV interviews
between then and April tenth, although they became more
and more difficult to avoid as coverage increased and time
grew shorter.

February eased into March while the media fire burned hotter and brighter. By the ides, few people in America had not heard about the girl who said she would fly, and everyone who knew about her had an opinion.

With each interview, Angel was more believable, as evidenced by two men who showed up at our house saying they were "from Langley" and wanted to "do some tests" with her. They couched their request in patriotic terms, but what it distilled down to was that they wanted to develop the next big thing beyond dolphins that had been trained to attach bombs to ship hulls. Check, please!

Our pathetic, fake-wing guy returned, but this time his benign "I love you" sign was replaced with the infinitely creepier "God meant for us to be together." Even with the two-hundred-yard restraining order, I didn't feel good about him.

Our family—with the exception of Charlie— watched again and again the inadvertently hilarious turn taken on a morning talking-heads show that usually stuck to dissecting political issues, but occasionally cast a weather eye on other current events. The topic of Angel's proposed flight attempt was tossed out and the five heads split into three factions: two thought, given the detailed planning Angel had spoken about on TV, it was actually possible she would fly; two—one of them the moderator—were skeptical that the attempt would even be made, preferring to believe the upcoming April Fool's day would reveal the entire event as a hoax; the accidental comedian was the fifth man.

He was dead set against Angel going through with what he called a "hare-brained stunt," and he railed against some unnamed authorities who were not stepping in to stop her. He wasn't quite foaming at the mouth, but he was jacked up with righteous indignation when he began the statement, "If God had meant for man to fly..." and then realized he had absolutely nowhere to go. The three-second silence before the moderator said, "With that we'll take a break," was filled with howls from one Emrys, two Evans', and two Fitzgeralds. Back at the Quonset hut, the pirates were also sharing our moment of schadenfreude.

April first passed without a big "only kidding!" from her camp, and the frenzy billowed around us. On the third, Angel withdrew from the public eye, refusing all interviews and appearances, and concentrating on final preparations. She had been working out every day for months, but now she stepped up her rigorous upper-body program. She was as strong and as buff as a slender girl could get, the small, rock-hard muscles of her shoulders and arms conjuring images of Sigourney Weaver in *Alien* or Linda Hamilton in *Terminator Two*.

Her abrupt withdrawal from view fanned the flames even higher, and with increased intensity came increased negativity. Nick came into the house after school on the fourth and was nearly in tears when he told me, "I fucked up, Mom; I really fucked up. I'm sorry." I steered him out of earshot of Shelby, whose eyebrows had lifted on hearing the forbidden word not once, but twice, and held his upper arms in my hands to steady him. At seventeen, he towered over me by at least six inches, but his face crumpled the same way it had when he was seven.

"Whatever it is we'll handle it. What happened?"

"This guy was waiting for me at my car when I got out of school. He said he was a reporter, so I gave him the standard no comment and unlocked the Jeep. Then when I got in and tried to close the door he grabbed it and held it open. I was pulling on the handle and he was asking me to confirm Angel was a fake. I yelled at him to let go, but he wouldn't, then he said he had proof her wings are not real."

That's when Nick got out of the Jeep to confront the man. Since Nick was twenty years younger and a thousand times fitter than the reporter, he knew he would prevail in a fight, if it came to that, but the other man had backed away, still taunting, though, that Nick's sister was a liar and a fraud.

"She is not! Don't you think I've seen her wings? They're real!"

"You're lying," the reporter spat back.

"Like hell I am! I've *seen* where the wings attach to her back."

"You've actually seen where the wings grow right out of her body?" the cagey reporter asked.

"Yes, lots of times."

"Her *naked* body?"

Too late, Nick saw the trap. Spinning around, he jumped in his Jeep, then, still hearing the man screaming questions at him, sped away and came home. I told him we should keep the ugly incident a secret—especially from Charlie—in the long shot hope nothing would come of it.

Three days later the tabloid the jackass worked for hit the stands with this headline: *Birdgirl's Brother Brags Of Nude Romps.* The vomit-inducing article said "reliable sources" supported a depraved accusation of inappropriate relations between Angel and her brother. Nick was said to have confirmed he had often seen her naked, and to have responded guiltily and angrily when queried about a sexual relationship between them before speeding away. Oh, and he also tried to run down the reporter, who only escaped serious injury by crouching between two parked cars. God bless the First Amendment.

By now, Angel almost expected this kind of attack, as it seemed to go hand in hand with the public interest and adoration, but for Nick it was a first. He was distraught, saying he wouldn't go back to school the next day, which was the Friday before Angel's Sunday flight. She put her arms around her convulsively sobbing brother, soothing him the way she had done that long-ago Halloween night, when a motion-detecting skeleton had terrified him with its death moan.

After Nick calmed down, Angel said her good-byes to Shelby and him. She would spend these last few nights before the event at the airport with her pirates, moving—along with a thirty-foot trailer—to the hang gliding field on Saturday morning. When the other children had left the room, she put her arms around me and held me tightly. Hugging Angel had been problematical for years, and to accomplish it one had to put an arm high up over her shoulder on one side and the other arm low on her opposite side, reaching around under the wing. As I stood there, cocked awkwardly at an angle so I could hold my little girl, her wings twitched rhythmically. She let go, stepping back.

"The car will be here at noon to pick you guys up."

"So early?"

"Well, it looks like we'll have a larger turnout than we planned on, so it might take a while to get through to me once you're within a few miles of the field."

"Do I need to arrange some sort of crowd control?"

"Done," she said. "Eleven off-duty cops for security on the field, and a few dozen civilian parking attendants."

"Jeez, what kind of numbers are you expecting?"

"We aren't sure, but we've added ten thousand more seats. I had to pay for an extra set-up day, so tomorrow morning the bleachers will start going in. We're renting a Jumbotron for the people near the field, and a bunch of large monitors for out in the parking area."

"Are you sure you don't want me to come with you now?"

"I'll be fine, Mom. You ride in the limousine with Shelby and Nick. You're cleared through to a nice little VIP area right in front." She hesitated, looking down. "And if Dad changes his mind, well, I want him to be there, too."

I put my hand on her cheek, and she nestled her chin into my palm. "He isn't going to change his mind, but the three of us will be there cheering you on. And won't Charlie feel like a big dope for missing it."

Once again, I had forgotten that parental no-no

about promising your child something you can't deliver. Nick and Shelby would not be going with me on Sunday.

Charlie came home an hour after Angel left, angrier than I had ever seen him. He stormed into the kitchen where I was making dinner and slapped the tabloid down on the counter in front of me.

"He was ambushed," I said, hoping to placate him. "Anything he said got twisted around. He's a kid and that reporter took advantage of him."

"You think I'm angry with *Nick?!* You did this to our family! None of this would have happened if you had stepped up and helped me stop her from doing this asinine stunt."

With that, my placating mood got sucked up into the stove vent over the boiling spaghetti water. I lost it and the two of us went at each other in rip-roaring, *Who's Afraid of Virginia Woolf* style. Charlie slammed out of the house and I slammed into the bedroom. After a while, Nick crept downstairs and finished making dinner for Shelby and himself.

I feel such stabbing shame now, thinking back on that awful fight. How could I have lost sight of the fact that Charlie, my poor, sweet Charlie, had first-hand experience with the loss by violent death of someone he loved? We never spoke about Mandy, but I knew a photograph of her with a smiling two-year-old Nicky on her lap still lived in the drawer of the nightstand on Charlie's side of the bed. How could I have forgotten what a sad ghost of a man he had been when I first met him? If only I had recognized his anger for what it really was—sheer terror—then it might have turned out differently for us. He needed me to gentle him, to reassure him, but I met his rage with my own.

Charlie walked out and didn't return until after ten. By then I had moved into Angel's apartment. After a sleepless night I went back to the house Friday morning to make breakfast for Shelby, and Charlie had already left for work.

That night we were both still bristling, but we kept the volume down and our tempers in check as he made it clear why he didn't want Nick and Shelby to attend Sunday's performance.

"Charlie," I said doggedly, but without rancor, "you know they've both been dying to see this."

"Of course they have. They want front row seats for something never before seen on earth. Who wouldn't? And who am I to say Angel won't actually pull it off? But let me ask you this: what if she doesn't?"

Why was he trying to frighten me? "Her team has gone over everything with a fine-toothed comb," I protested.

"And I'm sure the team that worked on the Challenger did the same. But they still managed to overlook that O-ring, didn't they?"

I couldn't answer because I was counting to try to stop my trembling.

"What if the plane crashes on take-off? What if her foot gets caught in that cage when they release her, so she's dragged through the air while genius-boy tries to figure out a way to land without killing her?"

The trembling was now accompanied by silent tears, but Charlie pushed on, dismantling the faith I had clung to, that Sunday would mean a triumph, not a disaster.

9

"What if Angel starts to fly and realizes she *can't* control her wings?"

And now Charlie was crying, too, but it didn't stop him from driving home his point.

"Or maybe she can. Maybe she's flying like a bird and an updraft or thermal or whatever the hell it's called hits her the wrong way."

I put my face in my hands as my weeping developed a soundtrack.

"If it is only one chance in a million that she falls to her death on Sunday, one chance in *fifty* million, are you willing to have Nick and Shelby witness it up close?"

By then I was gagging on tears, snot and fear, but I slowly shook my head no.

"When are you leaving on Sunday?"

"Noon," I choked out.

"Then I suggest you tell the kids you're all leaving at one. I'll keep them distracted while you slip away and, by the time they find out you're gone, it will be too late. They'll watch it here on television with me."

I nodded without looking at him, so Charlie quietly slipped out of the room. We were no longer officially mad at each other, but I knew there was no chance of being close or loving until after Sunday's flight. Once again, I spent the night in Angel's apartment.

I awoke Saturday morning to the sound of knocking on Angel's door. My head pounded from stress, crying and two nights of little sleep, so it took a moment to realize the knocking was on the door leading down to the gym. Then I heard Shelby's voice.

"Mom?"

"Come in, Shel; it isn't locked."

She entered and took in my puffy-eyed dishevelment.

"Are you okay?" she asked hesitantly.

"Yes, I just have a headache. I'll come down and make your breakfast right now."

"I ate. Daddy made waffles in the toaster before he went to work." *On Saturday?* "And I had coffee."

"Charlie let you have a cup of coffee?" I asked with amusement.

"Well, not a whole one. He put a couple spoons of his into my milk."

"That's how they get you hooked, kiddo. And the first one is always free." She eyed me with puzzlement as I swung my feet off the bed and stretched, suddenly feeling better. If only I could slog through until Monday morning, I could begin putting my family and marriage back to rights. I grabbed my robe and stood up to walk with Shelby back to the house.

"Hey, Mom?"

"Hey, Shel?"

"Was your mom and dad called Louise and John?"

I froze. "Ye-e-es," I said, dragging out the word and trying to keep a normal expression on my face. "Why do you ask?"

"They're on TV right now."

Angel had no television in her apartment, so I raced down to the house and into the family room where Shelby had left the set on. My parents were no longer on, but I was sickened to see that the TV was tuned to FCC—the Fundamentalist Cable Channel—a holy-owned subsidiary of The Brotherhood Of The Lord. Shelby had followed me downstairs, so I turned to her.

"How come you weren't watching cartoons?"

"I tried to get Nickelodeon on the remote, but I think I hit the wrong buttons. Then there were two old people with another man and he said their name. It was Fitzgerald, just like you and Angel, so I watched for a few minutes. Am I in trouble?"

"No, you're not in trouble. I wish I had seen the show, that's all."

"It wasn't very good. Louise was crying." *Yes, she would be.*

"Why don't you watch cartoons in your room, and I'll see if I can find Louise and John again."

"Okay."

As soon as Shelby left, I picked up the viewing guide from the previous Sunday's newspaper and found that the program which had already ended, the ambiguously named *Godsword,* would air three more times that day. I got dressed and had coffee, killing time until the replay at eleven, and wondering what hurtful things my parents would say about me that might trickle down and impact Angel.

While Angel was modeling for Whisper, The Brotherhood Of The Lord made several vicious attacks on her, both for the underwear posing and for having a pair of wings they believed made a mockery of God's companions, the *genuine* angels. They even claimed it was a sacrilege that she called herself Angel, as if she had emerged from the womb handing out little business cards she had produced in utero.

Most sane people saw the group's (I won't dignify them by calling them a church) attack as a way to get some free publicity at someone else's expense. I agreed, but since the attacks had been so vituperative, I did research on the Brotherhood and their H.M.F.I.C., one J. William Harper.

The organization was sexist, racist, anti-Semitic, homophobic and hypocritical. They condemned the three big Ds—dancin', drinkin' and divorcin'—and were opposed to every sex act that was premarital, nonprocreational or (God forbid!) enjoyable. They were staunchly antiabortion, but were ruthless in their policy toward any woman who had a child out of wedlock. Depending on which of their pamphlets you read, that child was either the punishment from God an unwed mother deserved or a sin by itself. They were a patriarchal testosterology that would have been thrilled to see burqas become America's next fashion trend.

In short, their heads were so far up their asses they could have fellated their own appendixes. But am I bitter? Who, me?

J. William Harper had been the head of BroOTL for ten years, during which time—in addition to condemning teen models to burn in hell—he had been challenged twice by the J.D.L. for denying the Holocaust. He slithered off the hook both times on the technicality that he had not flatly told his flock it didn't happen, he merely implied the media mountain had been based on an historical molehill. He was also questioned as a person of interest when three of his myrmidons beat a young gay man to death after one of Harper's particularly inspiring sermons on the threat posed by homosexuals. He famously wept on the news, not for the dead man, but for the souls of the three murderers, while denying he had intentionally provoked them to violence. The promise/threat he most often invoked was that the sword of the Lord is ever ready to smite a deserving sinner. He was exactly the kind of pastor my parents would admire, as they had always preferred the punishing fist of an angry God to the comforting hand of a forgiving Jesus.

And what was it they needed to be punished for, I wondered, as Sunday after sweltering Sunday of my childhood we stewed in our pews while being guaran-god-damn-teed of a one-way ticket to hell. By the time I left home, my father had been twenty-two years at the same furniture manufacturer, and my mother had always been a house-wife, so I seriously doubted they had some shadowy Bonnie and Clyde episode in their distant past. Why, then, their need to be so sadistically shriven?

Thirty minutes into the one-hour show, Harper brought my parents on and invited them to take a seat in his living room-like set. He had whipped up enthusiasm for their appearance that entire first half hour, promising to bring out two people who had intimate knowledge of the God-mocking girl who dared to fly like the angels.

Twenty years had gone by since I had last seen them. My father had less hair, my mother had more *her*. They looked old and meek, and Harper easily manipulated them to say what needed to be said to substantiate his righteousness.

Or perhaps they had worked out their routine in advance. However it was done, those three people were able to besmirch my daughter by airing the details of my own sins. Harper nodded sympathetically as he heard their sad tale of struggling to raise a moral child, only to learn that child was so steeped in sin and evil that they were—God forgive them—forced to cast her out of their house, swollen with the evidence of her filthy behavior.

Wow! Harper had to be cursing himself that the show wasn't airing during sweeps.

Harper took my weeping mother's hand and told her how much he empathized with her suffering. *Her* suffering. He told her she was very brave for taking a stand against evil. After all, when you have garbage in your house, he said, you don't let it stay there until the rot, stink and flies enfilthen (come on, folks, he *had* to have made that word up) your whole world. No, you throw it out and thank God you never have to see it again. He wrapped things up by declaring that the impious wings of their granddaughter were proof of their daughter's sinfulness and, therefore, a vindication of their action in throwing me out.

"These two courageous people," he smarmed into

the camera, "struck out the evil that sullied their lives in order to save themselves, as our Lord strikes down evil to save us all."

So, one day before Angel would attempt her flight, she and I were vilified by the head of a so-called church *and* by our own flesh and blood. My teen pregnancy was being clucked over as the final straw in an apparent haystack of previous sins. And Angel was my retribution.

I wanted vindication; I wanted equal time; I wanted the world to know the truth about what had happened to me during childhood at the hands of the two scripture-spouting prigs on Harper's show. There was garbage in our house, all right, and yes, it rotted and stank, but those fingers of accusation had been pointed the wrong way.

I remember reading a book by the daughter of a movie star from Hollywood's glory days, a book in which the daughter revealed the dark truth about what had gone on when cameras were not recording and witnesses were not around. At the movie star's funeral, the daughter was standing off to one side when one of her mother's closest friends walked over and spat in the girl's face.

No one wants to hear the truth, Angel had said a few years earlier. People only care about what you appear to be, not what you are. So a monster in a realistic smiley-face mask isn't a monster at all.

And frail, old, devout Christians can't possibly have once taken sick pleasure in the battering and tormenting of a little child.

It had been said, it was in the open, and there was nothing I could do to change that. The best I could hope for was to prevent Angel from hearing about the malevolent spew, at least until after tomorrow. I didn't want anything to upset her before she had to meet the challenge of pulling off her lifelong dream. I called Jack's cell phone and begged him to keep her away from any television that day and the next. I figured the straight news shows would give at least *some* attention to Harper's program, in view of the subject matter and the timing. Jack assured me they didn't even have a radio with them at the field, and that all of them— but especially Angel—were keeping their eyes on the prize. They had no interest in what was going on in the rest of the world.

I was so relieved. I didn't want her moment of glory to be lessened in any way by the petty lies and opinions of people like Harper and my parents. I wanted nothing to upset her or shift her focus from safely completing her flight. There would be time enough afterwards for her to hear how she and I had been trashed.

Charlie, who rarely worked on a Saturday, did not come home until seven. After watching *Godsword,* which had triggered so many painful memories of my childhood, I could have used the safety of his arms around me, but we were still polite strangers waiting for tomorrow to be over.

For the third consecutive night, I did not sleep in Angel's apartment.

Nick was playing video games up in his room and Shelby was helping Charlie put tomato plants in the backyard garden when I left, one hour before I had told the children we would all go. I settled back into the soft leather seat of the limousine, hoping I could nap on the two-and-a-half hour ride and compensate for my sleep deprivation. A glance in the mirror that morning had confirmed even the Shroud of Turin looked fresher than I did, and the employment of every professional makeup trick I had learned on the Whisper campaign had done only a little to mitigate my shroudiness. Oh, well. Nobody was going to be looking at me; Angel was the star on this cool April Sunday.

Earlier in the week, before Nick's press debacle, Charlie's meltdown, and my parents' television debut, I had gone out to the hang gliding field with Jack and Angel, where I saw the layout of the place and learned why it had been selected as the venue for Angel's first flight.

Wind measurements were taken at the field each day, with the records going back fifteen years. Those records had been studied by Jack before the date of the flight was set—April tenth being one of the most consistent days for optimum thermals. The field also had a single landing strip, long enough for Angel's Cessna 182 to take off. The entire operation was centered in a flat valley surrounded by gently rolling hills, the topography apparently contributing to perfect wind conditions for hang gliders. And, I hoped, winged girls.

Angel had pointed out where everything would be

on Sunday—the trailer, the plane, the bleachers and the stage where she would make her initial appearance.

"Be prepared, Mom," she had said, "we're going to put on a bit of a show for the crowd. Music, fireworks, the grand entrance."

"Good thinking. You wouldn't want to go out there and disappoint them by just, oh, I don't know, *flying?*"

"I know it's a news story and a historical event but that doesn't mean we can't give 'em a little razzle dazzle."

And razzle dazzle is precisely what the limousine pulled into at the end of my ride. We were flagged through the seething crowd by a series of young men in day-glow vests, inching along for twenty minutes before crossing the landing strip and pulling in to the area alongside Angel's trailer. As I got out of the car to wish my daughter good luck, I took in the scene only fifty yards away. Bleachers were already at capacity, and I knew from the long crawl through the crowds that thousands more would have to watch on monitors in the parking lot. Enormous speakers pumped out high-octane rock and roll that roared out to the surrounding hills, then returned in a wave only slightly less powerful than the outgoing one.

Vendors hawked snacks, drinks and souvenirs to the raucous attendees. T-shirts bearing a likeness of the familiar wings and the words "Air Angel" were sprinkled through the stands. I wondered if some young entrepreneur was behind them, or if Angel had thought of it as one more way to amp the mood.

A half hour till show time and the place throbbed like a stadium hosting a heavy metal band.

Jack brought me into the trailer where Angel was getting ready. The pirates moved efficiently as she stood in long-sleeved thermal underwear, waiting for the harness to be fitted onto her.

"This lady claims to know you," Jack said to her, and she turned to me with a big smile.

"Wouldn't the Schultzies pee themselves if they saw me in *this* underwear?" She was glowing like a bride, and her wings vibrated as though they sensed they would soon be airborne.

"Can't you keep those big suckers still?" Duncan asked. "I don't want to get whiplashed."

"Wing's gotta do what a wing's gotta do, Dunc," she replied.

Buddy and Joel got the harness over her head and settled on her shoulders. Straps were fastened across her chest above her breasts, and around her waist, then hooked to the heavier strap running down her back between the wings. The lighter straps of the bottom half of the harness were secured to three pairs of light cuffs at the tops of her thighs, above her knees and at her ankles. Right before she was loaded into the cage, one of her crew would tighten the dangling straps at her ankles—which she jokingly called jesses—that would winch up the back strap so her legs were held together. They would stay virtually immobilized until she released them for landing.

Once the harness was in place, Jack and Helen buckled on the wide cuffs that would lock her arms to the wings. The fastening eye on each cuff extended out about an inch, enough to stick through the hemmed slits in the backs of the flight suit sleeves.

The bantering between Angel and her pirates left no doubt about the affection they felt for one another, making me understand how far away I was now from the reality of her daily life. I was only her mother; these people were her *team,* the ones who were facilitating the realization of a fantasy launched so long ago from a tiny pair of membranous flaps.

The glamorous flight suit went on, followed by the sensor gloves. Once the gloves were secured to her sleeves, Helen pulled the cuff eyes through the sleeve slits, and Jack moved to fasten her arms to the bolted panels in her wings.

"Wait," Angel said. "Give me a minute." Stepping over to me she wrapped her arms around me, pinning my arms to my sides so I wouldn't have to do the lean-and-reach required to return her embrace.

"Whatever happens, I love you" she whispered in my ear, "and thank you for everything you've done to keep me safe and for always believing in me." I had barely enough time to breathe in the baby powder scent of her neck before she abruptly let go and stepped back.

"Enough sappy p.d.a.," she said boisterously. "Let's get this show in the air!"

The quiet moment was gone, and if I had told her then how much I loved her and how proud I was, I would have started crying in front of her crew, so I headed for the door, matching her exuberant tone.

"I'm leaving before all the good seats are taken." As I turned at the door, Jack was bolting her arms to the wings and Helen netted her hair so Joel could fit the rubber-lined helmet onto her head.

"Break a wing, kiddo," I called from the door, then went down the three steps to the ground.

Duncan walked me back across the strip toward a VIP area with actual VIPs in it, faces from billboards, talk shows, basketball courts, music videos and newscasts.

He brought me to a place about thirty feet in front of the VIP section where four folding chairs represented, literally, front-row seating for the event. He was sensitive enough not to ask where the rest of the family was—he knew how divided people were on the subject of Angel's flight—but I asked him to take away three of the chairs. When Angel stepped onto that stage and looked this way, I didn't want her to see any reminders of who was *not* supporting her. Better that she should see one person filled with pride and love.

With another ten minutes to wait, I had the time to take it all in. Behind me the bleachers resonated with the voices of fifteen thousand enthusiastic fans, many of them singing along with "*Born To Be Wild*," the Steppenwolf song currently rocking the house. Across the strip, the trailer was hidden behind the curtained stage, whose proscenium arch was formed by a giant pair of wings painted in browns and gold. *Fire all of your guns at once and ex-plode into spa-ace!* I knew Angel was probably making the move from the trailer to the back of the stage right about now.

Camera crews were set up on this side of the strip, stretching out in both directions a little way behind me. The Jumbotron, not yet receiving a live feed, flashed lighted messages: *Go, Angel, Go! You Fly, Girl! Look! Up In The*

Sky! Wings Rule!

A pair of helicopters circled overhead, ready to capture video of the historic event. I knew they were set to pull up and well out of the way the minute Jack began taxiing toward take-off. For safety's sake, there would be no close-ups of Angel as she flew. Steppenwolf segued into Queen.

The Cessna stood waiting, only about fifty feet from the side of the raised stage. I saw the fireworks stands, ten feet apart along both sides of the landing strip, ready to be set off the second Angel touched down. Their dual purpose was to dramatically punctuate the successful conclusion of her flight, and to distract the audience at the last second if her landing was less graceful than she wanted it to be.

Duncan and Helen emerged from behind the stage and took up their positions at the end of the strip about a hundred feet behind the plane. *We will, we will rock you. Thump-thump.* Duncan needed a clear sightline to Angel in case her glove sensor failed and he had to remotely trigger the release of her leg harness. Helen held the flare gun that would be fired twice, the first time for dramatic effect as Jack started the plane, the second to signal Angel her flying time was over.

She and the pirates had agreed on a maximum of two minutes from aerial drop to touchdown, as they couldn't afford any more time with the cuffs restricting the blood flow to her arms as she angled and controlled the wings. She would need her arms to work with even more strength and precision during that last fifty feet, when the wings would do a braking tilt-back at the same time she was dropping her legs to a forty-five-degree angle with her torso. Her boots hitting the tarmac would cause the full release of the lower-body harness, enabling her to straighten up on landing.

The music abruptly stopped. The Jumbotron screen held a shot of the stage, its dark brown curtains still. The crowd slowly quieted, although the expectant murmuring of so many people still created a din.

Jack stepped out from between the closed curtains, receiving a mild wave of applause. Everybody knew who they had come to see and he was not the one. His movie-star handsome face filled the screen as he stood scanning the crowd, and I saw he was wearing an Indiana Jones hat with one of Angel's primaries stuck jauntily into the band.

Without the music blaring, I could clearly hear the few people whistling or calling out, "We want Angel!"

Jack gave a slow smile and bowed. His plume may have been topaz instead of white, but he showed every bit of Cyrano's panache as he took his hat from his head and swept it in a low arc, the tip of the feather nearly brushing the ground. His bow must have been the cue, as the music kicked in once again. I smiled when I heard what song it was.

When I was a young teen back in the early Eighties, I loved the TV show *Adam Karnes: Hero For Hire,* mostly because I was majorly crushed on the cute actor who played the lead. The program was forbidden in our house because the main character flew around in the air for reasons I have now forgotten. My parents, going along with that if-God-had-meant-us-to-fly thing, said the show was sacrilegious, so I could only see it when I stayed over at a friend's house. What I most remember, aside from the shaggy blond hair of the star, is the theme song, a sweet little bubblegum tune that stayed up on the music charts for quite a few weeks. The song was called *"Dance In The Sky,"* and I used to sing it to Angel when she was a little girl. After she was old enough to understand the words, she sang it herself. It was the song she loved to sing in the tub, bathroom acoustics being kind to tiny, tinny voices. When she replaced fairies with dinosaurs, it fell out of her repertoire and, I assumed, out of her memory. Apparently I was wrong.

The song started as Jack straightened and moved to the side of the stage, and the curtains began to lift and part.

> *A cloud like a heart*
> *Is beckoning me*
> *To join in the waltz*
> *Up there*

As the curtains opened, Angel stood alone in the center of the stage. The crowd began to roar.

Can my feet leave the ground?
Can I fly to that sound?

She took three strides forward to the front of the stage, planted her feet wide apart and smiled up at the deafening crowd.

Will your love lift
My wings in the air?

And then my daughter did something I had never before seen her do. She threw her shoulders back and raised her arms, lifting and spreading her golden wings.

Oh, yes! I can fly!
And I'm going to
Dance in the sky

Tears filled my eyes as the wings stretched to their full twelve-foot span. The crowd was at a stratospheric decibel level, but I couldn't hear it. And all I could see was my beautiful, winged girl, the wind tousling the curls only the inner circle and I knew were not hers. When I had expressed concern that she wouldn't have the strength to fly, Jack explained that controlling the wings in flight required concentration, not muscle. Her arms would only be guides, the wings themselves doing all the work.

So those nights in the gym, that upper-body work, it had all been for this moment. Her shining moment.

She lowered her wings and walked to Jack, then the two of them left the stage and crossed toward the waiting Cessna. The music dropped back out as they neared the plane, but the enthusiastic crowd kept singing the words of the song.

Oh, yes! I can fly!
And I'm going to
Dance in the sky

They were standing alone at the side of the plane when Jack dropped to one knee to tighten the jesses. I watched him pull on the straps, looking up at her to ask if they felt right. They exchanged words, and then I saw that something was not going as planned. He reached up and pulled off the sensor glove on her left hand. I knew this had been the weak link in the plan from the beginning; that's why they had built in the remote as a fail-safe. I fought the urge to stand and go to Angel. If anything was wrong, I wanted this stopped. There would be another day for flying. I feared the pressure of the cameras and the crowd might persuade her to go against good judgment. Jack stood up with the glove still in his hand, blocking my view of her. What was happening? A moment later, problem apparently solved, he slipped the glove back on her hand and secured it to her sleeve. I willed my heart to stop racing, convincing myself Jack would have called it off even if Angel wanted to go on unless everything was absolutely safe.

7

    If the crowd had come anticipating excitement and drama, they were getting it big time, and then they received a bonus—romance. Jack took both of Angel's upper arms in his hands, bent down and kissed her. It couldn't have come as a surprise to her, as she tilted her face up and held the kiss with him for moment after moment, while the crowd chanted, screamed, whistled and roared.

    They broke apart and Jack climbed into the cockpit without looking back at her. Simultaneously, Buddy and Joel appeared from out of nowhere and popped open the big dove glove. Angel did a trust fall into Joel's waiting arms, Buddy grabbed her legs, and the two of them lifted her into the cage, tucking her wings in against her body. The door was snapped shut, tightly sealing Angel into her titanium chrysalis.

    Helen raised her arm straight up to fire the first flare, and as the brilliant streak of light shot high into the afternoon sky, the 182's big engine cleared its throat and growled into readiness. A dozen sparkling tendrils arced up and over, then began their descent, twinkling out before returning to earth, as the Cessna began rolling forward, right to left in front of the thundering crowd. Angel was tucked under the left wing of the plane, ballast under the right, so the audience could clearly see her through the open mesh of the dove glove as the 182 taxied by, gaining speed quickly. The two helicopters pulled up and away as the Cessna raced forward, turbo engine roaring toward lift-off speed.

I knew a few things about the plane the rest of the audience did not. I knew it carried very little fuel, partly because Jack did not intend to be airborne more than ten or twelve minutes—he would touch down right after Angel did—and partly because the combined weight of monitors, cages, ballast and a winged girl added five hundred fifty pounds to the lift load. The lighter weight of two nearly empty fuel tanks compensated for the heavier cargo.

The large quad-split monitor was in the cockpit on the second seat, and would receive two live feeds from the news crews on the ground and two from the helicopters. The choppers were both pirate hires, as Angel didn't want anyone in the sky with her who wasn't on her payroll. No flying paparazzi to buzz her midair. By keeping an eye on the monitors, Jack would know exactly when to go into his final approach so it timed perfectly with Angel's landing.

At the far end of the runway, the 182 hit sixty-five knots and left the ground. Jack held a steady ascent until the plane was almost invisible to those of us at the field, then he banked right, made a one-eighty and resumed climbing as he came back toward the field. He crossed above the strip, left to right this time, the ballast cage on the side fronting the crowd. Off to the right a considerable distance, then a left-banking one-eighty and he was well on his way to the two-thousand-foot altitude where the dove gloves would drop their payloads. Everything was calculated so that during the third leg of the climbing zigzag, the Cessna would reach the desired altitude as it crossed the strip directly in front of the bleachers. Angel wanted the drop point to offer the clearest visibility for the crowd.

Jack had zigged left, zagged right and, at the peak of the last zig, he popped the door on the ballast cage. The fifteen-thousand-strong gasp had barely even begun when, a moment later, the second cage opened and Angel tumbled into the sky.

The ballast plummeted, crashing into the ground on the other side of the landing strip; the Cessna shot up at a steep angle to clear Angel's airspace; but no one saw either of those events. All eyes were on the girl who claimed she would fly.

Her wings were tight to her body as she side-rolled out of the cage, and she instantly began dropping, dropping. Then the pivotal moment: the big wings snapped open and bit into the wind. Angel was flying.

She raked away to the right, the direction opposite the climbing path of her plane. I checked the second hand of my watch to begin a count, although I knew Helen had a stopwatch and would send up the second flare at the right time.

Angel's graceful movements in the air were sheer joy to watch, and I tried to imagine what it must feel like to experience them. She soared, catching a thermal, then did a slow, spiraling ring up maybe seventy-five feet. We were at thirty-two seconds by my watch.

Like a Fourth of July crowd watching fireworks, the audience oohed and aahed and gasped at each spectacular visual. At the top of her spiral, Angel arced over, head down, then plummeted into a heart-stopping stoop...one hundred feet...two hundred feet...scattered screams in the crowd...three hundred feet and still diving...now half the audience standing, many with their hands over eyes or mouth...four hundred feet...five hundred feet. Then I stood, terror choking off any sound I could have made. Six hundred feet down from the top of her arc, Angel did three very tight turns, spiraling down even farther, then raked away and up on another thermal. The crowd, released from its tension and fear, cheered, applauded, howled, stamped their feet and whistled, as she soared upward again. I glanced at the time: sixty-five seconds.

She had brought the people watching to the edge of an abyss, then yanked them back; they cheered her; they loved her; they believed she could do anything.

Sensing she didn't have a lot of air time left, Angel

banked into a very wide, flat figure eight, not the aerial show's most challenging maneuver, but certainly the most graceful, and one that gave people at both ends of the stands a good, long look. She slowly looped the big eight the entire length of the bleachers and back, staying well over the landing strip. She and the pirates had decided not to risk sailing over the crowd on this first flight.

She looked like some indolent golden hawk drifting in the sky as it selected from among the fast-food choices scurrying through the meadow below. The emarginated tips of her wings separated and opened into feathery fingers caressing the wind.

Helen fired the flare gun, signaling Angel it was time to begin descending. Over the noise of the audience, I could hear the buzz of the Cessna as it circled, waiting for her to land.

Seated as I was so far in front of the bleachers, and with no one on the strip or the field on the other side of it, I felt as though I were the sole witness to the fulfillment of my daughter's destiny. I shut out the screaming, cheering mob, and reveled in the sight of Angel tilting her wings up to slow her speed and increase their resistance to the wind. Her glove sensor worked perfectly, lowering her stretched-out legs the first fifteen-degree increment, as she slowly descended to three hundred feet. Drag from the massive wings gave her the appearance of floating, as her legs dropped another fifteen degrees at around two hundred fifty feet.

My eyes filled with tears—of joy? relief? love?—and I watched in awe. After a lifetime of wishing, dreaming and planning, my little girl was finally flying.

Right up until the moment she was falling.

I was not born until years after John F. Kennedy's assassination, but I recall my father describing to me the events which occurred in the days and weeks that followed it. The Zapruder film would not emerge for some time, so the public had only the knowledge of the event, no grisly, in-your-face visual of the man's death. Stately processions, well-behaved children, a stricken and stoic widow; these were the pictures that represented the aftermath, somber images that said, "Yes, death was here, but now it has gone," leaving the country to its dignified grieving.

That grieving process was jarred by a second death, famously occurring live on the television sets turned on in virtually every U.S. home. When Jack Ruby shot and killed Lee Harvey Oswald, he didn't know he had become a co-star of the news clip that would play again and again, jacked-up counterpoint to the dignified sorrow of official mourning.

Was that the precise moment America embraced the desire for eyewitness death? When those lurid photos from the 1930s—pictures of gunned-down gangsters sprawled in puddles of their own blood—became quaint reminders of a time when people had to settle for still photos taken after the good stuff was over?

Oh, we had always had a taste for it (witch burnings, lynchings) but news films like that of the Hindenburg fire and crash never provided us the delicious *immediacy* of watching one human being die right in front of our eyes. Sure, little people were falling to their death through the flames, but that was days ago, before the film got developed

and distributed to movie theaters. We wanted our death
now and we wanted it up close and personal.

Live TV brought that possibility into our lives, but
we didn't really appreciate it until a November day in the
Dallas police headquarters. Through the years our national
palate became more discerning, savoring the real-time view
of a space shuttle exploding or a S.W.A.T. stand-off, but
really feasting on any very personal public death. We curl
up on our couches wearing pajamas and sharing a bowl of
popcorn, and watch a high-speed police chase shot from a
news helicopter. Maybe the fleeing suspect will only smash
into another car and roll over a couple times, but maybe,
just maybe, the suspect will try to run from the overturned
vehicle and be gunned down by police. Darn, he's dropping
to his knees and putting his hands on his head as he is surrounded. Maybe next time.

Shame and humanity are slow to kick in at these
times. Well, we claim, they're bad guys doing dangerous
things. Okay, let's say that is a viable moral viewpoint.
Tell me, then, why was it all right for media outlets to play
and replay the horrifying images of innocent people jumping to their deaths from the upper floors of the towers on
that September morning? How many times did we see
those tapes replayed in the first hours after the tragedy? At
what point did someone in a control room or executive office
say, "Oh, Jesus, the families of those people are watching
this," and pull the video plug on that part of the disaster?
It was *jump-die-repeat*, until shame and humanity dulled
the collective appetite for more, then the images stopped
and were discreetly omitted from the documentaries and
dramatizations made later.

A convenience store clerk is shot to death on camera
by a robber; a hundred-year-old woman is caught on security tape as she is beaten with her own handbag by a huge
thug in the vestibule of her building; a police cruiser dash-
cam captures the hit-and-run death of a patrolman during a
routine freeway stop. And we see them at six, at eleven, on
the news magazine shows and online, not once, but over
and over and over, maybe with a little slo-mo thrown in.

In the days and weeks after April tenth, I watched

my daughter die a hundred times. For Charlie, Nick and Shelby, the first time had been more than enough. For me, though, having seen the realization of two of the three dark prophecies from my first eye contact with Angel, I knew my time was here, the time when I would have to ante up and play out the rest of the hand.

6

      I watched the videos of her death in those first days, until the periodicals hit the stands. The magazine coverage included a gamut of reactions that mirrored the range of opinions *before* she had flown. They varied from straight reporting to sensational reporting to exploitive reporting. The articles were sober, cautionary, questioning, gloating or cruel, depending.

      Time Magazine's compelling, non-judgmental cover the following week was a solid black background with an artist's rendering of the white chalk outline you see on cop dramas, showing the line extending out from an imaginary body in the shape of a large wing. On the opposite side, the outline was of a broken, twisted wing. Another magazine put a facsimile of a death certificate on its cover. Angel's full name was typed in as the deceased, and on the cause-of-death line was the single word: *hubris*. Even after the fact, people were forcefully stating their opinions.

      Charlie and the children withdrew to mourn, but I did what Angel had always done: I focused. I sat in front of the TV, switching channels when the one I was watching left her story for other news. I read what they wrote about her life, her miracle flight (although even in the immediate aftermath, there were those claiming it had all been a hoax) and her dramatic death. Much of it was true.

      Angel had faced a two-decade challenge: how can I fly? In the face of seemingly impossible odds, she whittled away at the obstacles in her path, determined to succeed even if not one other person on earth understood why she was compelled to do so.

      Could I do anything less to avenge her death?

Angel held the big wings at their maximum drag angle, slowing her descent as she triggered the sensor glove for the third time, lowering her legs the final fifteen degrees and putting herself in position for landing.

The crowd was on its feet again, their cacophonous response to Angel's performance rocking out toward the surrounding hills, then rolling back over us the same way the music had.

She faced the bleachers, wings spread majestically, floating down through two hundred feet, when her right shoulder and the upper arch of her right wing exploded in a shower of feathers and blood.

In my folding chair halfway between the Roman spectacle behind me and the Greek tragedy in front of me, I did not hear the sound of the rifle shot until it had made its return trip from the peripheral hills, its echoing thunder filling the sudden silence. The impact of the bullet had flipped Angel over in the air, so that even if she were still conscious, she had lost the ability to control her wings. With the left one now flat against her as she plummeted head first, and the right one trailing her falling body through an arterial geyser, the wings had lost their aerodynamic integrity.

I was on my feet and running toward the landing strip before the stunned silence of the crowd broke against the leading edge of their screams. There were no numbers high enough, no numerical sequences complex enough to prepare me as I watched my daughter tumble in the air and crash to earth, her gloves and boots rocketing off on impact, sailing away on their own short flights.

Even from twenty yards out, as I rushed to close the distance between us, I could see there was no chance of her having survived. I dropped to my knees alongside her shattered body while the audience mobilized. Most of the people from the bleachers were screaming in panic and trying to leave, perhaps afraid a sniper was shooting at random, but several hundred of them surged forward and rushed toward Angel and me.

There is a term used in falconry—mantling—that describes the actions a raptor takes to protect its dead prey from scavengers and other predators. The bird hunches down and spreads its wings in a protective tent that shields the kill from view.

If Helen and Duncan had been younger, if Buddy and Joel had been faster, they still could not have reached us ahead of the mob. As it closed in and surrounded us, people noisily jostling for better position, I threw my right knee over Angel's hip to straddle her, slipping in the spreading pool, and having to pull my knees in and plant them decisively in order to stay balanced. Leaning forward, I placed my palms flat on the wet tarmac to either side of her head, noticing as I did that a man stepped forward, picked up the sensor glove that had ended its separate flight about ten feet from Angel's body, and slipped it into his pocket before stepping back into the hushed crowd. That was one of the many "souvenirs" which began turning up on eBay within a few weeks, one of the many missing pieces of forensics that hampered the police as they searched for my daughter's killer.

Galileo notwithstanding, a feather will fall to earth more slowly than an anvil. Or an angel. The secondaries from the top arch of Angel's right wing had been blown off and sent skittering into the clear sky she had inhabited moments before. As I mantled her body as best I could, the first of those feathers began to rain down on the runway. People hesitantly plucked them out of the air at first, but as the crowd realized there was only a finite number of them, the tentative plucking turned to competitive grabbing.

Within seconds elbows were being thrown, as several men jockeyed for position under the same drifting feather. One man hoisted his wife onto his shoulders; she reached up and had almost grasped a cognac-colored bit of history when a second man leaped into the air, snagging the prize while knocking the woman over and to the ground. The husband decked the jumper and, like the old westerns where one punch sets off a melee including every cowboy in the saloon, the crowd around me erupted into a seething mass of mindless violence.

Angel and I were protected from the mob by a moat of gore which no one seemed inclined to step in. Then a movement caught my eye and, as I turned, I saw someone kneel at the edge of the moat, his hand stretching toward the tip of Angel's shattered right wing. As his fingers closed around a long, golden primary, I began to scream. He jerked back with his prize, and my shrieking voice rose in fury. In the distance another shrieking resonated—a police car siren? Those fighting at the edge of my bloody moat saw the man with the snatched primary pulling back. For a nanosecond I thought they would mob him and punish him for the desecration, but as the whining noise that competed with my screams drew closer, I saw the looks on their faces. Few feathers now floated in the air, but oh, so many still clung to the big, broken wings. With horror, I saw people inching into the moat, grimacing as the blood soaked their shoes, but willing to do what it took to secure a memento. That other sound screeched closer and I realized it wasn't a siren at all—my keening had layered a soprano harmony over the baritone voice of the Cessna's turbo engine—and I raised my eyes to the sky to see the 182 diving straight at me. The mob heard it, too, then saw it, and the pushing and shoving to secure one of Angel's golden feathers turned instantly to pushing and shoving to get the hell out of the way of a plane falling like the hammer of God.

I kept my protective position over Angel when the crowd scattered, preferring to die on the spot rather than abandon her body to the scavengers who had been cheering her only a short time before. As the Cessna continued its dive, I lowered my head and looked at Angel's face. At the last possible moment before impact, the 182 nosed up sharply and banked left above the scattering ghouls. Jack climbed and dived on us two more times, until even the most persistent scavengers gave up. By then I heard actual sirens—multiple police units and at least one ambulance— approaching slowly as they were stymied by the retreating mob and exiting vehicles.

The titanium helmet had protected Angel's skull and, as she had landed on her back, her beautiful face was undamaged, her expression not one of fear or pain but of repose. I leaned down to kiss her forehead and whisper that I loved her, but realized she already knew, had known it from that first glance in St. Luke's Hospital long ago. And so, rather than whisper what I needed to say, I told her what she needed to hear, softly at first, then louder and louder, until finally, after the blare of the music and the roar of the crowd, it was *my* voice that ricocheted off the hills, bouncing back and washing over the empty bleachers.

"You can fly!" I shouted again and again, and the echoing hills confirmed it: *You can fly! You can fly! You can fly!*

Our fake wing guy—whose name was Chester Aldovan (delete that, Jack, if you think it will cause legal problems)—was ruled out by the police almost immediately. Despite Chet's mother giving him an alibi, we knew from viewing the video that he had been in the stands that day. His turtleneck shirt, fake goatee and black beret *might* have convinced someone he was merely a time-traveling beatnik from the Allen Ginsberg portion of the 1950s had he not worn the same cheesy pair of wings he had put on for his many appearances outside our home.

Technically, Chet had violated the two-hundred-yard restraining order, but it seemed pointless to prosecute a field mouse with a jackal still at large.

No tickets had been sold, no security cameras had been set up, the only law enforcement present had been off-duty patrolmen hired for crowd control, so there was not a lot of good evidence for the detectives assigned to the case to follow up on. The news camera crews had made a few sweeps of the crowd to provide color for the human interest news story this was to have been, but at the time of the shooting, all cameras had been on the girl in the air.

Angel's body became the key piece of evidence in her murder, but, sadly, didn't offer much in the way of helpful information. All the normal trajectory-plotting equations were useless here, no human being having previously been shot out of the sky to provide guidelines. We assumed the gunman had been high up in the bleachers or standing somewhere among the parked cars behind them.

Her SRO autopsy produced the only concrete piece of forensics the police would ever find—a fragment of an outlawed bullet. First manufactured in 1990, Black Talons were originally marketed to law enforcement, but once they became popular within certain criminal circles—earning the sobriquet "cop killer" bullets—they were pulled from the market in 2000. Which was not to say, the detectives told me, that plenty of them weren't still around, archived until needed.

5

What made the Black Talon ammunition so lethal was its capacity to mushroom on contact with soft flesh, opening like the talon of a hawk and shredding everything in its path as it made its brief journey through a person's body. The Black Talon that had killed Angel—or at least caused the fall that killed her—had been most likely aimed at what hunters like to call the central mass: the heart/lung or "sure-kill" area. Whoever shot her had not previously tracked a flying girl in his sight, so he could not lead her movements as well as he might have led those of a flying duck, so the bullet went several inches off its mark. The Talon did not tear through Angel's chest as planned, but instead entered low on her right shoulder. I have read that coroner's report multiple times, but I suspect you are not interested in the proximal and inferior points on the bone, the coracobrachialis and teres major muscles, the brachiocephalic and lateral thoracic arteries. What you need to know is that the bullet pierced her body at a point four inches down from the center spot on the top of her right shoulder, clawed its way through veins, arteries, muscle and bone—including the scapula, the one we sometimes tell children is their wing bone—before exiting and obliterating the top arch of her right wing. Reviewing the video, the coroner concluded she was still alive as she fell, evidenced by the arterial blood pumping out in a series of spurts that went on till the time of impact.

In the months following her death, the police chased

even the thinnest leads—every one of those ghouls offering feathers dotted with Angel's blood was tracked down and interviewed. Most of the feathers had come from pigeons or turkeys, and the "blood" varied from the fake stuff sold in any novelty shop to honey with red food coloring in it. A few genuine primaries and secondaries turned up for sale, some with Angel's blood on them, but the sellers all turned out to be souvenir hunters, not murderers.

Four weeks after Angel's death, her body was finally released to me, and the last fight Charlie and I had was over what to do with it. He wanted a funeral and a burial in a place where he and the other children could lay flowers and grieve. Jack and I—for by then we were aligned— wanted cremation and an aerial scattering of her ashes. This was what she had told Jack she wanted, even leaving him a note to that effect, and it fit with everything I had known about my daughter. With a choice between being boxed and buried or being set free on the wind, well, there really was only one choice.

Charlie had never legally adopted Angel—we had not seen the need—so when he hired a lawyer to prevent the cremation, the judge ruled in my favor. Defeated, he left the courtroom, and shortly afterwards requested I move out of the house.

Jack and I took the Cessna up one last time (I sold it soon after to finance my quest) and sent Angel's remains on their final flight into a warm summer sky dotted with fluffy, pettable clouds like the bunnies in the pages of that first book I ever read to her. I released her ashes—and a handful of golden primaries from my imping kit—into the wind on what would have been her twentieth birthday.

Over that first year after she died, the leads thinned out, the case went cold and the public slowly lost interest. Angel had not lived as long as Marilyn Monroe, or done as much as Princess Diana, so her cult following was really more of a cultlet—small groups of teen girls who chatted about her online, occasionally wore fake wings in public and fantasized about flying.

Charlie reghosted. We were separated physically and emotionally, but neither of us did the filing to make it a legal separation. I lived in Angel's apartment, too busy to bother, and Charlie lived in the house, too shattered to care. Nick entered his senior year double-fisting longnecks and staying hammered. Shelby stopped speaking to me and would have sheltered with her daddy had he still lived in Charlie's body. She stayed more and more with Stacy at Katie and Pete's house, and I hear she has been living with them full-time for the last couple years.

And me? Well, I went out and bought me a rifle.

I waited twelve months to purchase the rifle, although I knew who I intended to kill within weeks of her death. My choice was a Savage 308, a high-quality firearm, certainly, but selected primarily because the name *so* reflected my intent. And, of course, it didn't hurt that there was that calming number after the name.

I decided on the synthetic stock, as it is lighter than wood and I am a fairly small-boned woman without (at least at the time) any experience handling a heavy rifle. The fifty-millimeter scope was probably more than I would need, but I figured, what the hell. For ammunition, I went with soft tips for maximum damage, although I hoped I would be able to quietly buy Black Talons.

Once I was armed with my Savage—purchased in another state—the next task was finding someone who could teach me to use it. And that is how Wiley Ritter came into my life. Wiley was a forty-five-year-old former Marine who owned and operated a shooting range. I had checked out several other places, chatting up the instructors, trying to get a feel for who was the right man for the job, but when I talked with Wiley and learned he had trained military snipers, I knew I had found Mr. Right.

In all the months he worked with me, Wiley never asked why I had bought the Savage or what I intended to use it for. I had worked up a half-baked story about proving to my deer-hunting father that I could handle my weapon and bring down a twelve-point buck as well as he could. Mercifully, Wiley's don't-ask-don't-tell policy precluded my having to put my acting ability to the test.

First he taught me how to shoot, then he taught me how to shoot with nearly perfect accuracy, and along the way—I believe Wiley was the tiniest bit sweet on me—he shared some tips from his sniper days. He taught me how to "lean into it" to counter the considerable recoil on the Savage, and he showed me a way to thread my left arm through the sling and wrap it before putting my hand under the floor plate of the magazine, giving me a firmer platform. And when we were to the point of refining my technique, he gave me a lesson on how to squeeze the trigger with the slowest, smoothest action possible. I remember that I had sighted in on the target, using my scope, and had my finger on the trigger, when I heard Wiley's deep voice a few inches from my ear.

"Sight alignment...sight picture...squeeze..." Wiley whispered in his southern drawl. "Sight alignment...sight picture...squeeze...let it surprise you."

It seemed strange at first, but within a short time I could almost hypnotize myself into stillness and focus with that chant. *Sight alignment...sight picture...squeeze...sight alignment...sight picture...squeeze.* Sometime in the mantra the tension on the trigger would ease into critical and the rifle would explode and recoil against my shoulder. The chant smoothed out my formerly jerky finger and became foreplay—preceding the main event, but very pleasurable on its own.

Wiley was impressed with how quickly I developed my skills, coming in as I did only once a week to his firing range, but what he didn't know was that I had my own don't-ask-don't-tell policy, and his was not the only range I patronized. Not wanting to draw attention to myself by practicing every day at one range, I spread my patronage over four, including Wiley's—although, at the others, I only paid my money and fired at targets for a few hours. I did this not only because I thought a once-a-week shooter would draw less attention than a daily shooter, but because the more people I came in contact with in that gun lovers' milieu, the better my chances of finding someone to supply me with Black Talons.

Sometimes I felt like the high school loser trying to score weed for the first time, but I continued to drop hints, figuring someone would know someone and my interest would be whispered in the right ear. Then one day a red-haired man in the shooting stall next to me came over when I had finished and struck up a casual conversation. His hints were subtle, his code abstruse, but I finally realized he wasn't hitting on me, he was offering to *sell* me something. The something remained unnamed, although he did ask if it was for the Savage. When I confirmed it was, he grinned and said, "Good. I wouldn't want to bring a size-ten shoe for a size-six foot," a statement I assumed referred to providing the right caliber ammunition.

And who was to be the lucky recipient of one of my contraband Black Talons? Why, Mr. J. William Harper himself. He had been my research subject since Angel's death, my reason for installing a TV set in her apartment within days, and his was the face I saw on every target at all my shooting ranges for eight months.

The house was in mourning when I slipped in early the day after the fatal flight. Charlie and the children had retreated to their separate rooms the previous evening, sick with the horror of what they had seen, grieving for Angel's loss. I closed the living room door, turned on the TV, tuned in FCC, lowered the audio so it would not penetrate beyond that room, then settled back and waited for *Godsword* to come on.

I didn't only listen to Harper's spew; I parsed out each word, every nuance of what he said. I sank in deeply, going under and behind his gestures, body language and inflammatory words. Oh, he was so-o smug and self-congratulatory, basking in his own prescience about God's intolerance for sinful acts—His willingness to strike down the sinner—but he was subtle and careful in his references to the infamous flight. He quoted scripture to make his point, but what I heard was, "Job well done!" He had not pulled the trigger, but he had inspired and provoked the person who had, I was sure of it.

I wondered if my parents were watching the show, nodding in approval of God's retribution. The picture of my mother shivering with excitement at the smiting of a sinner was crystal clear, but I couldn't bring my father's reaction into focus. He had always been the passive follower in their two-strong crusade, seeming almost embarrassed by her fervor. Even as a child I had sensed his less-than-zealous embracing of the righteousness my mother oozed, and I wondered why he went along with her insanity. Was he a henpecked wimp? Would the tornadic force of her twisted godliness have sucked in a stronger man? Or maybe the crime for which they sought redemption was not *theirs,* but only *his,* a sin for which he was grateful that she was willing—no, thrilled—to be the absolution point person.

4

As the months dragged by and the police followed lead after lead to dead ends, I filled Angel's apartment with everything ever written by or about J. William Harper. I ordered the complete DVD collection of *Godsword,* along with every sermon he had preached—the early ones only available on audio tape. I read all the news articles about the beating death of that poor gay man, the death in which Harper had been questioned as a person of interest. I carefully listened to the sermons he gave in the three months before that crime and, with my newly tuned ears, my ability to hear him the same way his myrmidons did, I detected his call to action—a call which would leave him as innocent as Henry II, who had never demanded the murder of Thomas Beckett, but had merely asked rhetorically, "Will no one rid me of this lowborn priest?" Hank had the superior power of persuasion, though, because four swordsmen cut Beckett down, leaving him to bleed to death on the polished marble floor of Canterbury Cathedral, whereas Harper had jacked up only *three* thugs to beat Daniel Sutton so badly that he bled out and died on the urine-stained floor of a gas station bathroom.

There were other cases, less well-known than the Sutton murder. And, of course, there was Angel. No chain of police-worthy evidence lead back to Harper in any one of them, only a microscopically thin wire that thrummed with his desire—a vibration interpretable only by the sensitive antennae of his insect soldiers. And me.

I bought the Savage in April, practiced with it four days a week through December, then put it to a higher and better purpose on a cold morning in January.

I began attending services at the mega church in
early November, paying cash each week for my round-trip
airfare, and spending Saturday nights in a nearby chain
motel. Horseshoe-configured rows of seats embraced the
long center leg of the massive cross-shaped stage—at the
heart of which Harper's pulpit and microphone stood—and
extended, bank after bank, right up to the nosebleed seats
under the curve of the domed ceiling.

I noted that the crowd always gravitated toward the
stage—the better to be close to the magic, I assumed—
filling the bottom rows completely, but leaving a few at the
top empty when the pulpiteer preached to a less-than-
capacity house. And the older, more frail members of his
flock were not as well represented on the Sundays when
bad weather was a factor. My crutches and bulky winter
coat became familiar to the ushers, scrubbed young men in
navy blue blazers who had initially offered each week to
help me to a seat, but who soon came to know me as the
independent old biddy who insisted on limping to a seat in
the uppermost row under her own power. My third Sunday,
one approached and invited me to join the group healing at
the end of the service, but I told him I was going to wait
until Easter service so I could receive the highest-wattage
God power Mr. Harper could send my way. The poor lamb
was either too dull-witted to detect my sarcasm or too polite
to acknowledge it. I came and went each week, clunking in
on my crutches, my gray wig topped with an old babushka,
my thick glasses perched on my nose. I noted how the most

senior of the followers walked and held themselves, then I tried to emulate their slow, stooping movements.

Late in January, when a blizzard was forecast to hit the southwest within days, I loaded the car with my 308, my crutches, my disguise, a thermos of coffee and a cooler filled with the makings for enough bologna sandwiches to feed me for two days. I rolled out on a Thursday morning and pulled into my usual motel late Saturday afternoon, the leading edge of the blizzard already knifing the city.

Just as Angel had never questioned her destiny, I now fully and sanguinely accepted mine. I ordered a pizza, tipping the driver lavishly for venturing out in the harsh weather, watched a *Becker* rerun, then went to bed early and slept like a baby.

The blizzard had done its part overnight, so I woke to the perfect day for my task—the crowd would be reduced enough for me to have several rows in the back all to myself. I belted the pillow around my waist, pulled on the heavy-gauge granny stockings, and slipped my feet into the worn, sensible shoes I had found for only a dollar at a thrift shop. For the last time I tucked my hair under the edges of the gray wig. The Coke-bottle-thick glasses would have to wait until I pulled into The Brotherhood Of The Lord's parking lot, as looking through them turned the world into an underwater funhouse. I tied the wrinkled babushka on my head and shrugged into the calf-length wool coat. I checked outside to be sure no one was around before I took my crutches to the car, not because I cared if anyone saw I wasn't really handicapped, but because my Savage was strapped securely to the inside of the right crutch.

I rode the empty elevator to the top level of the building, disembarking as usual and clunking my way past the security camera and the young ushers. They seemed pleasantly surprised that one of the oldsters would venture out in the frigid, sleety weather, but they waved me in with warm smiles. Inside, under the dimly lighted dome of the amphitheater-sized building, things were even better than I had hoped for. Easily a dozen rows of seats separated me from the nearest pod of worshippers. I knew once the show started, the ushers would close the doors and take the elevator down to the ground floor, where they would assist in the singing, healing and harvesting of the checks and cash.

I waited until the gospel singers had filed in from both sides, taken their places on the two outstretched arms of the giant cross, and begun their opening number. Their voices lifted to the rafters and covered any sounds I made removing my coat and the bulky pillow under it, setting aside my wig and glasses, and freeing my Savage from its crutch. I chambered the one round I intended to fire, sure of my marksmanship, thankful for Wiley's patient training and tricky playbook. I laid the rifle across my knees and settled back, waiting for my prey to appear.

Gabriel's trumpet could not have given a fanfare more enthusiastic than the one Harper got as he jogged out onto the main leg of the cross and trotted to his dead-center position between the two groups of sanctified singers. On any other Sunday, he would speak into his microphone for forty minutes, occasionally stepping back to let the choir whip up the crowd again, before striding down the length of the cross—which would by then be completely surrounded by the sick, the lame and the star-fuckers—so he could touch, bless and heal as many people as time and the Lord would allow. Perched in my aerie, high above the throb of religiosity, I knew today's program would be different.

Harper began speaking, and it was soon evident that Jews were this week's target. Only last Sunday it had been those scary homosexuals who were undermining our values, but they must have straightened themselves out pronto because now a Zionist threat had supplanted them. I assumed blacks were on the roster for next Sunday, as he rotated his targets with the predictability of a Swiss-made cuckoo clock. Abortionists, adulterers, gays, Jews and blacks, took their lumps on a schedule, but Harper could always slip in a wild card like a winged girl if the need arose. Women never caught the full splash of his spew—too many check-writing females in the flock, no doubt—but every sermon reminded them of their biblically prescribed role of meekness and obedience. *I got your meekness right here,* I thought, cupping the end of the rifle stock the way a man would fleetingly heft his own package to emphasize a macho point.

I knew from his gestures and tone he was preparing to launch into his big finish, so I stood up and prepared to launch into mine. Hoisting the 308 to my shoulder, I did the Wiley-wrap with my left arm, seated the gun securely, then did a slow, slow pullback on the bolt, the only way to open it without a loud, metallic *ka-chunk*. I put my eye to the scope, slowed my breathing, my heartbeat and my trigger finger with the silent mantra—*sight alignment...sight picture...squeeze...sight alignment...sight picture...squeeze...* I could almost hear Wiley's drawl in my ear: *Let it surprise you.* And it did.

Like a bowler who knows he has made his game-winning strike without even watching the ball complete its roll, I turned aside, laying the rifle across the seat that held the old wool coat, even as the booming report of the Savage thundered through the acoustically perfect dome—a basso profundo aria preceding the cacophony of screams which made up the final movement of that morning's soap opera.

No one looked in my direction, so unfocused was the echoing roar of the rifle, but I moved to the aisle and opened the door fully expecting to be tackled by the lambs in the navy blue jackets. The corridor was empty; all the action was on the ground floor. I headed toward the elevator, pausing squarely in front of the security camera and planted my feet wide apart, as Angel had done when she stepped out onto the stage before her flight. I had no big wings to lift in celebration, so all the video showed was my big smile and enthusiastic double thumbs-up before I hit the button to open the elevator doors.

The judge who sentenced me viewed that flash of showmanship numerous times before soberly citing it as one of her reasons for invoking the death penalty. I couldn't have asked for more.

Driving directly to the police station, I found a flurry of activity there as the news began coming in about the shooting at the BroOTL headquarters. People were rushing around everywhere, so when I asked to speak to a detective, I was impatiently told I would have to take a seat and wait. I had brought a book—Dorothy Dunnett's *King Hereafter,* which I highly recommend—so I sat amid the hubbub and read a dozen pages until I was approached by a tired-looking, overweight man in a suit from that place that guarantees it.

"Hi, I'm Detective Lind. I understand you wanted to talk to someone?"

"Yes. Allison Fitzgerald. Nice to meet you," I said, shaking his hand. "I have information regarding a homicide."

"All right, come on over to my desk. Can I get you a cup of coffee?"

"No thanks. I'm fine." He indicated a chair next to an older wooden desk, so I sat as he took his own seat and flipped open a little spiral notebook.

"Sorry about the wait. I don't know if you heard, but one of our local bigwigs was killed a little while ago."

"Yes, I know. I'm the one who shot him."

I was happy Detective Lind "caught the collar," as he had been requested to stay back and man the fort while the younger, hotter detectives were sent to swarm the BroOTL crime scene. By the time I had confessed and been booked, the other guys were drifting back in, only to learn that schlumpy Detective Lind was the hero of the hour. It feels good to do something nice like that for someone, and I was happy to make his day.

Over my protests, Mark Dennison paid a top criminal attorney to review my case and speak at the sentencing hearing. There had, of course, been no trial. Having been a bit player in two prior media circuses, I had no desire to take the starring role in a third. The lawyer's argument against the death penalty was based on a claim of maternal grief and temporary insanity caused by Angel's death, along with a plea that the good faith I showed by turning myself in and confessing should count for something.

Mark might as well have saved his money. The judge rightly pointed out almost two years had passed since my daughter's death, and that three separate psychiatrists had found me intelligent and competent—although, just between us, that second shrink seemed concerned when I told him I just didn't *get* Sudoku.

Which is how I come to be sitting here on death row, hurrying to tell Angel's story before time runs out. This is my fourth (and last) yellow pad, and they are all being left for Jack to read, burn, publish or lock away.

3

Perhaps you are wondering how Jack and I became so close, especially in light of my early suspicions about him. If so, I need to take you back to the day Angel flew, more than five years ago now, and tell you what happened once the ghouls had scattered under the threat of the diving Cessna.

I had maybe two minutes on the tarmac alone with Angel after the mob dispersed. Jack was landing without power, so Buddy and Joel stood by to help him if he needed it, fire extinguishers in hand. Helen's arm had been broken when she was roughly pushed back by the crowd while she attempted to get through to Angel. Duncan, who had also been trying to get through, saw Helen go down and opted to help her back to the trailer rather than continue fighting a losing battle to get close to us. With the pirates distracted elsewhere, the ghouls fleeing, and the police still a mile away, I was by myself when I left my protective crouch and stood up. Close as I had been to her, my hands and knees sliding in her blood as I guarded her, I had not really gotten a look at the whole picture, a picture which instantly came into focus as I stood up.

You've seen that image, I'm sure. Even the official crime scene photos somehow wound up on the internet, far superior, most people thought, to the multiple cell phone shots the people surrounding her body had taken, as the former did not have me hovering over her and blocking the view of the good stuff.

The broken girl—who appears to be sleeping on a red marble pallet that glows in the late-afternoon sun— sprawls awkwardly on her garnet bed, as small children do in their heavy, dream-filled sleep. One improbably large wing, the left, stretches out, its red-spattered tip seemingly pointing with accusation toward the bleachers. Her arm, still cuffed to the big wing, is relaxed, her fingers curled into a soft, loose fist. The torn remains of the right wing crumple against her back as if, in her dying, it had tried to snug against her body the way it had when I slipped a fin-gertip under it at St. Luke's Hospital so many years before. Her hands and feet are bare, gloves and boots having been ejected on landing. Those artificial curls surrounding her face, the ones that aren't yet soaked, shift with the slight breeze wisping across the runway.

There was the whole picture, the entirety I had not comprehended from my kneeling position over her body. And that's when I saw it, the thing that broke me. On the hand still bolted to her outstretched left wing, a diamond sparkled on her gently curled finger. In a ring she had not been wearing when her gloves were put on in the trailer.

When Jack dropped to one knee, he had not only fastened her jesses—he had proposed. And nothing had been wrong with the sensor glove; after she said yes, he had removed it to slip the engagement ring on her finger.

She had loved him enough to marry him, to fly trustingly into his arms to begin her own life. And now that life—any life—was denied her. What had my beautiful winged daughter ever done to deserve the kind of hatred that had brought her down?

It was the sense of *her* loss, not my own, that forced me back down to my knees beside her body, that set me to rocking and weeping, my bloody hands pressed over my eyes. When the pirates finally approached, when the police and ambulance made it to the scene, when Jack brought the plane to a stop and jumped out onto the tarmac, this is how they found me.

Because I was so close to her, I never really saw the bigger picture. To me Angel was always an ordinary girl who happened to have an extraordinary pair of wings. To the public, though, the people who never saw those original tiny flaps, who never ached along with her through the fairy and dinosaur flying fantasies, Angel appeared on the scene full-grown with magical wings—a creature from a fairy tale or a Greek myth.

I now believe the public was right and I was wrong. She was never ordinary. But the ember inside needed time before it could erupt into flame, as the crumpled pupa in its chrysalis needs time before it can reveal itself as a beautiful winged creature. Unlike a butterfly, however, she did not emerge from a chrysalis to fly with millions of others like her. Angel flew alone, destined—like so many chimerical creatures in mythology—to be the only one of her kind.

When Jack entered her life, a man with a degree in aeronautical engineering, a love of flying and an unequivocal desire to see her fulfill her dream, she had found the perfect consort. Even if Angel had been telling Charlie the truth when she insisted Jack was only an employee—and I'm not sure she was, even back then—the gods would have thrown the mythical girl and the bigger-than-life man together again and again until the flame caught. If Angel had stepped out of a Greek myth, Jack had leaped from the pages of a Raphael Sabatini novel, a dashing romantic hero in the style of Scaramouche or Captain Blood. Even when he knew the woman he loved lay broken on the runway, he had risked his life to scatter the scavengers, aiming the plane at them again and again, pulling up only at the last second to climb and dive once more, knowing all the time the turbo engine was sucking in not much more than fumes. The last ghouls were disappearing behind the bleachers when I heard the Cessna cough. Then silence as it glided down without power.

Had I reacted so negatively to Jack in the beginning because of his swashbuckling persona? Or my fear that he was a slick and dreamy con man who would sweep Angel off her feet and break her heart? I believe now that from the start I somehow *sensed* he was the one who would lead her to her destiny, and that terrified me the same way those long-ago visions in her eyes had frightened me into turning away before their full revelation.

The prison library is better stocked than you would imagine, and I have had for years now the leisure time to read as much as I want to. Sometime in year two of my death-row waiting game, I began reading the Arthurian legends for the first time. Here are stories of a man— perhaps a king—who lived at the end of the fifth century, if he ever lived at all. His story has been shaped, told and retold by dozens of authors and poets, my own favorite being Mary Stewart. So what about the man and his story is compelling enough for his legend to have survived fifteen hundred years?

Does Angel's brief life have the kind of legendary staying power the Arthurian tales do? Will authors and poets a thousand years from now weave stories around the myth of the winged girl, not caring if she once existed at all, needing only the concept of her to write their books? They are writing them now, I know, which is one more reason for me to set down the truth for anyone who cares to know it. The story I am telling may not have the drama and punch of the fabrications a fiction writer will bring to it, but it is the only true story of the life and death of Angel Fitzgerald.

If her legend survives, she will be Arthur, naturally, a soul tied to a destiny already in place at birth—Arthur, by the dark secret of his parentage, and Angel, by the presence of a tiny pair of wings. And as Arthur had his nemesis,

Mordred, she had her own in J. William Harper, a shadowy, ominous presence since she had been a baby. I had thought Harper entered our lives after Angel burst onto the scene as the lingerie model for Whisper, but as I watched the DVDs and pored over every news article in which Harper's name ever appeared, I found a piece from a now-defunct tabloid. The photo showed an eighteen-month-old baby girl with little bat wings, and the accompanying "news" story carried that hate-laced quote about demonic appendages. He went by plain old Billy Harper back then, but I knew from the tone and the language (the guy really needed to update his material) that it was J. William himself. So, like Mordred, Harper had always been the figure lurking in the shadows, biding his time, making sure that when he struck, the strike was lethal.

Jack, of course, is Merlin. Just because Arthur's life ended in tragedy, Merlin should not be blamed for leading him to his destiny. One could argue Merlin's destiny was to do the leading, and that his fate was as unchangeable as Arthur's own. Angel would have searched until she found someone else to facilitate her flying. The ending would have been the same, the only difference in the run-up to that ending being that she would never have known love before she died. And she did, however briefly, know love.

Jack is the only visitor I allow. We talk, mostly about her, and I fill him in on stories from her childhood, all the things she would have eventually told him over the course of their lives together. He tells me how they fell in love, and I have encouraged him to write the story down, for he knew her in a way I never could. He saw her in a way the world never would. I knew her fierce determination to fly, but I never understood exactly how she got from point A to point B in the process of figuring out how to do it. The graphs, charts and wing-structure analyses I had seen in her apartment were all foreign to me. Jack could explain them and I tell him he should. It is still too raw for him, he says, so I can only hope someday he will see the importance of setting the record straight about who she was, as I have tried to do here.

He tells me amusing things about my daughter that

have nothing to do with flying. I now know *she* was the one who sent the original e-mail to Whisper, who pretended to be the photographer of that ornithological journal. She knew about their upcoming campaign and rolled the dice to get money to finance her already-percolating flying plans. The puppet mistress had even talked Dr. Dolan into going along with her, into telling Charlie he had tried and failed to locate that photographer. She had banked on Whisper thinking it was a hoax, but wanting so badly for it to be true they would send a spy to check out the story. Her head had never been turned, not for a moment, by the glitz and fame of her short modeling career. It was nothing more than a means to an end.

I turned over to Jack all the personal effects I found going through Angel's things after her death, though not before I read and saw enough to know she had loved him. I wonder now why she never told me. Did she feel she was too grown-up to confide in her mother? Or was it, like so many of Angel's secrets, only part of a larger picture she intended to reveal on her own schedule?

2

As I looked through the notes they had written to each other—notes about airspeeds, angles of attack, lift loads and a private joke between them about something called the Beaufort Scale—I saw how they went from Ms. Fitzgerald and Mr. Emrys in their opening letters, to Angel and Jack when they were devising their plan, to Feathers and Wingman as they fell in love. She kept a journal, but I never opened it, figuring I wouldn't understand the flying stuff and had no business reading the romantic stuff. That also was turned over to Jack.

Tomorrow he is coming to pick up these yellow pads, so, although my right hand is stiff and I am all at once very tired, I need to keep writing for a bit longer. A little under two hours longer, to be exact.

In the Middle Ages, I have read, a woman—even a wealthy or highborn woman—could shelter within the stone walls of a convent and spend her life in a solitude punctuated by harsh living conditions, hard work, bad food and prayer. I am so much luckier than those Middle-Aged women, as living conditions within these stone walls may be Spartan but they could hardly be called harsh, a work shift in the laundry or kitchen is never more than four hours long, food is plentiful and is no worse than what a soldier would get, and no one forces me to pray, thank God. Stack my situation against that of the average M.A. nun milking a smelly goat at five A.M. after spending an hour kneeling on the hard floor of an unheated chapel, and it looks on the surface like a no-brainer. She would swap her moldy straw pallet for my thin prison mattress in a Londinium minute. But that transfer-seeking nun should closely read the fine print.

Convents could prevent the world from penetrating their walls. They were self-sufficient, refused entry for all but the most pressing reasons, and their news from the outside was limited to whatever could be spoken through a small opening in the gate into the ear of a frail and elderly nun—given the porter job because it was the easiest in the convent, and having the side benefit of her being mostly deaf.

Unfortunately, the world cannot be kept out of these stone walls. Though I steer clear of the rec room where the television set is on all day, I am updated frequently by my fellow inmates. Through them, along with the occasional newspaper, I learn that Angel is hounded even in death. The people who knew and loved her are all moving on in their own ways after five years, but the anonymous public will not let her go. One crackpot group tried to get a court order to exhume her body and prove her wings were fake. When they learned she had been cremated, they took it as almost slam-dunk evidence of a cover-up. And, of course, there are the men coming forward and claiming to be her biological father. I believe the number is up to six now, and all of them want DNA tests done on the blood dried on the feathers still held in police custody as evidence. Several of them are nut jobs offering to father other winged babies for a fee; several are trying to claim part of her estate; and one man, who would have been only ten years old when Angel was conceived, is either very bad at math or delusional.

Other stories leak through, too, about the faction hoping to get me off death row and the faction waiting to see me fry. I really don't mind being locked in, but I wish there were a way to lock the world out.

I would be a lousy raconteuse if I ran out of time before telling the whole story, so I had better start tying up loose ends. And I suppose this is finally the time to confess my sins, to reveal what my parents meant about my innate vileness when they guested on *Godsword,* why they were so willing—eager, even—to throw me out with the garbage and deny the existence of my child.

I was always steeped in sin. I know this because my mother said it to me so many times. As a tiny child I did not have a clear concept of what sin *was,* but I sure knew it permeated and polluted every cell of my body. I was a filthy liar; not just a liar, mind you, but a *filthy* one. I didn't want to be. I wanted to be clean and pure, but no matter how I tried, the sin was still there. Was I actually a liar? I don't know. I think back and can't recall having told any particularly egregious fibs as a preschooler, so I have to go on my mother's word that I did. What could those lies have been? Under-reporting cookie consumption? Padding the figures on the number of times I brushed my teeth that day? I ask you, what in the name of God can a four-year-old child prevaricate about that necessitates branding her a filthy liar?

I'm sure somewhere buried deep in my memory is the incident on which my mother based her claim about my untruthfulness. Although I cannot recall the incident, I clearly remember my reaction: I vowed I would never, *ever* lie again. Not even to get out of trouble at school. The problem was that, although I kept my vow, my mother didn't stop calling me a liar. I worked even harder to be scrupulously honest, knowing how much I must have hurt and disappointed her with my first lie if she wouldn't let it go. I would overhear her talking to her lady friends in the living room, my heart going out to her as she confessed her humiliation about my sinful behavior, accepting the yoke of failure on her part. Her friends would cluck in sympathy and reassure her the fault was not hers. I knew what they meant: the fault was mine. I kept my vow, if only to spare my mother the public embarrassment of having a filthy liar for a daughter.

How many years went by before I understood it did not matter if I were the most truthful girl ever? If I never told even the smallest, whitest lie? How much time passed before I realized my mother *needed* to cling to the concept of my lying because it was her justification for the punishment?

In our house the Bible belt was a literal term, and either parent would employ it when my sins called for something more harsh than reducing me to tears with threats and vile epithets. But it was my mother who, in her frenzied attempts to beat the sin out of me, often did not realize she was aiming the wrong end of the belt at me, that it was the heavy brass buckle she lashed through the air. Or maybe she didn't care. I mastered the dodge and duck; a bruise is one thing, but how would I explain away a broken cheekbone at school? I would have to lie, of course, and therein rests the chicken-and-egg conundrum. The dodging and ducking only confirmed my mother's belief in my guilt, as did crying. Could she *really* have thought it was sin that inspired me to avoid that chunk of brass coming at me? That an innocent girl would have taken the blow stoically?

Decades later I understand my mother would have had an orgasm if I *had* just stood still and let her play out her sick need, and I wonder how she fed the beast once her punching bag walked out.

The next phase of my sinfulness was puberty, when despite the churching and the beatings, my body manifested sin galore. It took the form of a pair of breasts whose only crime, in retrospect, was that they were larger and perkier than my mother's, and my full, full lips—lips begging for some unnamed "it" in my mother's view. Her over-the-top reaction to my new boobs and pouty lips made me thankful she didn't know the devil had planted hair seeds between my legs and the crop was growing in thick and dark.

By then I understood, at least on an intellectual level, that my mother was barking mad, but the old instinct to please and appease was strong, and so I guarded myself against the usual high school sins. I didn't drink, dance, date or drug. I didn't wear clothes that were tight, short or revealing. I wasn't a prude, and I didn't care what anyone else did, but I needed to keep the sin off me.

The beatings stopped the day the brass buckle was arcing down toward my face, my mother having chosen an overhand swing that morning rather than a lateral, and I grabbed the belt just under it and held on. She flailed and yanked, but I didn't let go, and as our eyes locked, we both realized at the same time that I was five inches taller than she was and that I would never let this happen again without retaliating. She sucker-punched me with her left fist— an uppercut that only got by me because my eyes were on the brass buckle—slamming my head back against the wall to which I had retreated from the whistling arc of the belt. Before I could recover, she was off, running to her bedroom and locking the door behind her. I had a knot coming up on the back of my head, but the belt was still in my hand and I knew I had been the victor. I threw that sinbeater in the dumpster behind my school the next day. My father never missed it, as he had stopped using it on me at the first sign of my budding womanhood.

I continued to sin through tenth and eleventh grade, bringing pornographic books into the house, daring her to try and stop me from reading them. Books like Darwin's *On the Origin of the Species, Coming of Age in the Milky Way* by Timothy Ferris, anything by Carl Sagan or Stephen Hawking, and every word written by Richard P. Feynman. I read biographies of Max Planck and Albert Einstein, just letting the sin boil and swell in me. I wanted to learn, to go out into the world and do something great with my life. In my own wingless way, I wanted to fly.

The breaking point came mid-September my senior year of high school. Without her Bible belt, my mother had been reduced to emotional ambushes, name calling and ever more creative threats of divine retribution for my numerous sins. One day she confronted me after school with a pair of my own panties, which she had pulled from the hamper and inspected for evidence of disgusting behavior. She shoved the cotton briefs in my face and I had no idea what she was screaming about.

Time and smartening up have given me perspective. I must have had a vaginal infection, and the stain would have been the dried remains of some sort of discharge, but my pious mother saw semen. I was innocent, of course, having never held hands with a boy, much less done whatever it was you did to get his fluids in your underwear. But, by then, I knew innocence was irrelevant. As Angel would tell me many years later, people see what they want to see. And my mother saw only sin.

She followed me to my room, waving the panties at me and threatening to show them to my father so he could see how right she had been about me all along. Closing the door on her hissing, spitting threats, I understood it was time to give up. They wanted sin, then by God, they were going to get it.

Chelsea, Heather and I hatched our plan to crash the fraternity party. They had done things like this before and gotten away with it, so I felt I had experienced sherpas on my climb to damnation. To give you an idea of how little

I knew of actual sin, the extent of my goal that night was to come home having tasted alcohol and having kissed a boy. And the rest, as they say, is history.

Time runs low, so I need to wrap this up. Whether there's a heaven and hell, a black void, or a holding tank for reincarnationists, I'll know in less than one hour.

You are probably wondering why no one has come to take the order for my last meal—I hear the fried shrimp is excellent—or to shave my head for the electrodes. And why no kindly priest has arrived to hear my confession, soothe me with prayer, and accompany me down a corridor of cells to my doom, as inmates call out, "Dead mom walking."

Oh, come on, you didn't really think I'd wait until the state got around to killing me, did you?

Crazy people are often charismatic, explaining
how so many crackpots through history were able to draw a
following. By the time someone noticed and said "Gosh,
Herr Schicklgruber, you sure have a heil of a lot of friends,"
it was already too late. So it was with J. William Harper.
No one with more than ten watts of brainage ever took him
seriously as a religious leader, but his magnetism ensured a
sheep-like devotion to him that kept on metastasizing. His
BroOTL empire collapsed after his death, so I guess there
was no one who could fill his big evil-clown shoes.

Am I sorry I killed him? You can bet your butt I'm
not. Thugs are thugs whether the brand name under which
they are marketed is Nazis, Inquisitors, Khmer Rouge, Ku
Klux Klan or Al Quaeda. I go to my punishment or reward
unrepentant.

No inmate in prison is popular, but some are more
well-tolerated than others. I am one of the well-tolerated
prisoners. Helpful and friendly, I have been careful to do
nothing here to suggest I should be on suicide watch. In
fact, people admire me for beginning my "memoirs" two
days ago, a sure sign, in their view, that I want to stay alive
and complete them. From day one I was a problem solver
and have been rewarded for that with more leeway than is
afforded the other death-row residents. I learned well from
Angel to play my cards close to the vest and bide my time.

I was the one who finally solved the problem of the
ubiquitous and tenacious wire grass in the exercise yard.
No matter how much poison the warden sprayed on it, no

matter how many times she had us dig it up, it kept coming back. I could have told her it was spreading by untouchable buds under the surface but, although that was true, it would have done nothing to further my cause or mitigate the grass problem. I asked for, and was given, permission to start a basic basket-weaving class, using the wire grass for raw material. I studied books for all the fundamentals, then learned more sophisticated techniques from Shar, a Moki Indian who is not only a triple murderer and former drug mule, but the daughter of an accomplished basketry artisan. Long before she was gutting narcs and stuffing Baggies of horse up her twat, Shar learned basket-weaving skills from her mama.

Before you could say "Back off, screw," the class was full and the wire grass was being pulled up and used as fast as it grew. We turned out straight-woven plaited baskets, handled carriers with fine joins, bee skeps, twilled twos and my favorite, using a technique that the Native Americans were known for: spiral-coiled construction.

We were not, of course, allowed to bring the baskets back to our cells, so we gifted them to visitors and traded them for favors from the guards. A few women raised money for their kids by perfecting a quick and dirty way to turn out large numbers of ribbed baskets with woven sides, then giving them to outsiders to sell for them.

I spent months making a large, lidded hamper for the warden, using the spiral-coiled construction Shar had taught me. The workmanship was better than anything you could buy at Pier 1 for under a hundred dollars, and the warden liked it so much she offered me money to make a second one. I declined her offer of cash and spent another eight weeks making a similar hamper for her sister.

It was only after making the second hamper that I asked permission to make a small basket for my own cell, something wide and open that could easily be checked by the guards during surprise inspections. I said I wanted to keep some photographs, letters and other mementoes in it. Which is how I came to have a twelve-inch diameter, six-inch tall open basket in my cell.

The unique feature of a spiral-coiled basket is that

it is made of one long element—in this case a thick braid of wire grass—wound in graduated spirals that are held in place by evenly spaced thread knots along the joining edges. These baskets are solid and aesthetically pleasing, but if one picks out the thread knots after the basket has been inspected by the guards for the umpteenth time, leaving only a half-dozen key knots to retain the shape, well, those last few threads can be undone in a flash, leaving not a basket, but an eighteen-foot length of sturdy braided rope.

Down to less than fifteen minutes before I release everyone who feels they still have some obligation to me. Mark Dennison can stop writing checks to lawyers looking for loopholes to keep me out of the electric chair. Charlie can let go of his anger toward me and move on. He's only fifty, and there must be some sweet, gentle woman out there who can love the ghost out of him as I did long ago.

Almost time to put a punctuation mark at the end of the sentence that has been my life. Most people end their life sentences with a period. Some, like Angel Fitzgerald and J. William Harper, go out with an exclamation point. Me? I think I have to choose a question mark. So much is left unanswered, unanswerable.

Would things have turned out differently if I had let that doctor remove Angel's wings? Or would she have spent her life sensing their loss, dreaming of phantom wings that could no longer support even the hope of flying?

What if I had left the Sigma Tau Gamma house when Heather and Chelsea did as their curfew approached? They begged me to leave with them, but that first wine cooler was delicious, and the second and third went down so easily, and for the first time in my life someone was telling me I was beautiful. How *could* I have left?

And if Angel is Arthur, and flying is the Holy Grail, and Jack is Merlin, who am I in this legend? Am I no more than the peasant woman in the forest who shelters Arthur from his enemies and keeps the secret of his birth until Merlin comes and takes him away, a minor figure easily left out of the story in future retellings?

How far might *I* have flown if my own wings hadn't been battered and broken in that first seventeen years?

A song has just now come into my head, one that I haven't heard or thought of since the day Angel soared in the sky like a magnificent, golden hawk, the girl/hawk in the poster there on my wall.

A cloud like a heart
Is beckoning me

TEN...NINE...

To join in the waltz
Up there

EIGHT...SEVEN...

Can my feet leave the ground?
Can I fly to that sound?

SIX...FIVE...

Will your love lift
My wings in the air?

FOUR...THREE...

Oh, yes! I can fly!
And I'm going to
Dance in the sky

TWO...ONE...ZE—

Embrace me, love, and let your
Great wings lift me up
From sere dune to misted sky.

> — Translated from the Gaelic
> ballad "Brèagh Slánach"

Dear Mr. Emrys... Jack,

It has been thirteen years since we last spoke, but I'm hoping you will remember me. You certainly had good reason to try to forget, as I recall doing my best impression of a flaming anal aperture during our final conversation.

Retroactive defense: I was a ten year old and, in the wake of my sister's death and the slow-motion collapse of my family, I needed someone to blame. Tag, you're it. Sorry.

Now, as the mother of two toddlers, and with a third little tax deduction on the way, I feel the full weight of my inability to provide more than the sketchiest details about the aunt and grandmother my kids will never know.

My dad and his second wife are living in an ex-pat retirement haven in Portugal these days, and he doesn't so much refuse to answer my questions as pretend not to understand I have asked them. He has moved on down the road and for me that road is a dead end, at least as far as my mother and sister are concerned.

Nick is another stone wall, although he did manage to spit out your name and grumble that you "got everything." I'm not sure what he means by everything, as all the money came down to him and me. The fact that most of his went blowing up his nose or filtering through his liver was his own choice.

I'm hoping the everything you got is in the form of letters, diaries or mementoes that you would be willing to let me see, assuming you haven't long since trashed them. If you have discarded what you had, can we at least meet for coffee? Maybe you can share one or two brief stories about Angel or my mother... something I could pretend are my own memories and pass down to my children someday.

I would so appreciate this favor, Jack, and if it's any consolation, before I started hating you so much, I adored you.

Sincerely,

Shelby Hart (née Evans)

I tried to remember the last time I had received a paper letter. Most of my students, I suspected, had never touched a postage stamp, much less written on something they would consider as quaint as papyrus. It reminded me of Angel: willing to use a computer to do research, but refusing to allow any of her own self to be reflected onto a hard drive.

"You can burn a piece of paper to cover your tracks," she would say, "but once you've sent your secrets out into cyberspace, you never know who's going to get their filthy little e-paws on them." Numerous Pentagon and bank hack-ins, as well as political scandals of the sexual kind have borne out the prescience of her claim.

Shelby's request was unexpected but reasonable, although it inadvertently revealed there were gaps in her familial knowledge much wider than she knew. I wrote back suggesting lunch at a place not far from the return address on her envelope, intending to hand over Allison's nearly two-hundred-page suicide note, which I had not shown to anyone else in the eight years since I skimmed it and put it on a high shelf in my home office.

I hoped her mother's words would fill in all the blanks for Shelby, as I had little else to add in the way of documentation. Angel's journals full of flight calculations, wing measurements and load-to-lift graphs were only dry, mathy reflections of her quest to fly, of interest only to an aeronautical engineer. There were a couple handwritten notes in the box with the journals, the kind of sappy prose a girl writes to a guy when she falls in love, and the goodbye letter Angel left behind for me before her first flight. All those memories had been packed away and relegated to a corner of my attic so long ago that I hadn't even dug out the box to inter Allison's opus when I acquired it.

I pulled the four yellow pads off the shelf, brushed away a layer of dust and slipped them into my briefcase the morning of our lunch. I had also polished up two light-hearted anecdotes, one about each woman, hoping those and Allison's pages would give Shelby the knowledge, if not the peace of mind, that she wanted. I knew there was a risk she would want more, that I'd have to pry up and tear off a couple scabs to satisfy her curiosity, and I had not yet made up my mind about revealing the secrets I had kept for so long.

That was six months ago, when I naïvely thought the only information to be passed on was mine to her, and that the only secrets were being held by me.

Even though I hadn't seen her in more than a dozen years I recognized Shelby as soon as she walked into the restaurant. Taller even than Angel, but less taut and angular, she had a subtle softness about her lanky frame, possibly from her pregnancy. Standing as she came toward the table, not sure whether etiquette called for a handshake or a hug, I lifted my hand in a gesture that could be inter-preted as a move to pull her chair out for her, if that's how she wanted to see it. Shelby smiled, took my hand and con-tinued to close the gap between us until she could lift her chin and give me a peck on the cheek. Without letting go of my hand, she pulled back and shook her head, still smiling warmly at me.

"Jack. Older than Methuselah and *still* lookin' très beau."

"Forgive me for not being flattered, but your last crush was a horse."

"Let's don't speak ill of Jasmine; she lives on a farm now and is a mother several times over."

"As are you, apparently," I said as we sat. "How far along are you?"

"Fourteen weeks. I'm in that brief doughnut hole between the throwing up and the lower back pain."

"Boy or girl?"

"No idea. We're not part of that whole amnio and sonogram obsession, so for all I know it may be a puppy. That's what the girls are hoping for anyway."

"And how old are they?"

"Three plus. Twins, but fraternal, so Kyle and I are mercifully spared all that dressing-them-alike crap."

The waitress approached, so I was given a reprieve from my rote inquiries. We ordered and, once our menus had been collected and we were left alone again, Shelby put up her hand to stop my next question, which would have been to ask what her husband did for a living.

"Well, you've managed to ask all the questions I'd expect at a ten-year reunion from a girl I barely knew in high school, but we both know we're not here to talk about me, my husband or my admittedly perfect children."

"Yeah, well," I said, staring down at the tablecloth and blowing any chance of projecting the casual aplomb I had been shooting for. "This isn't easy for me."

Shelby reached across the table, closing her fingers around my wrist.

"I was there, too, Jack," she said gently. "I know exactly how hard it is."

A large sweating busboy with a matching pitcher of ice water chose that moment to slosh our glasses full. It was a breather we both needed.

"The last thing I want is to make you uncomfortable or force you to relive anything that is still painful. I just need some sense of who my mom and sister were, and not the sensationalistic garbage you get when you Google them. I'd like my girls to have something to balance out the claims that Angel was a publicity junkie who faked a flight and that Mom was nothing more than a looney tunes vigilante."

"Is that really how they're shown?"

"You never searched them?"

"No. After Angel died, I kind of stopped interacting

with the world. Then when Allison did her Annie Oakley, I came out of my hole long enough to be her confidant those years she spent in prison, but after that there didn't seem to be any reason to look back or dwell on things."

"Then here I come along with my flashlight, trying to peek into your bunker."

"It's ancient history, kid. Grief and numbness fade. Or at least mutate into a new normal. In other words, you don't have to tippy-toe around me."

Our waitress returned, and once we were burger'd and BLT'd, Shelby went quiet, absently arranging lettuce, a tomato slice and pickles on her hamburger, then reclosing the bun. Finally, she looked up and spoke.

"If I ask anything that crosses the line, tell me to back off and I will."

"Fair enough."

She grinned at me, then launched into the half pound of beef in her hands. For the rest of the meal we exchanged light biographical material to catch ourselves up. She showed me a photo of Erin and Shannon, then talked about her husband Kyle, and I described going back to school for my Ph.D. at thirty-one and giving up flying for teaching.

As our coffees were set down and lunch drew to its conclusion, Shelby leaned forward.

"If you're sure nothing's off limits, there is one thing I was always curious about."

"And that was—?"

"Well, Angel was so amazingly beautiful and you were so drop-dead gorgeous that my imagination made you into sweethearts, but I never actually knew if it was true. I mean, I realize you were good friends and that you worked together, and I saw that kiss before the flight, but I also know how calculating Angel could be, so I figure there's a chance you two only did that for the crowd reaction."

I tried to smile, but everything inside me contracted into a dense pinpoint of emotion, a big-bang-in-waiting with Shelby's voice diddling the detonator.

"So, were you and Angel more than co-workers and friends?"

Ka-blooey! And a whole new universe of pain was born, as compressed particles of everything I had pretended not to feel for thirteen years exploded out from my heart and peppered the inside of my skin like searing buckshot, threatening to burn holes through me from the inside out. I must have flinched from the shock of it because Shelby grabbed both my hands and held them as if she were afraid I might punch them into a wall.

"Oh, God. Jack, I'm sorry. I'm so, so sorry," she said, tears filling her eyes.

The waitress chose that moment to approach our table with the check, but one look at the teary pregnant woman forcibly holding down the hands of the trembling old guy and she spun around so fast her crepe soles shrieked on the hardwood floor. I took two bracing breaths and met Shelby's worried eyes.

"She was wearing my engagement ring when she died," I said.

Her face crumpled, but she still gripped my hands. Now, though, it felt as if she were taking support rather than giving it.

"Jesus, I don't know anything, do I?"

"You were only a little girl."

She let go of my hands, sat back in her seat and let her shoulders slump. After a second she wiped at her eyes and smiled weakly at me.

"So, should I leave the lid on the worm can?"

"No. You have every right to learn as much as you want about your family history."

I reached down, flipped the latch on my briefcase and pulled out four yellow pads, which I put in front of her. "The last few days before she took her life, your mother wrote about herself, Angel, you, your dad, Nick and everything that happened to your family. I don't know why she left instructions for me to have them instead of your father, but I should have thought to look you up and give them to you years ago. It's your family and your story. I'm only an ancillary character."

She lightly brushed her fingers over the blank first page of the top yellow pad. "Wow, this is so..." She shook her head as if to clear it. "It was like one day they were both here and the next day, poof! Gone. Do you know I don't even have one of Angel's feathers? I used to pick them up off the floor all the time, even kept a few in a pencil cup in my room. But, after everything was over and I moved in with Katie and Pete, I guess I lost track of them, and now I don't have a single feather to remember my sister by."

"I'm sorry."

"Don't be." She patted the stack of pads. "You've given me back my mother and sister. Or at least the memory of them. Thank you, Jack."

I made a mental note to get the box out of the attic. I thought there might be some feathers in it I could give to Shelby, and even if I was mistaken, I knew the Indiana Jones hat Angel had bought for me to wear the day of the fatal flight was in it, and the golden primary feather must still be stuck in the band.

"I wish I had more to give you."

"This is over and above what I was expecting. I mean, I thought you might have Angel's diary, but this is much better."

"I did get the diary. But when I popped the lock and opened it, all the pages were blank."

Shelby laughed. "Oh, that wasn't her diary. That was her decoy."

"What?"

"Right after she finished the Whisper campaign she bought the diary and put it on her desk. This was months before her apartment was built and she moved out. The next day I sneaked into her room, found the key and opened the diary. There was nothing in it yet, so I locked it and put it back. I was a hideous little snoop and I must have left Gummi Bear goo or some other evidence of my covert op because when I broke into the diary a week or so later, an index card fell out with a not-so-friendly threat from Angel if I touched any of her stuff again. I was embarrassed she had caught me, so I never messed with anything of hers after that."

"Well, the diary might have been safe, but she still didn't write anything in it."

"I know! She switched over to one of those hard-cover ledgers she used to put all her flying notes in."

"Are you sure?"

"Oh, yeah. She'd sit on the couch writing, and if I so much as glanced over at her, she'd point a warning finger at me. I know she kept her personal diary in a ledger for the last year and a half before she died."

I sat back in my chair, stunned. I remembered the ledgers, maybe seven or eight of them. I had even glanced at a couple before stacking them in the storage box. Notes, drawings, equations, all related to flying. Was it possible one of them contained a diary, a record of Angel's thoughts about flying? Her family? Me?

"Shelby, I might have that diary. I stored all those journals thinking they were flight research."

I signaled the waitress for the check, and Shelby and I said our goodbyes. We agreed to meet again a week later, after she had read Allison's final words and I had had a chance to search for Angel's diary.

As soon as the piece of paper fell out, I knew I had found it. The paper was a glossy magazine page folded in quarters, with the following ad highlighted in yellow:

WANTED: FLIGHT GENIUS
Experience with ultralights a
plus.   Discretion a must.
Salary is negotiable and not
negligible. Box N-45.

Fifteen years ago ads like this cropped up once in a while in the classifieds of the three or four magazines dedicated to planes, pilots and flying. Invariably they were placed by retired gentlemen who thought they had designed the next big thing in aviation. They only needed to hire an aeronautical engineer or aircraft designer to polish the rough edges.

The ideas were weak at best and impossible at worst, but there was always somebody willing to take the guy's money and pretend to hone the design until it finally became evident even to the inventor that his idea wouldn't fly. I hated seeing people get bilked, so I usually answered the ads and tried to let the guys down as gently and quickly as possible after evaluating the drawings, mock-ups and models.

It was with that in mind that I went to a coffee shop to meet the mysterious individual who signed his letter "Fitz." I say mysterious because when I submitted my CV and a letter of interest to the blind box in the magazine, I also requested information about the kind of aircraft I'd be dealing with. Fitz's terse reply mentioned nothing but a potential monthly salary and a meeting place, so I assumed he thought his design was so hot it was in imminent danger of being copied or stolen.

The coffee shop was virtually empty, Fitz having set the meeting halfway between the end of lunch service and the start of dinner. As I glanced around for a likely candidate, there was movement at a table in the far corner and a tall, slender girl stood up and signaled to me. My first thought was that Fitz had been unable to make it and had sent his daughter instead, but as I crossed the room to her, two dark parabolas separated out from the wood paneling behind the girl and became a pair of wings.

In that last ten feet I realized who I was meeting and what Fitz was short for, even though she looked nothing like she did when she had been the supermodel every guy with a pulse had lusted after only a year or so earlier. I suddenly wished I had worn a better pair of jeans and a shirt with buttons.

"Mr. Emrys, I'm Angel Fitzgerald."

She looked as if she should be mall crawling with other teens rather than interviewing engineers, and the fine sprinkle of freckles across the bridge of her nose confirmed she wasn't wearing makeup. Remembering my response to those lingerie photos of her, I felt like Humbert Humbert, despite the fact that I wouldn't turn twenty-eight for two more months.

"Ms. Fitzgerald, it's very nice to meet you," I said, attempting to mask my stupefaction, "but all of a sudden I'm not sure why I'm here."

"Isn't it obvious?" she asked, turning around to give

me a full-on view of that draping heart of feathers. "You're going to teach me to fly."

All I knew about her was that she had wings and had been a model, but Angel knew virtually everything there was to know about my career, including some lower-level secret consulting I had done for the Air Force two years earlier, something that had not appeared on my CV.

She may have looked like a kid, but she talked and acted like a theoretical engineer and, although I had no idea at the end of an hour if she would ever fly, I knew I didn't want her to hook up with some unscrupulous person who would make big promises and take her money. She offered me a salary; I declined. Angel insisted, and I realized she wanted to keep things on professional terms, so I agreed to take a salary *only* after I had done enough research and tests to decide if flight was even a long shot possibility for her.

After we set up a work session for the following week, she shook my hand with the same surprisingly confident grip with which she had introduced herself, then left in the taxi that had been parked and waiting for her throughout our meeting.

> Dec. 15
> Yes! Finally! If any1 cn figure out
> how 2 gt me airborne it's this guy
> Emrys. Met wth him this aftrn. <u>Very</u>
> impressive. 2 prev. men padded
> resumes & asked 4 even more thn I
> was offering. (also, 2nd smarmy
> guy made a pass & he hd 2 be on th
> old side of 40. cringe!) J.E. left a
> few important things <u>off</u> his rez.
> Won't take money til he's sure he cn
> help me fly, so he's either totally
> honest or filthy rich. Judging frm his
> clothes & ride I'd go with honest.
> Movie Star looks/no M.S. attitude.

By the time I met with Shelby again I had read all of the diary, stayed colossally drunk for two days, then sobered up and tried to figure out how Angel could have lied to me the way I now knew she had.

In a single-malt stupor I cursed her, threw a bottle (okay, two) against the stone hearth of my fireplace for the satisfaction of seeing something shatter the way I felt my heart had, and railed at the injustice: hadn't I always been completely honest with her? Once I was sobered-up and subdued, however, I had to admit, if only to myself, that I had misrepresented the truth to Angel almost immediately upon meeting her.

She had done her research on me, but only as I fit into her plans, only professionally. Personally, she knew nothing more about me than what I had shared with her that first month, that I was single, that I loved to fly, owned a small plane and occasionally gave flying lessons.

What Angel didn't know was that I *was* filthy rich. Still am. My mother's family has owned and operated the Macleod Distillery near Loch Laggan forty-five kilometers south of Loch Ness and a ninety-minute drive north from Glasgow Airport for more than three hundred years. We, or rather they, as I'm one of the two black sheep who didn't choose to stay and work in the family business, produce one of the most coveted scotches in the world. When caller ID said "Brunei," you knew the order was private and would be in the hundreds of cases, so it was always a good time to ask for the latest high-tech gadget. Granddad Adair would have cursed me from the grave if he had seen those bottles of Usquebaugh twelve-year-old die a glittering, showery death as they smashed against the dry-stack limestone of my living room wall.

In addition to scotch whisky, the Macleod family has always produced an inordinate number of sons. Once Adair's wife Shea gave birth to the third boy, they assumed the dynasty was intact. After World War Two claimed both the older boys and tuberculosis took the youngest, Adair pressed Shea into action once again and she gave birth, at forty-four, to my mother Blair, then apparently hung up her uterus and refused to give my grandfather a fifth shot at patrilineal immortality.

When Blair was seventeen, a young Welshman

named Cade Emrys courted the Caledonian heiress and won her heart. Though Adair was suspicious of his motives, and there are those who say Cade only married my mother to ensure a lifetime supply of premium scotch, the two were a genuine love match and until his death from (surprise!) cirrhosis five years ago, they never spent a night apart.

Adair begrudgingly took my father into the business, but was relieved when Blair followed family tradition and pumped out four boys—Bret, Cameron, Leith and me—in the first eight years of her marriage to Cade. Grandfather decided he could tolerate the son-in-law until the grandsons grew up, but he never relinquished his power until my oldest brother Bret was ready to take over. He also set up four irrevocable trusts to block any attempt by my father to take control of our futures if something should happen to Blair.

Cade was an easygoing man who never bristled at my grandfather's rudeness and onerous control. He seemed happy enough to have a wife he adored, four healthy sons, a well-paying job and all the scotch his liver could process. I never once saw him drunk, but as I got older, I realized his good nature was bolstered by the peaty, smoky presence of Usquebaugh in the interstitial fluids that bathed every cell in his body.

About the time Bret took over from Grandfather, Cameron, the second in line, took off for America, leaving Leith and me to struggle with the intense internship Adair felt was key to having a strong, hands-on knowledge of the family business. And even though the Macleod Distillery had five shiny new germination vats with fully automated agitators to keep the steeped barley in motion, Granddad kept one of the original malting rooms so we could learn the old way of doing things. The locals operating the auto tanks and monitoring the space station-like control panels would snicker as Leith and I came in after school, carried our shovels into the old malting room and spent hours turning the steeped grain on the concrete floor.

Leith didn't mind, but I came to think Cameron had had the right idea. I petitioned my grandfather to let me attend college in the United States, telling him I would bring home a business degree and a familiarity with the latest technology that could be an asset to the distillery. Adair had two sons who were sticking so he didn't press me very hard on my sincerity, and I started college at sixteen, taking a double major in physics and aeronautical engineering. I was forced to enroll under the name on my passport, Llewellyn Emrys, enough of a burden in Scotland but a real bully magnet in the U.S., so I started going by Jack.

I never went back to work at the Macleod Distillery, although I made trips home several times a year to see my family. The size of my trust meant I never *had* to work, but I loved aviation so much I freelanced out on any interesting project I found.

So why didn't I tell all this to Angel, especially after we had become a couple in all but public acknowledgement? She thought she had a lot of money, and for an eighteen-year-old girl who'd earned it herself, it *was* a lot. But her couple million dollars could never have underwritten the challenge of getting her in the air.

Yes, I could have told her that renting wind tunnels, hiring a team, and designing and developing the specialized equipment we would need to test the viability of her flying would empty her accounts in very little time, but what purpose would that have served other than to throw one more roadblock in her way? I was drawn to the project before I became drawn to her and I had more money than I could ever possibly spend. It was a no-brainer to step in without letting her know she wasn't shouldering the full freight.

This all sounds very patronizing in retrospect, that I let Angel believe the other four members of the team were working for the salaries she was paying them, when I was giving them three or four times that amount to ensure their dedication to the project and silence about it, but at the time I didn't see it as a lie of omission.

I consider myself an honest person, but I justified lying to Angel for the greater good, the same way she and I justified lying to her family, to Allison in particular, and to the entire world. We had reasons that made sense to us at the time, but now I'm seeing they were rationalizations that don't hold up to scrutiny.

Several years into my prison visits to Allison, she asked me if I knew the fairy tale called Briar Rose. Not having grown up in the U.S., I had never seen the movie *Sleeping Beauty*, so I didn't recognize the story as she told it. After many years of longing for a child, a king and queen have a baby girl and they plan a feast to celebrate her birth. Through an oversight one of the wise women of the kingdom is left off the guest list, and when all the other wise women save one have bestowed their blessings and gifts upon the infant, the uninvited woman steps forward and curses her, saying on her fifteenth birthday she will prick her finger on the spindle of a spinning wheel and die.

The court is horrified, but after the woman leaves, the one remaining wise woman who has not yet given her gift steps forward. Unable to negate the awful curse, she is at least able to lessen it from death to a deathlike sleep of a hundred years, to be broken only by true love's kiss. The king decrees all spinning wheels in the kingdom are to be destroyed, and his soldiers sweep the countryside, chopping and burning until every spinning wheel is gone.

On her fifteenth birthday, long after everyone has forgotten the curse, Princess Briar Rose goes exploring in her father's castle and discovers a room she has never seen before. An old woman inside works at a device Briar Rose doesn't recognize and when she asks the woman to show her how to use it, she pricks her finger on the spindle and falls into a century of slumber.

As Allison told me the story, she was wistful, almost sad, and I thought she was talking about destiny, and how it can't be changed. I assumed she was reflecting on a belief that Angel was destined to die at the pinnacle of her life's achievement, flying, and nothing could have been done to stop it. Now I wonder if I got it right.

Perhaps Allison's point in telling the story was the king might have saved his daughter if he had been honest with her, if he had shown her a spinning wheel and told her of the dark prediction instead of keeping her ignorant.

Did Allison regret not having told Angel about the prophecy she thought she had seen in her newborn's eyes? Would the path of Angel's life have taken a different turn if she had known her mother believed there was danger in her flying? Or would she have disregarded it as superstition or motherly overprotection? Allison died not knowing what would have happened had she told Angel the truth.

Allison and Angel were no longer around to reconcile the dishonesty we all shared in and carried guilt about, but Shelby was alive and deserved the truth. All of it. Her mother's words would open the door, but it would be up to me to shine a light inside, and if that light illuminated my own deceptions, I would have to own up to them.

Shelby was already in a booth when I got to the restaurant. There was no awkwardness that second time and, as she stood and hugged me, I realized how long it had been since I had shared meaningful physical contact with anyone. My right hand went to the nape of her neck while my left crossed her back; she snugged into my shoulder the way Angel used to do, and it felt so right it almost hurt. When she pulled away I saw she was affected, too. We were beginning to bridge the gap left by the deaths of Angel and Allison.

On the table were the four yellow pads with slips of paper marking a large number of places where Shelby had questions. We sat and she put one hand on the top pad.

"This was tough. I mean, I'm glad to have answers, but Jesus, it wasn't an easy read."

"I know. And I'm ready to discuss anything in it."

The waitress approached and we ordered our first of many cups of coffee that day. Shelby fidgeted with a paper napkin for a few moments, so I reached over to put my hand on hers.

"Where would you like to start?"

"Nick," she sighed. "I've been such an asshole to him for so long."

"Well, you made it sound last time like he's been a little difficult to deal with."

"Yeah, but why not? He was only four when his mom died. My girls are barely three and a half, but they sure as hell would suffer if I ceased to be in their lives. And my dad. Why didn't he ever tell me he was married before?

Talk about being out of the loop."

"I'm sure he managed the truth the way he felt was best."

"I'm his daughter; he should have told me."

"When? When you were six or seven? What would that have done but make you feel insecure that Mom and Dad weren't the rock-solid, together-forever couple you saw them as? Or should he have told you when you were ten or eleven, when he was trying to deal with Angel's death and with your mom's spectacular flameout?"

"Okay, okay, he had good reasons. But Nick should have told me. I treated him like a loser for not sucking it up and handling things better because I thought we had the same losses and that he should have been the big brother for me to lean on. Maybe I could have been stronger for him, or at least nicer, if I had known."

The coffees were set down in front of us along with a few sealed mini cups of cream analog. Shelby busied herself with sweetening, whitening and stirring, then placed her spoon on her saucer and looked at me.

"Will you talk to him?" she asked.

"Nick? Of course," I replied. "But now that you know, why can't you talk to him yourself?"

"Too much bad history, I guess. He knows how I feel about the drugs and alcohol, and he hates me for not letting him be around the girls. With Dad all but out of the picture, I've pretty much deprived Nick of the only family he has left."

"He never got married? Or hooked up with anyone long term?"

"No, and not that I know of."

"Give me his phone number and address and I'll see him as soon as I can."

"Just be kind to him. You don't have all the recent history with Nick, so maybe he'll stand down his defenses long enough for you to broker détente," she said. "I guess reading about my own losses made me realize I want my big brother back."

Her voice broke on those last few words and she cleared her throat to pull back from the edge. I put my hand on hers again and she squeezed it one time to prove she was okay.

"I'll do everything in my power to repair the siblingectomy."

She smiled and began asking me questions about what Allison had written. I hadn't read the stuff in eight years so my memory had to be refreshed before I weighed in on many of the points. An hour and three coffees in, her comments touched on a big lie, one of the secrets Angel and I had held together.

"What I have trouble believing is how calm Angel was that day. I mean, it was her first attempt to fly, she had a huge audience, and yet she seemed completely cool and confident."

"Because it was *not* the first time she had flown."

"Wait a minute, that's impossible. Mom said—"

"Shelby, your mother wrote what she thought was true, but Angel lied. To her and to everyone else. In fact, we *both* lied.

"Wow," she said softly. She shook her head, as if the reframing of her past had confused her, then briskly slapped her palms down on the table. "Okay, the puppy is standing on my bladder, so I need to take a pee break."

As she stood up quickly and crossed to the ladies', I wondered if she really had to go or if she needed a break from me and my maybe-unwelcome truths. What I know about pregnant women could fit inside a contact lens case, so it could have been either one.

> March 7
> Tmrrow's th big day. We move past theory & in2 reality. Or at least possibility. Wind tunnel shd verify big honkers capability of carrying me aloft. JE all business & imersed in prep. I wonder if he ever notices th person <u>between</u> th wings?

The closest wind tunnel that met my specs was over six hundred miles away, so I rented a Hawker 400XP for a few days and flew us there. I would have felt better with a doctor on board in case something went wrong, but Angel said no to bringing Dr. Whittaker into our circle, afraid he couldn't be trusted to keep our activities secret from Allison. I would have to make do with our youngest team member after Angel. The first assignment I'd given Joel in January when I began assembling our group was to take an EMT course. He had gone full time for six weeks, so Angel thought he had come aboard only a week earlier.

I also didn't tell her the van Buddy was driving to the location—ostensibly to transport the modified massage table she would lie on for the tests—also carried an oxygen tank, a portable defibrillator and a box full of emergency medical supplies. There was no need for Angel to know how worried I was about the risk she would soon take. I told myself I was merely being cautious and professional, but I knew already how much I wished she could pull her focus off flying long enough to notice the guy who was working so hard to get her in the air.

Carpet was too heavy to cart and would have been difficult to attach to the walls, so we went with industrial bubble wrap, the kind with air cells as big as eggs. Three thick layers completely covered all but the outtake vents on the back wall of the tunnel.

I had chosen a low-speed wind tunnel with a fixed throat, as most facilities are geared for supersonic or, at the very least, subsonic testing, and use a variable throat to control air speeds. The problem with those is that the changes take a few minutes while the walls of the tunnel expand or contract. I wanted to be able to kill those fans instantly if Angel got into trouble.

In addition to paying an enormous fee to use the tunnel, I had to play up my military credentials and impose on two highly placed men to give me references so we could have the facility to ourselves. It was a make-or-break day and we all knew it.

As Buddy and Joel bolted the table down, Duncan set up the cameras. While I familiarized myself with the controls, Helen walked with Angel like one of those ponies that calms a thoroughbred before a race. Angel paced, her wings lifting and twitching as if anticipating the challenge.

When all was ready, Angel lay face down on the narrow padded table, wearing a pair of goggles and an old leather pilot's cap buckled under her chin. To minimize drag, she wore a leotard and ankle-length tights. Her feet were bare. Her wings draped to the floor on both sides of the table, and I manually angled them into position to catch the wind.

At ten miles an hour, the primary feathers on the tips of her wings fluttered against the floor. At twenty, they rose up off the floor several inches. At thirty, all the feathers riffled in a front-to-back undulation. At forty, the big arcs above her shoulders began to rise slowly, taking the rest of each wing with them. Angel's chin and torso were lifted up as the wings configured into a flight curve, but her hips and legs remained on the table as we hit fifty. Then the left wing tilted too far; in a heartbeat, the flat surface of the underside took the full force of the wind and she was kited off the table, flung across the room and slammed into the wall. The sickening crunch was audible even through the thick glass of the control booth, and as I hit the kill switch and ran into the tunnel, I was afraid she had broken every bone in her body.

"Angel! Can you hear me?" I pulled up her goggles to see if she was conscious. Her eyes were open but unfocused as she sat with her legs splayed out in front of her and her wings collapsed against the wall. I shouted at Joel to start checking for broken bones, then put my hands on the sides of her face. I was frantic for a response, but tried to keep my voice calm.

"Angel? Angel?"

She met my eyes, slowly focusing, then blinked hard two times, as if shaking something off. A big goofy smile lit up her face and she said something too softly for me to hear. I leaned in closer.

"Angel, I couldn't hear you. What did you say?"

"No broken bones," she whispered.

"We can't be sure until Joel checks you out. I know I heard something break."

"Jack."

"What?"

She raised her right hand and hooked her thumb back at the wall behind her.

"Bubble wrap, dude," she said, and I realized the sound I had heard when she hit the wall was a few dozen plastic air cells popping. She started to laugh softly, her shoulders jostling against the smooshed wings, then one by one the rest of us joined in, first from relief that she wasn't hurt and then from exhilaration, as each of us realized that with a lot of tweaking, we might be able to pull this off.

> *March 8*
> *Totally crashed but so worth it!!!*
> *They work! My wings have lift &*
> *now I know 4 sure I'm going 2 fly.*
> *JE was 1st 2 me after I hit th wall.*
> *Was half dopey from th impact, but*
> *not so out of it that I failed 2 notice*
> *how nice it felt when his hands were*
> *on my face & he was saying my*
> *name. Funny, all those times he*
> *touched my wings, checking thm*
> *out & measuring thm, I didn't feel*
> *anything. His eyes looked worried.*
> *& blue. Dark, beautiful blue, like 2*
> *little skies I could see myself flying*
> *in2.*

After leaving three messages, I realized Nick was not going to return my calls, so I drove to his apartment around eleven on Saturday morning. He looked awful when he opened the door: stained undershirt, sweat pants and a two-day beard.

"Hello, Nick."

He stared for a few seconds till recognition animated his face.

"Hey, Magic Jack, come on in," he slurred, as he slung his arm back in what was probably supposed to be a welcoming gesture.

The place was as dark and untidy as any undergrad bachelor digs I had ever been in, and the cloud of funk that hit me as I stepped inside seemed to be comprised of body odor, cigarette smoke, old Chinese food and, not to put too fine a point on it, ass.

"Sit down, man. Mi casa es your casa," he said, knocking an empty pizza box off a chair for me. He then flopped down on the couch, not bothering to push aside a towel that looked to be equal parts terrycloth and mildew. Shelby had been right; he was a total mess.

"So, Nick. It's a little shy of noon and you look a wee bit drunkish, if you don't mind a candid observation."

"Yeah, well, in the memortal words of Kris Kristof-ferson, the beer I had for breakfast wasn't bad so I had two more for dessert." He barked out a laugh that transitioned into a purposely protracted belch. "What can I do you for?"

"I saw Shelby last week. She thinks you could use a little help."

He snorted with amusement. "Good old Shelby. I can't imagine what she meant. Look around. I'm a snappy dresser, I have a be-yoo-tiful apartment and life's good. I'm gonna get another beer."

"Thirds on dessert?"

"No. You said it was almost noon, so this one will be an apéritif before lunch. Can I get you one?"

"Actually, I brought my own."

I went to my car and took a bottle of Usquebaugh thirty-year-old from the case I always carry in my trunk. One of the things I learned from Adair Macleod was that a premium scotch works better than a lock pick for opening doors.

Back in Nick's apartment, I set the bottle down on the littered coffee table between us, pulled out my penknife and cut the leather thong on the embossed hangtag, then slit the foil collar. Nick took his beer out of his mouth long enough to lean in and check the label.

"Shit, man" he said, sounding impressed. "What'd you do, rob a king?"

"Any chance you have two clean glasses, or should I slip it into a paper bag so we can neck-suck it?"

Nick scrambled into the kitchen and came back with a brandy snifter and a juice glass. I poured, sat back, and then proceeded to ride with him to perdition. It didn't take as long as I thought it would because of the multiple beers he'd already had, and I refilled the snifter again and again while we talked about sports, movies and politics. I swirled that original pair of digits in my juice glass, occasionally touching it to my lips to support the illusion we were drinking together.

Two hours later, after Nick had knelt at his toilet to puke and pray for a good long time, he was on the couch sobbing his guts out.

"I want to help you, Nick, but you're going to have to talk to me. What the hell is going on with you?"

"Yeah, that's the big question, isn't it? What's wrong with Nick?"

He swayed slightly, still reeling from his ride on the ninety-six proof Tilt-A-Whirl. I waited.

"You want to know what's wrong with old fucked-up Nick? Let's see. Oh, I don't know, how about his mother died. Then his sister died. Then his mother died. *Again.*"

If in vino there is veritas, in single malt there is veritas cubed. With his dad pulling up stakes and moving out of the country, and Shelby keeping him away to protect her children, Nick felt everyone he had ever loved had abandoned him. Which bore out his suspicion that he was worthless and gave him permission to trash himself.

He was fixable.

I have always been immune to the kittenish, wide-eyed helplessness of a certain type of woman, much preferring to spend time with ladies of a more confident, brainier persuasion. Maybe because my grandmother and mother were both sword-point sharp. Or perhaps I was influenced by the twenty-three-year-old post-grad speech-and-language student I hired my first year of college, when I wanted so badly to sound "American." Within six months she had relieved me of my Scottish accent, as well as my virginity, and I wasn't sure which I was happier about.

Angel's intelligence was unquestionably strong. For someone with only a recent high school diploma, she had sussed out much of the groundwork for her future flying long before she brought me aboard. When I hired the rest of the team we built on a sound foundation, rather than having to start from scratch.

The confidence she displayed came, I assumed, from her year as an internationally known celebrity. Now I know from my second read of Allison's legacy that Angel went into that job with a pre-set ability to at least *appear* confident, even around older, more experienced people like the corporate stooge the company sent to talk a naïve teen into shilling a product on their terms.

I would have been attracted to Angel even if she hadn't been so physically beautiful, especially with my daily exposure to her as we worked all summer developing the wing cuffs and lower-body harness that finally allowed us to get a fair test in the wind tunnel. We all knew flying was possible for her by then, if we could only come up with a way to get her in the air.

Through hot afternoons, we pitched and discarded a hundred ideas. Because of the formidable lift of her wings, we ruled out having her jump from a plane like a para-trooper. Much too likely she'd have loft before the plane cleared out of her way. Pulling her on a tow-rope platform behind a truck until she lifted off turned out to be impractical as well as dangerous.

And then one day I recalled having seen old films of the X-15 being launched. If I remembered correctly, it had been unable to take off on its own also. I asked Duncan to call some of his former Air Force colleagues, and within a week we were all sitting in front of a TV watching video dubs of a 1961 X-15 flight. As the experimental rocket dropped from the underwing of the B-52, instantly clearing the mother ship, we all knew we had found our solution. I sent Duncan to evaluate aircraft, Helen and Buddy off to do initial research and design for a drop system, and Joel to scout isolated places where we could do test flights away from the prying eyes of the public.

When everyone had cleared out except Angel and me, I watched her pace from one end of my living room to the other, wings twitching and a look of sheer delight on her face. I cleared my throat loudly to get her attention, and she stopped to look over at me.

"What?" she asked.

"Who does a guy have to kill to get a paycheck around here?"

Her face lit up even more and she crossed to me in three long-legged strides.

"So you *do* believe it's possible?" she asked, her voice shaky with excitement. "You think I can fly?"

"I do. So cough up, sister."

She laughed and stepped close as she raised her hands and slapped both open palms against my upper chest several times to punctuate her words.

"Didn't I tell you? I knew I could fly!"

She was lost in her excitement, but all I could think about was the feel of her hands through my shirt as they stayed where they were after the last triumphant slap. There was no coy come-on in the gesture, and the effect was more like an exuberant Golden Retriever jumping up and putting its paws on my chest than a woman trying to initiate intimacy. I had seen nothing from her all summer to indicate she favored me any more than the other members of the team, but I knew I was a goner and I had to declare myself, regardless of the outcome.

I brought my own hands up to cover hers on my chest and looked down into her eyes. Her smile faded, the wings went still and, even though my brain was telling me I was making a mistake, I leaned down to kiss her, moving my hands to the sides of her upper arms as I did.

I had kissed enough women to have a pretty good idea of the response range, but this was unprecedented for me. Zero. Nada. Zip. Her lips were tight and unyielding, and her body went rigid under my grasp. I stepped back and dropped my hands to my sides.

"I'm sorry," I said, afraid I had compromised a perfectly good working relationship. "I shouldn't have done that."

"Why not?" she asked, sounding genuinely confused.

"It's pretty obvious the attention is unwelcome."

"No, it's welcome. It's totally welcome."

She looked almost afraid and very near tears, and all I could think of was how joyful she had been before I

pushed my libidinous agenda. Then her last words finally
processed through my besotted brain cells. She had turned
nineteen two months earlier. Was it possible?

"You've never kissed anyone before, have you?"

Suddenly tears were in her eyes, and she tried to
turn away to hide them, so embarrassed was she.

"Oh, God, I'm a crappy kisser!"

I got my hands on her shoulders before she could
pivot far enough to throw me a wing block, and turned her
back to face me, my own confidence reanimating.

"Not crappy, merely inexperienced."

"Where is that hole in the ground when I really
need it to swallow me?"

My heart was liquefying with the need to hold her.
"You don't have to pucker; that's only in cartoons."

"I kiss like Daffy Duck," she wailed, but she kept
her eyes locked on mine. I leaned down until my forehead
rested against hers and she was forced to close her eyes.

"Soft lips," I instructed. "Relax."

"Quack," she replied in a plaintive voice.

She didn't kiss back, but her mouth softened under
mine and the muscles of her upper arms relaxed in my grip.
We slowly pulled apart, maintaining maximum eyelock.

"Better?" she asked, tentatively.

"So-so," I said, grinning.

This time the slap on my chest was sharp enough to
sting. "Bastard."

I pulled her tight against me, trapping her hands
between us.

"Don't worry," I said. "Flying is hard; kissing is
easy."

Angel came up on her toes to meet me halfway and
that third kiss was a keeper for me. I assumed it was good
for her, too, as her wings vibrated so much they made us
both tremble. At least I think it was the wings causing it.

> *August 26*
> *My 1st 3 kisses 2day! 1 second, 5*
> *seconds & 20 minutes long. Don't*
> *know what finally made JE notice*
> *me. Called Stacy 2 tell her th news.*

She asked if he did tongue. Dis-
gusting! I told her no & I would nvr
do that. She laughed & said 2 call
her when I changed my mind. Told
her goodbye 4ever then & she
laughed even more. We know how
2 fly me now & I'm going 2 buy a
plane. Well, maybe not 20 minutes
but it must hve been at least 10.

Shelby invited me to the house for our next Q&A. She wanted me to meet Kyle and the girls, so I got enough information from her to hold up my end of the conversation, at least through dinner. Shannon was unicorns, Erin was stickers, Kyle was accounting.

My social skills were atrophied, as the last time I had had dinner with a family, other than on my visits back to Scotland, was when Angel and I joined Charlie, Allison, Nick and Shelby that last Thanksgiving before she flew. I was a little nervous, so I came armed: roses for Shelby, Usquebaugh for Kyle, and surprises for the girls.

"Erin, Shannon, this is your Uncle Jack. Go ahead, say hello."

Erin solemnly held her tiny hand up to shake mine, but Shannon eyed me suspiciously.

"Hello, ladies," I said. "It's very nice to meet you."

Shannon glanced up at her mother, then back to me. "If you're my uncle," she said, in a voice like a cartoon mouse, "why come I never saw you before?"

"Because I have been on a secret mission. I can tell you about it, but you have to promise not to tell anyone else." I got down on one knee to be closer to their level. "Can you two keep a secret?"

"*I* can," Shannon stated firmly. Erin bobbed her head up and down rapidly.

"You guys take Jack in the living room while I put these in a vase and check on dinner," Shelby said on her way to the kitchen. As soon as she was gone, Erin leaned in close to my ear.

"What's the secret?" she whispered.

I carefully checked in all directions to make sure no

one was listening, then spilled the beans in a stage whisper.

"I've been hunting unicorns."

Erin gasped and slapped her two little hands over her mouth. Both girls went big-eyed, but Shannon looked stricken.

"You *kill* them?" she asked, bottom lip quivering. I had forgotten how literal children can be.

"No, no, no, I hunt them to take their pictures for storybooks." They exchanged a glance, each trying to see how the other was reacting to the magnitude of my mission.

"How many did you see?" Erin asked in a conspiratorial tone.

"Well, none so far, but that's because I usually hunt them in the winter and it's very hard to see them against the snow."

Erin bought it, but Shannon's eyes squinted at me and she put her hands on her hips in a perfect miniature of female exasperation. "Do you *really* hunt unicorns?"

I whipped out the proof from my pocket, identical sheets of mostly unicorn stickers, with a few rainbows, hearts and kittens thrown in for good measure. Their eyes got big again and I noticed Shannon's were the same blue as her mom, but Erin's gold-flecked, dark brown eyes looked like Angel's. As I handed them each a sheet of stickers, Shelby came back into the foyer.

"Cheez Louise, girls, are you going to keep him on his knees all night?"

As I stood up, each of my hands was captured by a smaller hand and I was led into the living room. When Kyle came home a little while later and Shelby brought him in to introduce me, Shannon was sitting on the arm of the chair and Erin was in my lap slowly twisting my tie into a silk pretzel while I regaled them with unicorn trivia. When they saw Kyle, they were off me and running toward him with happy "Daddy" squeals in unison. I stood to shake hands, but he already had a girl on each arm, so we nodded and smiled.

"Very nice to meet you, Jack. We'll go wash up for dinner and be right back." I could hear Shannon and Erin whispering excitedly to him as he carried them out of the room, and I knew the security of all unicorns was being compromised.

"You don't have to be nice to them if they bother you," Shelby said. "Just drop kick them across the room. That's what we do."

When I assured her they hadn't been bothering me, Shelby cocked a skeptical eyebrow. But they really hadn't. In fact, it had been curiously comforting to feel their intense focus as I spun out the b.s.

During dinner the conversation alternated between adult and child topics. I learned that Kyle and Shelby had met when he went to work for Charlie's accounting firm the summer Shelby was there earning extra money between eleventh and twelfth grades by doing filing and general gofering. When Charlie decided to move to Portugal five years ago, he let Kyle take over the firm on a fifteen-year buyout. Shelby and Kyle got married after she graduated.

The twins enlightened us with the revelation that Jason Pacheco flushed crayons down the toilet at preschool and tried to wipe his boogers off on other kids' arms. Then, a duet: "Ee-uww!"

My contribution to the conversation was a brief summary of my late college return to get my doctorate, and a couple classroom anecdotes gleaned from my mostly dull time as a physics professor.

After the meal, Kyle offered to bathe the girls and put them to bed so Shelby and I could talk. Shannon held her arms up for Kyle to carry her out of the room, but Erin hung back long enough to peel a rainbow off her sheet of stickers and press it onto the back of my hand. She giggled as the hairs on my hand popped up the sticker a quarter of an inch, then she looked at me to see my reaction. I was once again painfully reminded of how much like Angel's her eyes were.

I told Shelby about my visit to Nick, leaving out the part about getting him drunk so he would open up to me. We agreed he should be allowed to read what Allison had written, that it might give him a sense of inclusion he had long since lost, but when I broached the idea of Nick being invited to her home for a visit, she was defensive.

"Not a good idea, Jack."

"Why? The drugs?"

"Call me overprotective, but I don't want the girls shooting up their first heroin before kindergarten. I mean, you gotta save something for middle school."

"O—kay," I said, understanding there was maybe a soupçon of parental overreact going on. "First, it was blow, not a rubber strap and a dirty needle, and second, he hasn't done it in years."

"You believe him?"

I tried hard not to make it sound provisional when I answered in the affirmative.

"Probably didn't stop until he ran out of the money Mom left him."

"No, he stopped when your dad left him."

I only took one psychology course in college, but you don't exactly have to be Freud to realize that a boy who feels abandoned and overlooked will do almost anything to get his father's attention, even screwing up badly enough to get negative attention. Shelby had all but moved in with Stacy by the time she was thirteen, so Nick was left alone in that house with the ghost of Charlie Evans. Nick's initial attempt to get his dad's attention was the drinking, the one, unfortunately, that has stuck. Flunking out of college was gambit number two, and an openly flaunted cocaine habit was his trump.

Normally, it's the people who can't see the ghosts, not the other way around.

"After your father got married and moved away, there was no more need for Nick to be so self-destructive. He stopped doing coke the day Charlie left."

"Then why does he still drink?"

"He's an alcoholic. Your brother has a disease, and he has no more control over it than if he had cancer."

"Jack, if you had children, little people relying on you for their protection, you'd know why I'm so uneasy."

"I don't need kids of my own to know not to put a child at risk," I snapped. Shelby looked up at my sharp tone and I backed down immediately. "What if I come with Nick? For a family dinner like tonight. If he causes even the slightest trouble, I'll haul his sorry ass out of here and you can give up on him without a shred of guilt."

We were interrupted by two girl-comets hurtling straight at Shelby to say good night. She turned to defend her bulging stomach from a direct hit.

"Hey, careful! Don't hurt the baby."

"Puppy, puppy," crooned Shannon, carefully patting the bump, as Erin climbed onto the chair arm to nestle against Shelby's side. Kyle came in with his sleeves rolled up and a towel draped around his neck.

"Okay, who wants a story?" he asked.

Both girls shouted, "Me! Me!" But it was their mom who got up to take them to bed, telling Kyle I had a proposition to lay out. The girls said good night to me and, after Shelby's prompting, I was noisily smooched on both cheeks and enveloped in the sweet scent of baby powder.

Shelby led them out, their bare feet flapping on the hardwood floor beneath the ruffled hems of their nightgowns. Erin turned for a last impish smile at me, then I was left alone with Kyle.

He was less hesitant about Nick than Shelby had been and, fifteen minutes later when Shelby returned, we all agreed to a test dinner the following weekend. I would accompany Nick and guarantee his good behavior.

I brought the four yellow pads with me when I went to Nick's apartment the next day. Like Shelby, he had not known of their existence and was eager to read them.

"You'll probably have a lot of questions for me after you read what your mom wrote. Shelby does. Anyway, so I don't have to tell my stories twice, I thought you and I might go over there next Saturday for dinner."

His look was half suspicious, half hopeful. "She said it was okay?"

"Yes."

"Are there conditions?"

"I'm your date."

"And I have to behave myself, right?"

"That would be the requirement with *any* invite, wouldn't it?"

"And what does Magic Jack get out of all this?"

"A free meal. Your sister's one heck of a cook."

"You told her I'm not doing drugs?"

"I did."

"But she didn't believe you."

"She was skeptical." He snorted derisively, but I knew I was making headway. "She has every reason to be, but you can remove all her doubts."

"Right."

"Stay sober and play nice. Repeat a couple dozen times and you might get your baby sister back."

"The million-dollar question is, does she want *me* back?"

"More than anything," I said, knowing that's what he needed to hear. I stood up to leave and gave his head a playful whack. "Saturday, then. I'll be here at five-thirty. And Nick? Try to do a little better than this undershirt and sweat pants look you've got going on."

"Bite me."

He was reaching for the top yellow pad when I let myself out.

The operation was getting too big to stay in my house, so we rented a Quonset hut and moved everything there, including the Cessna Angel bought toward the end of September. We hoped to have all the gear tweaked and the plane refitted with the dove gloves in time to make a secret test flight with Angel before the end of the year. After three promising teases in the wind tunnel we were anxious to go for the real thing.

You've already read Allison's account of the various bits of technological magic that helped put Angel in the sky, so I will say nothing more about them than that they were developed, tested and reworked throughout September and October.

Now that I believe I understand Angel's reason for being here, her message to the world, if you like, I need to veer away from the flying campaign and write about our relationship. This is intensely personal information and I have not revealed a word about it all this time, from respect for her memory, from the pain it causes when I recall even small details, and because I have always adhered to the rule that a gentleman does not kiss and tell. But if you are to weigh in on whether or not my supposition about her purpose is right, if you want to understand the *entire* story, you need to know what happened between Angel and me.

After that first hesitant kiss near the end of August, we both knew we would become lovers, but there was much going on with the flight prep and we knew we were young and had all the time in the world, so we moved ahead very slowly. It wasn't from reluctance to proceed, but a savoring of each precious moment that paced us.

Logistics were always in play. Angel couldn't comfortably sit in a movie theater, but if she did she had to sit in the back row to keep the tops of her wings from blocking someone's view. I had to accept the fact that I couldn't put my arms around her easily to pull her close. And even the tamest tussle left her with bent or broken feathers.

So, we adapted. We rented DVDs and watched our movies at home. When I wanted to hold her, I learned to step in front of her face to face and slip my hands around her waist and under the wings. And Angel taught me how to do the upkeep on her feathers that Allison had taken care of in the past.

The first thing we had to rule out was spontaneity. Angel was different from any woman who had ever lived, and each new step in our romance had to be calculated and engineered. Including sex.

I had had frank sexual discussions with partners *after* making love, but I had never before had to work with a woman to figure out *how* to make love. And since Angel was the neophyte and I was the experienced man of the world, it was up to me to blueprint our first time. Take out your *Kama Sutra* or your *Joy of Sex*, imagine a huge pair of wings on the female in each illustration or photograph, and you'll see what I was up against. Literally.

The work was not unpleasant, however, and even the failures and miscues brought us closer. At least they did after we had finished laughing.

Angel could not lie on her back. Her wings might

have looked feathery and delicate in those lingerie ads, but they had substantial mass that caused her spine to arch up painfully if she tried to stretch out supine. We ruled out the missionary position.

She could lie on her side by pushing the bottom wing behind her, so one night while we were fully clothed and watching TV on the couch, I suggested yet another fact-finding experiment. Spooning with Angel turned out to have two drawbacks. The first was that I had to lie on the wing that was pushed back from underneath her, and no matter how carefully I moved, feathers got bent and broken. This was not an aesthetic issue; she needed all her feathers in working order to fly. The next day I spent hours with the imping needles and glue putting that blasted wing back to rights. That would have been enough to scratch the spoon position off the list, but there was also the little detail that, unlike with the average woman where I could spoon her and kiss the back of her neck, curving around Angel's body meant I got a mouth full of fluff. And not the good kind.

Angel helpfully suggested spooning with me in front and her behind, and I had to explain that although it would solve the wing problem, it would create a penis problem. These discussions were not as romantic as chilled wine and twinkling candles, but they were a necessity.

I had been reluctant to suggest what we finally chose for our maiden flight, as it seemed sexist and crude to lie back like a pasha, point to the vertical and say, "Hop on, babe." She was a virgin, she was the girl I adored, and I wanted her first sexual experience to be loving, gentle and pain free. Having a woman straddle me like that had always felt like raunchy rodeo sex, and I'm not saying I hadn't liked it; but I felt it was not first-timer material.

On a Saturday evening in early fall, with candles flickering on the night stands and Harry Connick, Jr. on the stereo, I lay back on my bed and waited for Angel to come out of the bathroom. I had done an initial tear on the condom wrapper for fast retrieval, and slid it under the edge of my pillow, when the light visible under the door to the bathroom went out, the door opened and an angel entered the room. No airbrushed *Playboy* centerfold could have speed-bumped my breathing the way the sight of her naked body did in the candlelight.

As she put one knee up on the bed, I reached for her upper arms and pulled her forward so that she stretched out along the length of my own body. I put my right hand behind her head and guided it into the nook between my neck and shoulder and, as she relaxed, I felt those big wings softly settle on either side of me.

The murmured words were, I'm sure, as sweet and intense as they always are between lovers. The touches as unselfish, insistent, teasing, inquisitive, gentle, surprising and painful as they have been since the beginning of time. As it has always been, the most beautiful, sensual woman in the world joined the handsomest, most virile man for a ramp-up to a perfect union. In other words, those details are not for you to read.

After kissing and molding our bodies to each other for what felt like hours, Angel put her palms flat against my upper chest in an intimate replay of her contact with me the day we had kissed for the first time. She pushed herself up to a seated position with her knees pressed into my flanks, and her wings sprawled out to cover the bed. I placed a hand on either side of her hips and exerted enough pressure to show her what to do. Her quads tightened as she followed my lead and lifted herself up, and I rolled the condom on in seconds. My hands went back to her hips to make sure she didn't lower herself onto me too quickly. The mutual teasing had been going on for more than a month, so we were both eager to play out the sexual endgame.

The action up until then had unfolded the way it always does, but once we started moving together, everything changed. I rolled my hips, gently at first, while she got used to having me inside her. Her eyelids fluttered closed, her chin tilted up, her body movements instinctively complemented my own, and *her wings began to lift off the bed.* Sloggy and languid at first, those twin parabolas rose steadily, feathers whispering against the silk sheets until even the trailing primaries had been dragged clear of the mattress. Angel was lost in her own slow rhythm, but I was riveted by the dazzling blaze of gold as the candlelight danced on the undersides of her rising wings.

Here was the picture from the magazines and bill-boards, the lovely winged girl spread wide. But those had been fantasy images created by winches, grommets and fishing line. Now, perhaps responding to a minuscule tic of purpose buried deep within a single strand of DNA, or at a cellular level, surfing the power of Angel's arousal, the wings rose and extended out on their own.

I knew logically there was no way for them to lift. I understood there were no muscles to pull them up and out as they spread across my bedroom, as they stretched to their full twin arcs. Strangely, my technical analysis of the rising wings did not distract me from the sexual finish line I was inexorably arcing toward.

As Angel panted shallowly, her feathers manifested an oscillation ripple, first in small waves the way they had always done when Angel was angry or excited, and then with increasing intensity as the wings rose higher. At their peak, they held for a moment in two wide, vibrating curves, the ends of which flattened out and shivered against the ceiling, and then they slashed downward, shattering a Lalique decanter of fifty-year-old Usquebaugh and over-turning the curio cabinet in which it had been displayed. Before the crystal shards had hit the floor, before the malty reek of two liters of four thousand dollar-a-bottle scotch filled the room, the wings sliced upward, this time with no delicate trembling of feathers against the cedar beams, but with a solid, ominous thunk, violent contact which propelled them downward once again.

Crashing noises exploded all around us as the wings raged in the confined space, knocking picture frames off the walls, and firing wine glasses into fatal trajectories against the windows. They seemed to drive Angel to faster, bolder movements, and it felt as though my fingers digging into her hips were the only thing bringing her back down onto me after each lift of her tensing thighs. She was no longer an inexperienced girl tentatively seeking her rhythm; she was primordial female riding hard to her own release and I was first man, ramming it home with all the force I could pull up from the selfish depths of my being.

My teakwood watch box smashed into the ceiling, showering us with Patek Phillipes, Breguets and Piagets, but neither of us felt the shrapnel. The frenzy of the wings intensified, driving us relentlessly. Angel clawed my chest and I bucked her up off the bed with violent thrusts. What sounds we made were guttural, incomprehensible. And still the wings whipped furiously, pushing us to go farther, to feel what no two people had felt before.

Like medieval flagellants straining toward ecstatic release under the bloody cuts of the flail, Angel and I were ravished by the avalanchine slashing of those massive feathered scourges. Candles in leaded glass chimneys stood on the night stands, out of range of the most forward fury of the wings, but the flames had been extinguished once the wilding began. And so it was in filtered moonlight ghosting through the French doors that I bore witness to Angel's first climax.

Her intake of breath was the ragged and protracted restart gasp of a near-drowning victim. Her head snapped back, she threw her arms straight out to the sides, and her body went rigid. The wings ceased to thrash, freezing in position straight out from her shoulders, and for a moment nothing moved except the spasming walls inside her that wrenched me over the precipice. Angel shuddered violently and I watched that motion transmute into her wings. When the last wave exited her trailing primary feathers with a shivery twitch, her body went boneless as she and her great wings collapsed on top of me.

> *September 29*
> *Finally, last night & I hve no words.*
> *Not true. I hve 1 word...Jack.*

The blazer and slacks Nick had on when he opened his door had seen better (and cleaner) days, but it was obvious the poor guy was trying. He pulled the sides of his jacket out and sketched a curtsy.

"Is this good enough to keep from embarrassing you, G.Q.?"

"I've picked up worse-looking dates." That wasn't

entirely true, as the chimpanzee who had done up his tie was apparently aiming for a lumpy, three-inch Windsor knot.

He turned to grab his keys from the hook by the door, but I snagged them first and tossed him mine instead.

"I'll lock up. You go start the car," I said.

"And what color would your Oldfartmobile be?"

"Black. And you'll find it double-parked alongside your Scheissewagon."

As soon as he rounded the corner I pulled the door closed and left the keys dangling from the lock. The retired narcotics cop I had hired was down the block, waiting for us to pull out.

The twelve-cylinder roar of the Ferrari engine filled the night as Nick gunned it in neutral, and I climbed into the passenger seat. Behind the wheel, Nick looked like a rumpled, happy version of the sixteen year old I had met so many years ago.

"I don't suppose this is a gift," he said with a grin.

"Buckle up and drive."

I made him stop twice. Once for two little bunches of flowers for his nieces and once for a bottle of sparkling cider. He was bristling as we got in the checkout line.

"I assume this is so I don't get drunk and puke on you," he said, challenge and hurt vying for first position in his tone.

"It's for your sister who can't drink alcohol because her inconsiderate husband pumped her full of people."

He relaxed, relieved that the focus was not always going to be on his shortcomings.

The girls were thrilled with their nosegays and their second surprise uncle in a week. Nick was nervous at the start, awkward with Shelby and intimidated by Kyle, but I poured on the Emrys charm like WD-40 on a stuck lock and before long everything was moving smoothly.

When Kyle opened a bottle of cabernet, Nick looked at me for guidance. I declined to indicate either permission or denial, but when I took a glass he did, too. Halfway through the meal Kyle offered to pour a second round and Nick asked for the sparkling cider instead.

Erin and Shannon left with Dad to take their baths, and Nick and Shelby and I moved into the living room to talk about Allison's last written words. The siblings shared a sense of guilt for having cut their mother out of their lives after Angel's death. They both had followed Charlie's lead in blaming Allison, but time might have softened that view had she not publicly executed a man.

I had spent more time with Allison than anyone else outside of that prison, and more time with Angel that last year of her life than anyone on Earth. I was the conduit to a past Nick and Shelby had been cheated out of, and was willing to answer all their questions. There were certain topics I didn't intend to discuss, but Nick and Shelby would never know to ask about them.

Nick was skeptical about my ability to predict wind patterns at the place where the fatal flight occurred, and I complimented him on the catch. It was complete bullshit, a story Angel concocted to mask the real reason the flight was set for April tenth.

Once we had completed our three secret test flights in the last quarter of the year and were ready to set the date for the public debut, Angel pulled me aside to lay out the facts of life. She wouldn't fly right before her period when she might have PMS, and she wouldn't fly *during* her period in case she had cramps or what she called a general feeling of "offness." She told me she always felt strongest in the ten or twelve days immediately after she stopped menstruating and, since the wings were controlled only by the strength of her arms, we sat with a calendar and counted days on and days off until we had our perfect wind day.

Nick and Shelby loved it. That was the sister they had known and loved, always working the angles, always a step ahead of everyone else. They started telling stories that predated my appearance on the family scene, so I sat back and let brother and sister connect without any third party interface.

While they talked, I discreetly checked my phone and found the text I had been hoping for: no weed, no seed, no blow. Good. That meant the narc had cleared out and the cleaning crew had begun.

I noticed Shelby wearing down, so I suggested we leave. At the door she stepped up to Nick and put her arms around him, catching him off-guard.

"I'm so happy you came," she said.

"Thank you for inviting me," he replied, genuinely touched.

They pulled apart and Shelby smiled at him. "We should do this again very soon."

"Okay," Nick said, "but can I come alone next time? You probably don't know it, but this guy's a great big homo and I fear for my chastity."

Shelby laughed and kissed him on the cheek.

On the drive home, I suggested we stop for coffee, partly because I wanted to talk to Nick alone, but mostly because I wasn't sure if his apartment makeover was complete yet.

I told him he had done well at dinner and that I was sure Shelby would begin opening up to the idea of his continued presence in her life. He responded with one of his typical snarky remarks, but I could tell he was relieved he hadn't screwed up and secretly pleased I had noticed and acknowledged it.

Leith and I spent most of our childhood scrabbling for the attention or approval of Bret and Cameron. My grandfather's favor and, to a lesser extent, my father's, were sought and fought for, but it was the big brother seal of approval we so desperately wanted. Our older brothers were like us, only bigger and better, and we didn't care if they occasionally whacked us in the head when parental eyes were directed elsewhere or pointed out our many shortcomings, as long as they were in our lives, showing us a picture of the boys and later, men, we wanted to be.

As the youngest child, I never had anyone other than our two dogs to look up to me, to seek guidance from my wisdom, and I was unprepared for how satisfying it was to have Nick want that big brother seal of approval from me, so different from my response to the impersonal validation requests of my students. He was almost thirty, but had been alone and confused so long he was desperate for an influential force in his life. And it looked like I was it.

"So, can I ask you a question?"

"You just did," I replied.

"Are you, like, rich?"

"Yes."

"Were you rich back when I first met you?"

"I was rich the day I was born."

"That's funny."

"Why?"

"Dad thought you were after Angel's fortune."

"I kind of suspected he did."

"Then why didn't you tell him the truth?"

And so I told Nick the story, giving my reasons for lying to Angel, if only by omission, about my finances. I hoped Nick's assimilation of the facts wouldn't send him down a thought path leading to my being responsible for his sister's death, but I was ready to take the heat if it did. She never would have flown if I hadn't paved the way with cash.

Nick stared into his coffee cup for a long time while I braced for the indictment, but when he finally looked up and gave me an evil grin, I knew, regardless of what he felt, he was only going to bring me up on the lesser charge.

"So it turns out Magic Jack is a sexist, patronizing jerk," he said with genuine pleasure. "And Shelby and I always thought you were Mr. Perfect."

I let Nick ride the enjoyment of my fallibility for a minute before bringing up the subject of his drinking.

"Hey, *you're* the one who got me drunk last week, and don't pretend you weren't sucking it down yourself."

"Oh, I drink. And I've been drunk. In fact, I've been hell-rowdy, upchuck-your-entrails, walk-around-with-your-zipper-down drunk twice in the last thirteen years."

He silently calculated, then narrowed his eyes at me. "Thirteen years ago was when Angel died," he said.

"And after the police finished with me that night, I went home and stayed blackout hammered for three days."

He fidgeted with his napkin, tearing off tiny pieces and placing them in a pile, the same way Shelby had at our second meeting. "You said twice in thirteen years. When was the second time?"

I had resolved to be honest with Nick and Shelby, to

illuminate all the dark nooks and crannies at last, but when it came right down to it, there were some crevices best left unlit. Even spackled over and sealed from view forever.

"Let's say a more recent personal loss," I hedged. "But enough about me. Let's talk about you. Specifically, your alcoholism."

"I don't think I'm an alcoholic," he replied without a lot of conviction in his voice.

"Oh, you're an alcoholic, boyo, believe me."

"And who made you the fuckin' expert?"

"My father and one of my brothers. Look, Nick, you *are* an alcoholic. You know it, I know it, so the only thing left to decide is what kind of alcoholic you're going to be." He had been expecting a frontal attack, so this threw him.

"And what are my choices?" he asked, playing along.

"From my experience, there are only four ways to be an alcoholic. A, you drink hard and steady, kind of what you've been doing, and you blow out your liver, your loved ones and your life, in that order. B, you keep up a low-level but steady intake, enjoying an ongoing buzz that still let's you function in society with reasonable ease. C, you stay completely off the juice for months, then reward yourself with a weekend bender. Or D, you never take another drink."

After a long, thoughtful silence, Nick gave me one of his bad-boy grins. "B sounds pretty good to me."

"I'm not surprised; it's a popular choice. That's the one my dad selected. The problem with A, B and C is they all have the same outcome. The only correct answer is D."

"*If* I decide I don't want to be an alcoholic."

"That ship has sailed. You'll always be an alcoholic. But if you choose D, you can be a *nondrinking* alcoholic, which is the only way to go. I'm only asking you to think about it."

When I pulled up in front of his apartment building, Nick got out and came around to the driver's side. "Hey, you never gave me back my keys."

"They're under your welcome mat."

"I don't *have* a welcome mat, dickwad."

"You do now, asshole." I gunned the engine and the

Ferrari sped away.

All previous cleanups after sex had been limited
to a shower and a change of sheets, but my first intimate
encounter with Angel required brooms, mops, vacuum
cleaners and the replacement of a wide swath of scotch-
soaked wallpaper.

We woke in the same position in which we had gone
to sleep or, more accurately, passed out of consciousness,
me flat on my back and Angel collapsed on top of me, her
face against my neck, her wings draped harmlessly to either
side of us. Any thought of a morning repeat died a quick,
limp death as I scanned the room without moving my head.
Something telegraphed my being awake, as Angel rolled her
head to the side and smiled at me. We discovered we were
glued together with my blood when she raised herself up,
reopening the scabbed-over gouges her fingernails had left
on my chest and torso, causing me to yelp with pain. She
sat up on me, wincing, and I couldn't believe the damage to
her body. The blood streaked across her breasts was mine,
the blood on the insides of her thighs was to be expected,
but the bruising on her shoulders, upper arms and hips was
horrifying. I had never knowingly left a mark more serious
than a hickey on a woman before, and I began my apologies
while she surveyed her wounds.

I wouldn't let her off the bed until I had retrieved a
pair of tennis shoes for each of us. Carefully crossing to my
closet, I stepped over broken glass, pieces of my watch box,
picture frames, the corpse of a really nice German stereo
system and what seemed like a million feathers, all while
inhaling air that would have failed a breathalyzer test.
Once shod, we crunched our way to the bathroom where we
held each other in the warm spray of multiple shower jets,
alternately bathing each other's battle scars as tenderly as
possible, and weeping at the sight of them. When we had
gingerly toweled dry, we put on the footgear again and went
back into the bedroom to assess the damage.

As we surveyed the destruction our pandemoniacal
coupling had wrought, I was the first to speak. "Damn. I'm
good."

She cocked an eyebrow at me and said dryly, "I'm assuming it isn't usually like this."

"Bingo."

When we began cleaning up, I furtively gathered the timepieces that might give away my secret, leaving only a Casio dive watch for Angel to find, a gift from Bret and his wife when I was in Scotland the last time. Those two hearty souls expected me to go Loch diving with them in a country where summer is more of a myth than an actual season.

It was several weeks before either of us was up for another go, and by then my bedroom had been stripped of breakables, flammables and miscellaneous impedimenta, while Angel's nails had been filed down to blunt ovals. Sex was never again as dramatic as that first time, primarily because there was nothing for her wings to smash and hurl around the room, but what we felt each subsequent time was the same as on our maiden flight together—powerful, perfect, breathtaking physical love.

The Friday after Thanksgiving, Angel made her first flight. Though we had theories and equipment out the wazoo nobody knew for sure what would happen that day. We were out in the middle of nowhere in order to keep our big secret, but that also meant it was a two-hour drive to the closest hospital. Helen took off smoothly from the vast pasture I had paid to have mowed a week earlier, while the rest of us waited at the corners of an imaginary rectangle, the better to ensure someone would be within a few dozen yards of Angel when she came down.

My biggest worry was the landing. I would have felt better if Angel had been able to make a few parachute jumps in advance of her first flight, if only to master the bent-knee landing. Because her wings would still be spread wide on impact, there was no way she could do a hit, tilt and roll. And her arms were locked to her wings, so they wouldn't be able to assist in balancing her. It was going to be up to her to find her footing immediately and keep the wings from propelling her into the ground.

Helen dropped her out of the dove glove at around a

thousand feet, the wings snapped open like champs and Angel had the feel of things within seconds. We had all agreed there would be nothing fancy on the debut flight, but instead of gliding down as we had planned, Angel did one short swoop upward before returning to her downward drift. Duncan popped the leg harness for the first partial release at the right time, repeated for the second two pops, and Angel came in positioned perfectly for a landing.

In the final seconds, the wings flared, jerking her arms back violently. She lost her balance and when she came down, she hit hard. We were all running toward her while she was still tumbling forward, cuffed arms unable to slow her pinwheeling momentum.

When I got to her she was crying so hard she was gasping, her right shoulder sickeningly dislocated. I knelt down and cradled her head, yelling for Joel to check her over, to see if there was anything other than the shoulder to deal with. The suit had ripped at the knees and there was some light bleeding there, but the dislocation was the worst of it. Buddy held her legs and I turned her head away from the action when Joel snapped her shoulder back into place. I asked the others to give us some space, so they all moved off to flag in the Cessna.

I rocked her as she wept, kissing her hair and whispering, "You did it, Feathers, you flew. God, I love you so much."

She said something, but the words were muffled against my chest, so I held her a few inches away from me and asked her to repeat it. She was choking and gulping, but I could make out her words.

"I didn't have to do it, Jack. I didn't have to fly."

Nick joined AA and started coaching basketball at a youth center. I bought gym memberships for him and his sponsor, a guy only two years older than Nick and seven years sober, and they started working out together three or four times a week. Nick quickly lost his drinker's pallor and began muscling up, looking more and more like the teen athlete he had been when I first met him.

As Shelby's pregnancy advanced, I relocated our

get-togethers to my house, where the efforts of a chef and maid precluded her having to lift a finger. She and Nick continued to bond, and evenings always started out with them asking me questions about Allison or Angel, but ended up with the two of them sharing stories about their childhood, stories that had the power to bring back memories of their loved ones.

Kyle and I got to be friends after he admitted he had wanted to be a pilot when he was a kid, and that gave me the impetus to get recertified. I had not flown a plane since the day Allison and I scattered Angel's ashes in the sky, but it only took a few hours for me to get my skills back, so I took Kyle up for his first flying lesson.

The two little rugrats and I got along famously, and Nick and I were even entrusted with baby-sitting duty a couple times so Shelby and Kyle could have an evening out.

Somehow I was being absorbed into a family.

I carried her high up against my chest to keep from stepping on her wings as I walked toward the motor home we had rented for the trip. Once inside, I laid her gently on the bed, found Duncan's bottle of Vicodin and made her swallow one with water. She was still crying, but more softly now, as I filled the rubber ice bag with cubes from the freezer mini-trays, then wrapped it in a dish towel and used my T-shirt as a tie to hold it against her shoulder. Before she drifted into sleep, she murmured once again, "I didn't have to do it. I didn't have to fly."

Outside, the group was waiting for me, anxious to know how she was.

"The good news is she's sleeping. And other than a sore shoulder, I think she'll be fine."

"Is there bad news?" Helen asked.

"Yeah. I don't think she wants to fly again."

"Are you joking?" asked Buddy.

"No. She keeps saying that she wishes she hadn't done it, or she shouldn't have done it. Something like that."

"At least I got it all on video," Joel volunteered. "In case she still wants to go public."

Buddy and Joel left to ferry the plane back while

Helen and I took turns driving the motor home and Duncan watched over the sleeping girl. We got back to the Quonset hut around nine that night, and the guys were waiting for us with a full coffee urn and a dozen deli sandwiches. Angel still slept, so we left her in the motor home and bedded down on the Army cots we had bought for our late-night work sessions. I lay awake wondering if the flying odyssey was over, and where Angel and I would go from here.

At 6:00 the next morning, the door clanged open and Angel strode in like Boadicea facing down the Roman ninth legion.

"Good morning, pirates!" she shouted, bringing all of us fully awake.

She wanted to know how soon she could fly again, and when I spoke with her privately, trying to get a read on what she had said the day before, Angel brushed it off as nothing more than rambling from the pain. It was the first time she had ever deliberately lied to me.

> Nov. 27
> Th same!! Exactly th same!
> Coincidence? Need 2 fly again
> ASAP 2 see. Flew 37 secs.
>
> Dec. 14
> Amazing! I'm right. I know I'm right.
> Flew 91 secs.
>
> Dec. 17
> Yes! 3 out of 3. Can't wait to tell
> Wingman. Heck, can't wait til we tell
> th world! Flew 2 mins 15 secs.
>
> Dec. 20
> Worked out th date wth JE. April 10.
> Tell him now or aftr "1st" flight? No
> more flying til then. Crap!

Reading the diary entries did not give me a clue what Angel had meant. Whatever it was, she obviously decided not to tell me until after the public debut flight. Why did those entries nag at me? What was I missing? And why had she said she didn't have to fly?

Something happened to her that first time she flew. I mean the real first time, something that seemed to plunge her into despair and make her regret having flown. And yet she was eager to fly again. With only a little more than two weeks of recovery from the shoulder injury, she flew in the middle of December and again three days later. Both times she was jubilant and flushed when she landed. What was I missing?

The videos from those first secret flights were long gone. I had asked Buddy and Joel to destroy them after Angel died, right before I convinced my brother Bret the Macleod Distillery needed a corporate jet, and provided him a pilot and a mechanic. Duncan passed away about a year ago and Helen is in a facility for Alzheimer's patients, so there was no one left to talk to who had been there and no evidence to examine. The only existing images of her flying were the ones from that fatal day. Would viewing them give me an answer?

I downloaded the two-minute clip and watched her die for the second time. My throat constricted, but nothing jumped out at me. I watched again and still, no hints. Yet I felt sure something was hidden in plain sight.

I slowed the clip to half speed and as I watched it again, something went *ping* in my brain. Half speed again, and that same *ping*, only sharper now. I stopped, went out for a walk to clear my head, and tried to figure out what my subconscious was seeing that my eyes weren't. No luck.

Back at the computer, I went through the clip at one quarter speed. The slow rollout from the dove glove, the unfurling of her great wings, her heart-stopping stoop and hot-dogging spirals. That big, fat lazy eight from one end of the field to the other. The descent: legs lowering in increments, arms bringing the wings up for controlled drag, back straight for landing, then BOOM! Her wing explodes and she's falling. The *ping* in my brain repeated steadily, as if to indicate I was getting warmer.

I went back to the start, advancing frame by frame. *Pingping.* Her form was perfect for landing. *Pingpingping.*

Those massive wings stood perpendicular to her body. *PINGPINGPINGPING.* Angel's arms, cuffed to the wings, stretched out to her sides. ***PINGPINGPINGPINGPING.*** Her chin lifted, her back arched—AND FREEZE!

I stared at that frozen image and oh, God, I knew where I had seen it before.

When I was a wee laddie, my Grandma Shea would rock me on her lap and sing Gaelic ballads to me, though I never understood a word of them. Grandpa Adair knew English was the language of business and, unlike so many of his generation, he encouraged the discarding of the old and the adopting of the new.

By age four I was already taking heat from Bret and Cameron for still being a baby on Granny's knee. None of us knew back then about the three boys of her own Shea had lost before our mother was born, and even if we had we probably wouldn't have cared, because if there ever was a dependable truth in the world, it is that boys, especially in groups, are inconsiderate little pricks.

At five I exercised my burgeoning independence by abandoning Shea to join my brothers for manlier games. I understand now the loss she must have felt at my leaving, though she graciously let me go. She must have known I was the last she would dandle, as she had been middle-aged when my mother was born and great-grandchildren were still many years away. Yet she let me run to my rough-and-tumble play, when she could have easily manipulated me with guilt to keep me on her lap another year or two.

As I got older and would run into the kitchen to her, parched for a glass of lemonade, crying with a bloody nose or hungry for whatever confection she was turning out that day, she would always be singing those old Gaelic ballads while she worked. Then one day when I was around twelve, I went into the kitchen as she peeled potatoes at the sink, intending to sneak up behind her and shout something to make her jump. She was softly singing one of her favorites, "Brèagh Slánach," which translates to "Lovely Salvation." Something in her voice stopped me from going through with my lurch and shout, and when I stepped back to a hidden place in the pantry, I saw she had tears on her cheeks.

I found a translation of "Brèagh Slánach" to see what had made her cry, but it was just a sappy love poem. I wondered if my grandmother had had a lover before Adair. Was she pining for a man long gone?

Some years later I came upon the ballad again and finally understood that the words were not about a lover, but about love itself.

> "Embrace me, love, and let your
> Great wings lift me up
> From sere dune to misted sky."

The ballad is about the power of love to raise you from an arid existence to a place closer to Heaven. I believe this is what Angel discovered, what she, and only she, could prove. When Angel wept after that first flight, it wasn't only from the pain of a dislocated shoulder, but also from the shock of enlightenment. What she felt when she flew was what she felt when she and I made love. That's what she meant when she told me, "I didn't have to fly." All that time, effort and money only led her to the same experience she could have had at any time in my embrace.

Her message would have been, I believe, that every one of us has wings. Dormant, metaphysical wings, to be sure, but stimulated and given lift by the power of love in its perfect physical expression, capable of bringing us to that lovely salvation we all yearn for. Even in childhood the seeds are there in dreams and fantasies of flying, seeds that will germinate once the hormones of puberty kick in.

When I went into the motor home to check on her a few hours after that first flight, she was sound asleep. As I was about to exit and rejoin Helen up front to continue the drive home, I saw an envelope propped up on the dresser, an envelope with my name written on it in Angel's hand.

My dearest Wingman,
*   I have failed. I know this because if I had flown successfully today, I would have burned this letter.*

First, know it is not your fault. I have been compelled to travel this path for as long as I can remember, as if an unseen hand gently pulled me along to a specific destiny. And the few times I attempted to resist that pull, the same hand, more roughly, pushed me from behind.

I don't know why this powerful force has pushed and pulled me all these years only to let me die on my first flight. I always believed there was some mystery I was being led to, a secret for me to discover. I guess I was wrong.

I hate that I have left you. I hate that you will blame yourself. But please know I would have found a way to fly, <u>had</u> to find a way to fly, whether I had ever met you or not.

What I <u>wouldn't</u> have done if I had never met you was known love. An uplifting love that made me feel cherished and protected. I love you, Wingman, and I know you love me, so grieve only as long as you absolutely must, then move on. Let your perfect love give wings to someone else.

Feathers

P.S. Tell my mother not to bury me. Please, please not the ground. Whatever is left after the flame, let it fly.

There was no way to reseal the envelope, but I put it back where I had found it. When I retrieved the box with Angel's diary, the box Shelby believes I have been searching for unsuccessfully for months, the envelope was taped to the inside cover of the diary. It read like a goodbye letter that first time around, but now when I read it I realize Angel had premonitions about her destiny, an understanding that something awaited her, even if she couldn't guess what it was.

I believe Angel got her answer on the first flight, confirmed it on her second and third, and planned to share the message after her public flight, when the whole world would be listening. The message would have been: love one another, seek out and cherish the partner who gives you wings to lift you up, to let you fly.

Left-handed children were once forced to write with their right hands, subverting their natural—you might even say God-given—direction, the same way certain segments of society now try to subvert physical desire. No matter how much sex is demonized from the pulpit, cautioned against by prudes, every kid who hits puberty feels that powerful hand pushing them to find *the one*. Few are lucky enough to get it right on the first try, and many, sadly, never find a flying partner at all, but the hormones rage and the hand pushes hard for each of us to find our perfect other.

Was this an ancient truth Angel had inadvertently rediscovered? Do "Brèagh Slánach" and the story of Briar Rose exist to remind us love is always the answer? Maybe along the line we stopped believing and needed a new voice to refresh our memory. But what of the people who responded so vituperatively to her? Did they sense Angel would inspire a joyful freedom that could undermine their power bases of fear, guilt and shame? Perhaps her biblical name and heavenly wings made her an even greater threat.

Is that why they had to shoot the messenger?

As Nick and Shelby got more comfortable with each other, they no longer needed me to keep the conversational ball rolling. I had answered all their questions about Allison's written legacy, although I still hadn't figured out how to tell them I had found Angel's diary without showing it to them. And if I supposedly hadn't found the diary, I couldn't very well say I had found my old imping kit with dozens of Angel's feathers in it. I wanted to give Shelby the feathers, but not until I worked something out on the diary.

I had honestly answered their questions, but I had not told everything I know. Then, two weeks ago, I was forced to come clean about the last secret that impacted them.

Nick and Shelby were going out for the evening, so Kyle asked if I wanted to join him and the girls for dinner.

I parked outside the franchise restaurant and waited at the door while Kyle parked and got out of his car with Erin and Shannon. We were approaching the reservations desk when Kyle's cell phone rang, so I signaled him to take the call while I got us situated. With a little girl holding each of my hands, I followed the pimply-faced teen maitre d'uh to a table and asked for two booster seats.

As I got the kids settled and handed each of them the combination coloring book and children's menu, Kyle came rushing over to the table.

"We've got to go," he said. "Shelby went into labor and Nick's driving her to the hospital." He started to lift Shannon out of the booster seat while he was talking, and I stood to get Erin.

"Hey, I'm hungry," Shannon whined.

"Me, too," Erin added.

"Wait, Kyle, why don't you leave the girls with me and I'll get them fed and home. They're only going to be in the way at the hospital."

"But I have no idea when I'll be back."

"Exactly. So I'll stay with them until you do. Hey, I've slept on couches before, you know."

"If you're sure—"

"I'm *really* hungry now," griped Shannon, clinching the deal.

"Okay, okay."

"Take my car and give me your keys," I said, handing him the keys to the Ferrari.

"I can't drive that road rocket," he protested.

"Well, you're gonna have to because I need your SUV with the car seats. And I need your house keys anyway, so chop-chop."

Kyle fished out a heavy key ring and tossed it to me. "Bye, girls. Daddy loves you." He speed-kissed each of them and was gone.

"Bye, Daddy," they called to his back.

I picked up the adults' menu, peeked over the top of it and said, "I thought he'd never leave," setting off peals of giggling.

During that dinner I learned creatures that don't

have hands, such as chickens and fish, can still provide fingers for a child's dining enjoyment. I also learned Erin's favorite salad dressing is thousand eyelash, and Shannon has to painstakingly squeeze a thin line of ketchup down the length of each individual french fry, carefully staying between the lines, before she can eat it. And I learned a Caesar salad comes with tomatoes, cucumbers and not the slightest hint of anchovy when you order it in a place where primary colors go to die.

I left a lavish tip for our waitress as a thank-you for taking Erin to the loo when she announced in a voice louder than you would expect from such a tiny person exactly what she needed to do in the "baffroom".

Back at their house I thought it would be PJs and a story, but they insisted they needed their bath. I tried to give skipping it a naughty and attractive ring, as bathing two four year olds would be way out of my comfort zone and skill set, but they glared at me with matching stubborn expressions. In truth they both needed a bath. Shannon's straight, light brown hair was tipped with ketchup from leaning over her plate as she Van Gogh'd her fries. Erin's shorter, darker hair had stayed out of her food, but when she had tipped her head back to show me how a mama bird drops a worm into baby bird's mouth, the chicken finger she was using as a worm stand-in missed her face and slid down into the neck of her T-shirt. I couldn't ask the poor waitress to make another restroom run and Erin shrieked when I attempted to retrieve it, so I knew beneath her clothes was a soggy strip of fried chicken lubricated with honey barbecue sauce.

I filled the tub while they skinned down to their birthday suits and Shannon squirted some cotton candy-smelling liquid under the faucet, so we were bubble city when I lifted each girl by the wrists, dangling her over the suds so she could dip her toes in the water and make sure it wasn't too hot before I lowered her in. I handed each one a wash cloth and told them they were going to take turns playing the mommy giving a bath to her little girl, which they thought sounded like great fun, so I sat on the floor with my back against the wall while they splashed enough water over each other to rinse away the ketchup and honey barbecue sauce.

Ten minutes of shrieking, splashing and squirting later, they were clean enough, so I held up a towel and asked who wanted to get out first.

"No-o-o," Erin wailed. "You have to wash my hair."

"But I don't know how and I might get shampoo in your eyes."

"That's okay. Mommy buys the don't-cry shampoo." She handed me the bottle and, although she had paraphrased, I saw it wouldn't blind her if I made a mistake.

While Shannon sat at the far end of the tub surfing a one-legged Barbie over the peaks of the diminishing suds, I washed Erin's hair. I put one arm in the water and had her lean back on it, then I picked up a plastic cup that had been on the edge of the tub and began dipping water and carefully sluicing it through her springy curls. She looked up at me with complete trust as I squirted shampoo on her head and briskly massaged it into her hair, then she sighed and closed her eyes, her long lashes fanning out damply on the delicate skin beneath them.

Perhaps if Angel had lived, she and I would have had a little girl who looked like this, with maybe a wee bit of me thrown in. A child who would have trusted me to hold her head up out of the water, to keep her safe. Someone to run to me when I walked in the door, the way Erin and Shannon do when Kyle comes home, their little faces lighting up for Daddy. As I rinsed the shampoo out of her hair, I realized Erin had fallen asleep on my arm.

They were more or less dry and in their nightgowns when Nick called about 8:15. "Yo, Jack, it's a boy!"

"Shelby okay?"

"I guess so. The doctor just came out and gave us the news, so they're gonna let Kyle in to see them both in a few minutes. I've got an early game tomorrow so I'm not going to hang around."

"Well, tell Kyle the girls are fine. I'm putting them to bed now. And tell him congratulations."

"Roger that," he said before hanging up.

"Attention all cute girls," I said. "This means you,

Erin and Shannon. Guess what? You have a baby brother."

"No puppy?" Shannon asked, clearly disappointed.

I suggested a brother had some advantages over a puppy, and we began coming up with reasons to be pleased with the news.

"When he gets big," I said, "he can give you rides on his motorcycle."

"And he can tell on Jason Pacheco when he tries to wipe a booger on me," Erin added helpfully.

It was long after midnight when I heard the key in the lock and jolted awake on the couch, a drying streak of drool on one side of my chin. Kyle looked drained when he handed me my keys.

"Hey, new dad, congrats," I said quietly.

"Yeah," he answered. "Look, I'm beat and she needs the bag she was supposed to take with her to the hospital. Would you mind running it by there on your way home?"

"No problem. Where is it?"

He left the room without answering and returned a minute later with an overnight bag he handed to me.

"Jeez, man, get some sleep. You look wiped."

"Yeah," he said, rubbing his eyes with the heel of his hand.

I thought I would drop off the bag at the nurses' station and leave, but when I told them who it was for, they said she was expecting me.

"Knock, knock," I said softly at the open door to her room. Shelby was sitting up, lightly dozing. A bassinet was on one side of the bed, an empty chair on the other.

"Jack?"

"How are you doing?"

"Come on in."

"I'll only stay a minute, then let you get some rest."

"No, I want you to pull up a chair and stay awhile. But first, why don't you take a peek at your godson?"

I went around to where the bassinet was and leaned over to peer through the clear plastic dome at the tiny baby inside. He was sleeping on his stomach, a newborn's diaper swallowing much of his bottom half.

"Need more light?" Shelby asked dryly.

I didn't. The soft glow from the reading lamp above her bed filtered through the plastic, illuminating the tiny triangular flaps. Cutting my eyes toward Shelby, I saw her staring at me with an unreadable expression.

"Anything you'd like to say, Jack?"

"I'm sorry; I should have told you."

"You're right, you should have. But we've got all night, and I need to make some decisions tomorrow, so why don't you sit down and tell me now."

And that's when she learned Angel's wings had not been a gift from a mystery sperm donor at a frat house gang rape, but a product of her own family's gene pool.

During that fall and early winter when Angel made the three secret flights and she and I began our love affair, we also traced the origin of her wings. It began with a casual comment from her about the circumstances of her birth. She had the bare details of the encounter that had resulted in Allison's pregnancy, and she wondered if she should do another DNA test on each of the men, given that biotechnology had advanced significantly in the years since the last round of tests.

"Are you a hundred percent sure they came from your biological father's side of the family?" I asked.

"You think my mother's lying?"

"I've met her maybe a half-dozen times, so I don't know what Allison's capable of doing. But if the wings come from her parents' family, might she have preferred to throw the blame on a conveniently anonymous father?"

"But then why wouldn't she have had them cut off when I was born? Two tiny scars on my back and I would never have known."

"We're spitballing in abstracts and hypotheticals here, so we're not going to come up with anything more than a wild guess. If you really want to know where your wings came from, we'll find out."

"How?"

"I know a guy."

I was being a cocky bastard, showing off for my girl,

and I wish now I had kept my mouth shut, but I did in fact know a guy. With Angel's enthusiastic approval, I hired one of the most discreet and talented private investigators in the country.

I had met Will Sanders when Bret called me a few years earlier about an Usquebaugh knockoff turning up in American liquor stores. The bottles, our signature leather thong and hangtag, even the embossed silver foil collar were identical, but the stuff inside was shit scotch and threatened to undermine our brand name in the States. The authorities had been unable to track down the culprits and, since Cameron had moved back to Loch Laggan, I was the go-to brother on U.S. soil.

I brought Sanders in and within two months there were indictments against fifteen people, including a former Macleod Distillery employee my grandfather had fired years earlier for nicking stock from the aging house and doctoring the records to hide the missing whisky.

Sanders was no less impressive on my second go-round with him. He found the documents, the doctor and the grave.

Allison never knew she had been a twin, and that her brother had been born with wings. The surgeon who removed them was long-retired when Sanders found him, but he readily recalled the event. Not so much because of the removal of the tiny flaps—he routinely took off extra digits, vestigial tails and other superfluous biologica—but because of the mother's reaction to her newborn son. She was repulsed by the anomaly, refusing to hold or name the child. The doctor had thought once the offending flaps were removed and the young mother spent time with her babies, the natural maternal instinct would kick in and she would realize she loved both her infants. She was sent home with the twins and three days later the boy was dead.

The death certificate he had signed claimed SIDS, but the doctor, when pressed, admitted the baby appeared to have starved. He speculated that the mother, unable to bring herself to nurse the infant she reviled was also un-willing to feed him formula from a bottle.

Angel read the report in silence, then asked me to

come with her to visit the grave. She was furious when she saw the untended plot with only a cheap, flat marker with the family surname and the year.

"So the bitch kills him, gets away with it, and then doesn't even bother to *name* him before she sticks him in the ground?"

We discussed telling Allison, but Angel was afraid to add any more to the burden of guilt and grief her mother already carried. She didn't see what would be gained by giving Allison the information, and I went along with her decision. Now, having read Allison's account of her hellish childhood, I see why her crazy mother abused her the way she did. After all, Allison spent nine months in utero with the unnatural boy, and some of the taint must have rubbed off on her.

Angel paid to have the grave cleaned up and lovely flowers planted around it. She replaced the cheesy little plaque with a marble marker. The engraver was not surprised by her instruction to carve a pair of wings above the name Baby Fitzgerald, but he had clearly never done anything like what Angel requested for the lines under the name: *Brother to Allison / Uncle to Angel / Starved to death by his mother.*

Afterwards, Angel told me, "I hope the granny from Hell stops by someday and sees that she is loathed."

When I finished the story, Shelby sat in silence for a long time.

"Kyle was horrified when he saw them," she finally said. "And when the doctor prescribed the usual, he wanted to sign a surgical release on the spot."

"Jesus."

"I told them to get the fuck out of my room. And when the head nurse refused to wheel the baby in here and leave him so I could make sure no one hurts him, I called the hospital administrator and threatened to sue his ass off."

"No wonder they let me in after visiting hours."

She smiled and squeezed my hand, saying, "So, the baby has wings and his mother has balls, but I haven't yet decided what to do."

"Am I to understand I'm here as advocate for the wings?"

"Yes. The prosecution has made its case loud and clear, so if anyone is going to speak for keeping him intact, it's you."

My theory was still new, and I didn't know if it would sound plausible to her, but I explained it anyway. I said I had found the diary and I would give her the pages supporting my belief, along with Angel's goodbye letter about her sense of having a purpose that would be expressed through the wings. I did not offer to show her video proof that Angel was having an orgasm when she was shot. Shelby listened to it all without comment, then told me she would carefully weigh what I had said, so I got up to leave.

"I forgot to ask. Does he have a name?"

"Yes."

BIRTH ANNOUNCEMENTS

Jim and Joyce Witkowski are the parents of a daughter, Joy Ann, born last Sunday at Madison County General. Joy Ann weighed 5 lbs 14 oz and is the Witkowski's first child.

Kyle and Shelby Hart are the parents of a son, Gavin Angelo, born last Friday at St. Luke's Hospital. Gavin weighed 7 lbs 6 oz. The Harts have two other children, twin daughters Shannon and Erin.

Leroy and Coral Johnson are the parents of a son, Tariq, born last Fri-

**day at Silverton Memori-
al. Tariq weighed 8 lbs 2
oz and has one brother,
Derrick.**

Shelby isn't sure she believes in my theory, but
Gavin is keeping his wings for now. I'm not even sure if I
believe my theory, but if Angel *was* a messenger of love, I
have been an ineffectual first disciple, confining myself to a
sere dune since her death instead of searching for love
again and proving her message.

Charlie Evans got it right. He was slammed with
grief when his first wife died tragically, but he kept himself
open to love, finding it with Allison. He was six or seven
years older than I am when Allison killed herself, but if
Shelby is to be believed, he has pushed through the pain
once again to find love. Charlie is a man who wants to fly,
who knows his wings will be unfurled only in the embrace
of another person.

Today my life changes. I have given notice to the
university I won't be back next semester. Or ever. I wasn't
that great a physics teacher anyway, as my heart was never
really in it. Besides, I'm going to have too much to do in the
coming years to stand in a classroom droning on about
quarks, regardless of their charm.

I'm forty-two years old and I want to fly again, in
my own plane *and* metaphorically. If there is a chance I
can float once more in that misted sky so close to Heaven,
then I will reopen myself to loving and being loved.

I have promised Shelby I will be there for Gavin
every step of the way, to share what I alone can tell him
about the joy and responsibility those tiny flaps will bring
into his future life. And if I do not live long enough to see
him become a man, to learn if there *is* a message and if he
is the messenger, he will have these pages to guide him.

I will go back and clean them up, explain better
where I have truncated or obfuscated, delete anything that
sounds like my own personal nattering or wallowing, but
there is no rush. I should have at least sixteen years to edit
and rewrite all this.

Shelby and Nick now have the feathers that were in the box, but I am holding onto the Indiana Jones fedora and the journals with all of Angel's flight calculations and will turn them over to Gavin when the time is right.

I solved the diary dilemma by making photocopies of each page, one for Shelby and one for Nick, through the entry for March 27. I claimed this was the final time Angel wrote because of the frantic activity in the run-up to the fatal flight, my last lie to them. In reality, everything was locked and loaded early enough for our entire team to take it easy that last few weeks.

Angel once said she liked writing on paper because it can be burned to keep a person's secrets, so tonight I help her keep that final secret. I also forgive her and let her go as I feed the last seven diary entries to the flames.

March 28
Per shd hve started yest or 2day. Weight & body fat very low right now 4 th flight, so maybe that's causing th delay.

March 30
Getting worried. Per still hasn't started. Ate a ton 2day. Maybe a couple extra lbs will bring it on.

April 3
Eating like a pig. 3 lbs up, still nothing.

April 6
10 days late. Crap! Do not want 2 fly during my per. Stopped stuffing myself. Now I want it 2 hold off til <u>aftr</u> my flight.

April 7
No PMS but threw up this A.M.

April 8
Had Stacy sneak me in a preg test. She waited outside & I told hr it was neg but I didn't really pee on th stick. 2 scared.

April 9
Peed on th stick. I'm preg. Can't tell
Wingman til aftr tmrrow or he'll call off
th flight. I <u>WILL</u> fly tmrrow & aftrwrd
I'll tell him <u>evrythng</u>!!

DO YOU LIKE MYSTERIES?

Please check out
MURDER IN ONE TAKE
MURDER: TAKE TWO
and
MURDER: TAKE THREE
a series by April Kelly and Marsha Lyons

All three are available on Amazon and other online
outlets. Read sample chapters, outlines of the books,
and author
information at flightriskbooks.com.

Please turn the page if you want to read more
about these mysteries

MURDER IN ONE TAKE

Det. Blake Ervansky is first on the scene when an Oscar-winning star is shot by his ex-lover. As lead cop on the case, Ervansky has everything he needs to put away Ali Garland: motive, weapon, videos of the murder and a dozen eyewitnesses, one of whom is his partner of less than 24 hours, Sgt. Maureen O'Brien.

This is LA, the beating heart of showbiz, though, so nothing is as it seems, even Ervansky's new partner. Ali Garland appears to have been justified in defending herself with lethal force, but could this wide-eyed ingénue be the architect of an airtight double fake? Has she really pulled off the perfect murder?

Ervansky and O'Brien will only unravel her skein of deceit when they turn to the same Hollywood magic that convinces audiences aliens can phone home, talking clown fish do search and rescue, and every hooker is just a nice girl waiting for the right millionaire.

2014 FIRST PLACE WINNER!
Mystery / Suspense
Kindle Book Promo / LuckyCinda
International Contest.

MURDER IN ONE TAKE: "...all the intrigue of Hollywood's big-budget blockbusters."
—*Kirkus Reviews*

MURDER: TAKE TWO

What has six legs, black stripes and kills people? A homicidal magician and the biggest tiger in his world-famous act. Murder will be hard to prove, though, as the dead guy never existed, all the evidence seems to have been eaten, and the victim's corpse isn't the only thing that has magically disappeared.

When Maureen O'Brien vanishes at a funeral, P.I. Blake Ervansky learns about her shocking former life, a past he doesn't think he can live with. Then, before he can tell her their partnership is over, a call from a client in hysterics reveals that a recently-solved case has come messily unsolved.

Putting aside their own differences, Maureen and Blake circumvent a corrupt sheriff and draw closer to the truth, until Blake finds himself in a deadly game of cat-and-mouse in which he's the mouse, and the cat outweighs him by 400 pounds. It's a cage match he won't survive unless the skills Maureen acquired in her dark past can neutralize the killer before Blake becomes cat chow.

MURDER: TAKE TWO: "Tight and sharp-witted."
—Kirkus Reviews

MURDER: TAKE THREE

When movie action hero Micah Deifenschlictor is accused of murdering his longtime agent, private investigators Maureen O'Brien and Blake Ervansky are offered a small fortune by Micah's attorney to prove her client's innocence.

Blake and Maureen uncover evidence that eliminates Micah as a suspect in less than a day, earning the huge paycheck for very little work. When the case boomerangs back to them, however, the detectives realize they may have been duped into participating in a cover-up.

After secretly reopening their investigation, Ervansky and O'Brien are drawn into something much larger and darker than mere homicide, something that will bring unimaginable grief to Blake's life, not only changing him as a man, but irrevocably altering his relationship with Maureen.

2014 SHAMUS AWARD FINALIST!
Best Indie P.I. Novel

WATCH FOR APRIL KELLY'S NEXT BOOK

THE LAST FIRST KISS: STORIES SHORT AND TWISTED

AVAILABLE JANUARY 2015

For author biographies, sample chapters and a
complete list of books please visit
www.flightriskbooks.com

36731311R00159

Made in the USA
Charleston, SC
12 December 2014